THE FOX
&
THE FORTUNE

Further titles in this series from Severn House

THE FOX AND THE FAITH
THE FOX AND THE FURY
THE FOX AND THE FLAG
THE FOX AND THE FORTUNE

THE FOX
&
THE FORTUNE

Dan Parkinson

This title first published in Great Britain 2000 by
SEVERN HOUSE PUBLISHERS LTD of
9–15 High Street, Sutton, Surrey SM1 1DF.
This first hardcover edition published in the USA 2001 by
SEVERN HOUSE PUBLISHERS INC of
595 Madison Avenue, New York, N.Y. 10022
by arrangement with the Kensington Publishing Corporation.

British Library Cataloguing in Publication Data

Parkinson, Dan
  The fox and the fortune
  1.   Seafaring life - History - 18th century - Fiction
  2.   Historical fiction
  I.   Title
  813.5'4 [F]

ISBN 0-7278-5628-6

F
1357131

To those who go down to the sea,
whether in jaunty sailing ships
or in the no less lofty vessels
of their imaginations.

Printed and bound in Great Britain by
MPG Books Ltd, Bodmin, Cornwall.

Prologue

With coming of spring in the year 1778, came also the turning of tides. The fledgling British Empire, still in its infancy as a world power and spread thin by years of widespread conflicts—first under George II and now under George III and his ruling party—had lost the chance for a quick resolution of the uprising in its American colonies. Now the question in Lord North's administration was how much could be salvaged by negotiation from strength . . . and how much strength was there.

The best efforts of the brothers Howe toward a compromise of interests had failed, and there was war. Clinton and Cornwallis had failed—as British muskets facing American rifles had failed—to either strangle the northern colonies or neutralize the southern ones. Burgoyne's plan for a quick end to the insurgence had failed, and the Howes' occupation of Philadelphia had proven to be less a victory than a hugely unprofitable exercise in defense. Months had become years as the fighting went on, and even the House of Lords now admitted that the situation was rather beyond tidying up.

Where the colonists had fielded little militias, now there was a Continental Army afield, trained under the eye of Von Steuben and directed by Braddock's own protege, General Washington. This army had emerged from a long winter at Valley Forge to wholly disprove the Crown Party's fiction of dealing with a minor annoyance on American shores.

Where there had been privateers pitted against the king's White Fleet, now there was a small but aggressive American

Navy, carrying the battle across the Atlantic to British shores. And now the rebellious colonials had allies. France was enthusiastically involved with the Americans, and Spain — though less enthusiastically, seeing the Anglo colonials as a future threat to Spanish holdings — was yet allowing the supply lines to remain open.

Now also, the rebels in their various colonies had a common identity. The Continental Congress was once again at work in Baltimore, and the Articles of Confederation had been approved for ratification.

Half a hundred colonial battle flags had given way to a new flag — red and white stripes, thirteen in number, with thirteen stars on a field of blue.

In Paris, the Americans Franklin, Deane and Lee worked out final negotiations for a full treaty with Louis XVI. In London, Lord North introduced bills of reconciliation, hoping to avoid further French intrusion into American affairs.

In the great houses of Wilmington and Baltimore, where men gathered to discuss such matters, it was said that Clinton would succeed Howe at Philadelphia and would abandon the city within months. It was said that a king's Commission had been appointed to discuss peace terms. It was said that France — and some mentioned Spain as well — was the salvation of American hopes. It was said also that any man who trusted Spain had stones between his ears, and that France was hardly better, being solely concerned with its own interests and with twisting the lion's tail.

And it was said that never in living memory had there been a time that offered such opportunity for the making of fortunes . . . though the means to do so in such unsettled times were precariously unreliable.

The lines between patriotism and treason, just as between privateer venture and piracy on the high seas, were extremely fine in times when no established authority was at hand to explain and enforce the difference.

One

Where cloud-tattered moonlight touched the crisp tops of waves, silvering the long crests that marched in lock-step measure like so many Prussian grenadiers striding through the sea, two vessels beat landward across the tidal stream. Great shadowy silhouettes, elaborate and sleek, they thrummed and whispered as wooden hulls clove the waves. Their running wakes were bright foam on dark waters. Taut rigging hummed and keened among high sails aslant to take the faltering wind.

Foremost of the two was a solid four-master, a merchant vessel riding low and laden. By her greater size and high-stacked sails, a landsman might have said she was the faster of the two and able to leave her pursuer in her wake. A mariner would have known otherwise at a glance. The merchant vessel was losing her race. Slowly and relentlessly she was being overtaken by the dark shape less than a mile astern.

Any sailor of the time, seeing that pursuit, would have shaken his head at the inevitability of what must follow. For the dark ship in pursuit was a deadly vessel, a ship designed for the chase and for the kill. Larger than a brig, it carried the massive, elaborate sailing gear of a warship — a ship-rigged vessel of frigate class — and the glinting muzzles of great guns, spray-sheened, glistened at its flanks and along its ranked ports.

At his stern rail, Captain John Shelby Butler squinted as he steadied a glass to study the big, dark predator following in his wake. He knew the ship, and he knew the intentions of those aboard. Back there, coming on apace on the moon-scudded

7

water west of Bahama Deeps, was *Valkyrie*. And commanding her was the French Acadian freebooter, Francois Thibaud.

There was no question — no question at all — what Thibaud had in mind. Thibaud was a pirate, *Valkyrie* was a killer ship and the merchantman — alone and laden — was a ready prize.

Beside Butler, Timothy Leech rested big arms on the rail and nodded. "He's comin' on, Cap'n," he growled. "He'll have closed to half a mile by the time we make the cay yonder. He'll have them twin long-twelves aimed right up our stern, an' not a soul about to say him otherwise as he sees it."

For a time, Butler did not respond. As turning winds tugged at his sails aloft, making tackle blocks rattle overhead, he glanced up, deep-set gray eyes thoughtful. With her deep holds full of Ian McCall's goods — ranked cotton bales mostly with a small-hold complement of tobacco, fabrics, wines and spices — *Pride of Falworth* plowed water like a scow . . . or seemed to, dropping her nose listlessly as her high sails began to luff. She lost a knot of way as Butler listened to the rumble of waves against her timbers, then another.

Without looking at his first mate, Butler returned to his glassing of the pirate chasing him. "Hands to those fore and main sheets, Mister Leech," he said. "Let's at least show him that we can keep our canvas trimmed."

"Aye, Cap'n." Leech stepped forward to the quarterrail, past a grim-faced helmsman, and bellowed, "Mister Strode! Hands fore an' foremain to trim to the wind! Stand by aftermain and mizzen."

On the sloping foredeck, men scurried to comply. Leech planted big hands on his hips, watching the shadows of them there. When he was satisfied he returned to the stern rail. "Our . . . ah . . . 'temporaries' are losin' heart, sir," he said. "As they see it, we're dead men already, an' runnin' just delays the obvious." His teeth glinted within his beard, a fierce grin that aimed itself at the dark pirate ship harrying *Pride of Falworth* toward the shoals of an unnamed and uninhabited cay south of the Florida shore.

Butler felt the slight shudder in the decking beneath his buckled shoes as the helmsman turned to look back, breaking his concentration on steering to the sails.

8

"Mind your helm, Mister Trice," the captain snapped. "You can look at the pirates later."

"Aye, sir." The helm took up rudder, and again *Pride of Falworth* leaned to the weight of slanted sails.

Butler turned to glance forward. The cay loomed dark ahead of them, a low, brushy island rising from moonlit sea. On the charts it had no name, being only one of many little islands that extended in a curving chain from just south of New Spain's barrier peninsula to the curving deeps where the Gulf Stream flowed.

Butler reckoned distances, his ears hearing the whisper of waters along *Pride's* hull and the muted melody of wind in her sails. "Put a sounder in the fore, please, Mister Leech," he said. "One of our regulars, of course."

"Aye." Leech nodded, already striding away. At the quarter-rail he called, "Mister Strode, who can you spare to sound afore?"

There was a pause; then the bosun's voice came back to him. "Mister Summers or Berroth, sir. Or one of the fo'c'sle hands."

"Send Mister Summers to the spreaders to sound," Leech called. "Have Mister Berroth stand by aport with log and line."

"Aye, sir."

Captain Butler's cold voice came from behind the big first mate, "Our pirate is luffing just a bit back there, Mister Leech. He may intend to stand off and let us foul ourselves in the shoals."

"I wouldn't think he'd turn cautious now, Cap'n." Leech squinted, a touch of concern in his voice.

"Nevertheless, he is slowing." Butler pointed. "I wonder if a bit of entertainment might sharpen his attention. Gunners aft, if you please, to man the nines."

"Aye, Cap'n." Leech's grin returned, big teeth glinting among his whiskers in the mottled darkness. He turned and called, "Gunners aft, man the stern chasers! Linstocks an' slow fuse! Look alive!"

Just over half a mile astern, *Valkyrie* had slowed by a knot, lying back, although still overtaking the merchantman. Butler held his glass on the predator. *Thibaud is in no hurry now,* he thought. *He expects that I shall skirt around behind that island and try to*

9

buy some time by playing at dodging games. He is wondering whether to just stand off here and wait for first light to flush me out. "They say that Captain Thibaud is a man of temper," he mused, aloud. "They say he has no patience with those who try him."

"They do say that, Cap'n," Leech agreed. "It's his French ancestry, I shouldn't wonder."

Shadowy forms appeared at both quarterdeck ladders, hurrying aft — men with tubs and pails, with swabs and coiled lines and muted lanterns. Six men . . . two gunners and four gunners' mates. Butler nodded his approval. Terrence Boyd and Chad Ames were peerless gunners, as capable with marine artillery as any man aboard the warships of the great fleets. Nor were they the only good gunners *Pride of Falworth* carried in her complement. Though few beyond himself and Leech knew of it, *Pride's* crew of regulars was a vastly different mix of men than might be found aboard the usual merchant vessel of the time. The ship carried twice as many first-rate gunners, in fact, as the number of old guns she had. And the captain's private muster of hands was nearly double the number of men a four-mast bark required.

Most of them presently were not aboard. The majority on the ship now — eighteen of the twenty-six men working her decks — were new hands, temporaries . . . a motley lot of beached seamen hired on only weeks before at an obscure port on one of the contested islands.

The gun crews swarmed aft along *Pride's* quarterdeck and hauled in her twin nine-pound stern chasers to check loads and freshen prime.

"Misters Ames and Boyd," Butler said.

Their faces came around, half-lighted by the glow of muted lanterns. "Aye, Cap'n?"

"What do you make the range of that vessel yonder to be?"

They peered across the intervening water, glanced at each other, and Chad Ames cleared his throat. "Maybe a thousand yards, sir. About that. Twice our accurate range with these old pieces. Even if we had twelves — as the pirate yonder surely does — we'd still need to close a bit for good effect."

Butler nodded. He knew ranges and limitations as well as they did. "But a lofted ball might carry that far, might it not?"

10

"Oh, aye, sir," Ames agreed. "Might even drop a shot on his deck, with a bit of luck. But a spent ball won't do more than annoy that bloody cruiser, sir."

"Then, by all means," Butler said, "let us see if we can annoy him. You may fire for effect when you are ready."

"Aye, sir." Glancing at each other again, the gunners went to their guns and began lofting the muzzles of them, using pike poles and quoins. By the time they were satisfied with their elevations, the nine-pounders were pointed at the southern sky, standing at rakish angles like a pair of stubby color standards.

The gunners took up their smoldering fuses and aligned on a place above *Valkyrie*, then looked around.

"Proceed," Butler said.

"Aye, sir." With visible shrugs the gunners made final check of notches and lowered their smoking linstocks. Fuse touched primed vents and the nine-pounders bellowed in unison. A cloud of sulphurous smoke rode for a moment astern of *Pride of Falworth*, then drifted across her starboard flank and out to sea.

"Reload and fire again," Butler said.

The guns were run in for swabbing and loading, and Butler raised his glass. He trained it on the dark ship in the distance.

"Something for him to wonder about, at least," Leech said, leaning against the rail. "He's seen our muzzle blasts. I wonder what he thinks we're doing."

"He likely wonders what *we* think we're doing," Butler said, in a cold voice that carried no amusement. He handed the glass to Leech. "Your eyes are younger than mine, Timothy. Tell me what you see."

Leech steadied the glass. "Nothin' yet, Cap'n. That's a long way for a ball to . . . aha! First shot's in the water off his port bow, maybe fifty yards out. Nice plume it made. Where's the other? I don't see . . . by Georgie's broad belly, Cap'n, I believe the lads dropped that ball on his deck! There's a scramble there, an' they've opened some lanterns."

"Well done," Butler husked, nodding toward the gunners. "Would you wager you might do it again?"

"At the right odds, Cap'n." Terrence Boyd grinned. "Now, if we heated the balls first . . ."

"And set him afire?" Butler snapped. "I wish to annoy the

11

gentleman, Mister Boyd. Not burn his ship."

"Oh. Ah, aye, sir. Right. I kind of forgot there for a moment . . ."

"Just do it again, gentlemen, if you can."

"Aye, sir."

Again the twin nines thundered, this time bracketing the distant frigate with tiny-looking plumes of spray. They were doing no real damage, Butler knew. With nines, at such a range. . . .

"He's adding sail," Leech said. "I'd say he has decided to close and deal with us here and now."

"Very good." Butler nodded, turning away. In the fore, a distant voice was calling depths at intervals of a minute or so. And now a second voice, closer, began calling out the readings of log and line. *Pride of Falworth* was making five knots in four fathoms of water, the depth beneath her keel slowly decreasing.

"Trim all yards by the wind, please, Mister Leech," Butler ordered. "Go amidships and direct the helm from there." He peered across dark waters at the looming cay ahead. "The lads know now that we're coming, and bringing company with us. Bring us around the leeward shore, as we discussed, please."

"Aye, Cap'n."

"Send Mister Trahan aft to spell me on deck. I shall be below until we round the cay."

"Aye, sir."

In his little cabin belowdecks, John Shelby Butler closed his gallery shutters and removed the hood from an oil lamp. By its light he spread a chart on the table and traced patterns on it with his finger. The present course line had not been extended since a final daylight reading at eight bells—hours earlier. At that logging, *Pride* had been on course north, not yet in sight of the cays. She had been making six knots on a port reach, and the pirate vessel had been some five miles astern, hull down on clear waters.

Now with the cay dead ahead, he had no need of instruments to locate his course. He knew exactly where he was, and where he was going. Long months of careful planning and preparation were about to pay off.

The cay was inked-in on the chart, a bean-shaped little island with a sheltered cove on its north shore. Two previous courses were marked on the same chart, both dated within the past three months. And both of those also had homed on the same little cay.

"Provisions," he muttered, tracing the first one. Then he moved his finger to the second. "And personnel."

Satisfied, he sat on the bench beneath his shuttered galleries and opened a bound-wood chest. Idly, a cold smile playing at his lips, he withdrew and unrolled a pair of ribboned foolscaps: his commission as a ship's master, issued by the Commonwealth of Virginia, and his charter as master of *Pride of Falworth*, issued by Squire Ian McCall, the vessel's owner. Rolled inside this second document were his standing orders as master, and his latest charge — to carry cargo to the Indies, execute trade on behalf of his sponsor, and then to return to Chesapeake.

A six-month cruise, at most . . . dated nearly a year ago.

One by one, he held the papers over the lamp's wick, then watched them as they burned to ashes. In his mind was the face of Ian McCall, the merchant-patriot. Butler smiled a frosty smile as he addressed the image. "You think me lost at sea, Squire? Have you set bounties yet, to reclaim your properties should they surface at the pirate ports? Have you set your trusted Evan to find me — or word of me — at all cost? I know you have done so, of course. After all, business is business, as I've heard you say so often."

On impulse he opened one of the shutters and looked astern at the dark sea, and the dark ship that rode there. It would do no harm now to show a bit of light to the brute, Thibaud. The pirate knew where he was, and was racing to overtake.

"I served you well, McCall," Butler muttered. "John Shelby Butler served you with honor, and you've turned a nice profit from my labors. Too much, for too long, for too little return. The times, they do change, Squire. Mayhap, if you'd been freer with bonuses now and again . . . mayhap if you'd seen fit to transfer title of my ship to me after six good voyages, as some wise owners have been known to do . . . then again, maybe nothing you could have done would have mattered. You've lost your ship, Squire, and you've lost your faithful captain. John Shelby Butler is no more, only Jack Shelby."

He put the chest away, stamped out the embers among the

13

ashes at his feet, put on a fresh coat, then donned his sword and buckler. Through the soles of his shoes he could feel *Pride* coming aport, swinging through the wind to slide past the little cay's hidden cove. He tensed slightly, enjoying the thrill of imminent action. The coming about would allow the pirate to come within easy gun range. Now everything depended upon *Pride*'s playing the role of a surrendering ship—just long enough for *Valkyrie* to come abreast of that cove.

"What I do now is *my* business, Squire," he breathed. "And as you say, 'business is business.' " Hooding his lamp, John Shelby Butler closed the cabin, and Jack Shelby went on deck.

At first bell of the morning watch—half an hour after midnight—the private warship *Valkyrie* overhauled the merchant *Pride of Falworth* in shallows off the north shore of an unnamed cay, and fired across her, bow and stern. The merchant ship immediately lowered its colors and waved lanterns in signals of submission.

Less than eight minutes later, armed sailors aboard four stout launches—put out in secret from the cay—heaved grapples across *Valkyrie*'s after rails and swarmed aboard, cutting down the surprised pirates who tried too late to defend their deck.

At second bell of the watch, Jack Shelby and his officers stepped aboard the marauder and took command. Standing on the pirate vessel's blood-slick deck, the man who had been John Shelby Butler had the pirate Thibaud brought before him. "Your career has ended, Thibaud," he announced. *"Valkyrie* is my ship now. I shall waste no time with you or your crew. You are at an end. You will be first, to set the rest an example in valiance if it pleases you to do so. How you take your death is up to you. I am master of *Valkyrie* now, and I warrant I can use her far better than ever you did."

Hard hands lifted Thibaud to his feet and dragged him to the starboard beam where he was doubled over the rail and held motionless. Timothy Leech did the honors, with a belaying pin from *Valkyrie*'s fifes. With one well-placed blow he shattered the pirate's skull.

Then three by three, the remaining pirates were hauled to the lee rail and brained with clubs. Splash after splash echoed as

14

their bodies followed that of their captain into the dark, voracious sea. Beyond could be heard the splash of oars where boats plied between ships.

"I can't say I relish the next part, Cap'n," Timothy Leech said as a dozen of their regulars put out in a launch to cross to *Pride of Falworth.*

"Nor do I, Mister Leech." Shelby shrugged. "Neither the men nor the ship. Still, it must be done as we have planned and no less. *Pride* must disappear for good, and we no longer have use for our temporaries, who have already seen far too much. Mister Strode has his orders, though, to make it clean and painless if he can."

Leech looked across at the silhouette of the merchant ship that he and the man beside him had sailed for so long. He felt no real regret, though. It was only a bark. "There's the cargo, as well," he muttered.

"Bales and odds," Shelby said. "Commodities. Too much trouble for what it's worth where we'll be dealing. The ship must be scuttled, and properly. Open a seam or two and let her drift toward the deeps. Nothing need ever be known of this night, Timothy, and best not. But there will be plenty of plunder for us elsewhere. We shall be rich men, Mister Leech . . . every man of us who survives."

"Aye, Cap'n."

"See to the finishing of this business, Mister Leech, then assemble hands for an inventory of *Valkyrie.* This is a fine ship, and we need to know her well."

"Aye, sir." Leech started away, then turned back and raised a big hand in grinning salute. "To piracy, Cap'n."

"Aye, Mister Leech." Jack Shelby nodded. "To piracy."

Aboard the bark, Mister Strode and his mates went about their tasks in businesslike fashion. While sounds of chopping and splintering rang from below decks, the "temporaries" were rounded up, then herded to leeward rails, and the slaughter that had been done aboard *Valkyrie* was repeated . . . this time upon surprised, innocent men. More corpses splashed into the dark sea.

When it was done, Strode looked around. "Was that the last of them, Mister Summers? The count should be eighteen."

15

Owen Summers shrugged. "I didn't count the buggers. I thought you were counting. But that was all of them."

Dickie Trice came from below. "Her seams are open, an' she's takin' water, Mister Strode. Slow an' steady, like you said."

"Then, let's get back to our new ship." Strode nodded. "We're out of the merchant business, lads. From now on, merchantmen are *our* business."

Two

She was a grim and furtive ship, creeping southward across the flowing gulf stream, avoiding the main shipping lanes and eschewing encounter of any sort. Though fully rigged and well-gunned, a cruiser of the class called snow, she played a hiding game in this season, for she had not the strength to challenge nor the manpower to defend. Her name was *Fury,* and the men aboard her numbered fewer than the guns at her ports — fewer even than the sails that her swift rigging could carry.

Fury was a fugitive ship, escaped from Crown custody and fair game for any vessel that might spot her. And those aboard her, though not a man of them had charges remaining against him — those who once had were now exonerated by proper court-martial conducted at sea — were fugitives as well because they had taken her and flown.

At first light of a clear morning *Fury's* foretopman spotted sails in the distance ahead. Sails odd-set and oddly abank, but sails nonetheless. He steadied himself on the snow's trestletrees and squinted, shading his eyes against the confusing light of the eastern sky to his left, then cupped his hands and called, "On deck!"

Amidships, Charley Duncan — first officer now by act of his captain — raised his eyes. "Yes, Mister Fisk?"

"Sail ahead, sir! Hard down a point on the starboard bow!"

Duncan glanced aft, where Victory Locke manned the helm. There was no one else on the little quarterdeck, and Duncan felt a stab of guilt. It was his watch, and that was where he belonged. But there were other things needing attended to,

17

and little enough time to do them. And now a sighting from the foretop. Duncan strode forward to the rise of the deck, where *Fury*'s jaunty bowsprit grew from the planking. He peered into the distance ahead. Low mist obscured the sea from deck level. He turned, looking aloft where the form of Purdy Fisk was silhouetted against dawning sky, ninety feet above.

"What do you make her, Mister Fisk?"

"Hard to tell, sir!" the topman's voice floated down. "Might be a merchantman, but there's something amiss with her settings. She shows sail, but no handling. She looks adrift."

"Very well, Mister Fisk. Keep a good eye on her." Duncan hurried aft, where a half-dozen hammocks were slung along the rails. He tried to remember which of the off-watch might have had the most sleep, then gave up on it and went to the nearest one. The man in the hammock was snoring, and he shook him awake. "On your feet, Mister Quarterstone, if you please. We have sail ahead and need a second lookout."

Pliny Quarterstone sat up, rubbing bleary eyes with hard fists. "Fine thing," he grumbled, "waking a man from a dream like that."

"Like what?"

Quarterstone got to his feet, sighing as he came awake. "Oh, you know. Like that. What other kind is there when a man's been at sea for three months?"

"We haven't been at sea *all* that time," Duncan reminded him. "We did pay call at that island, if you recollect."

"But there wasn't anybody there, Mister Duncan, if *you* recollect. Just a bunch of goats. I'm not the sort of gentleman to dream like that about goats!"

Duncan nodded, understanding, then cocked a thumb toward the mainmast's soaring port stays. "Be that as it may, Mister Quarterstone, we need a second spotter aloft. Mister Fisk is watching a sail yonder, and we need someone to keep a sharp eye for any others."

Quarterstone stepped to the rail, swung up and around the after stay and set his feet on ratlines, nimble as a spider on a web, then hesitated. "We could do with a bit more help on this blessed barge, you know. Forty-five ables is fit complement for a snow. Not fifteen."

Having spoken his mind to the morning, the sailor swarmed aloft, climbing like a monkey to disappear into the intricate silhouettes of the maintops.

There was a chuckle at Duncan's shoulder, and the first officer turned, coming to attention. Patrick Dalton stood there, tall and tired-looking in the gray light. Duncan hadn't heard the captain's approach.

"Morning, sir," Duncan started. "Mister Quarterstone is only a bit out of sorts, is all. He was a'bunk just —"

"I understand," Dalton cut him off, looking aloft. "And he's right, of course. We do need more crew. There is a limit to what the best of men can perform. What is the sighting?"

"Sail, sir. Ahead and a point astarboard. Can't make much of it yet.

"Whereaway?"

"Hard down, Mister Fisk said. Just tops in sight. Maybe twelve miles or so?"

"A fair guess, depending upon the size of the vessel. Can he read it?"

"He isn't sure, sir. May be a merchantman, but he says it looks askew and drifting."

Dalton nodded. "I see Mister Locke is alone at the helm."

"Aye, sir." Duncan scuffed a shoe in embarrassment. "All's been quiet, sir, and I was takin' the time to splice some line. We're down to pickings in the lockers."

"Very well, Mister Duncan. I realize our condition. We'll have to make port soon, no matter who's looking for us. But please take the deck now. I shall relieve you at the bell, and you can have your breakfast."

"Aye, sir. Goat again, sir?"

"Don't think on it, Mister Duncan. Pretend it's partridge. It helps."

"Aye, sir. Although with Mister Wise on galley duty, even partridge might taste like goat."

Duncan headed aft, and Dalton looked around him at the deck of his ship, stifling a sigh. Almost three months had passed since *Fury*'s escape from a Crown escort . . . and from the humiliation of a custody flag atop her lanyard.

Escape had meant freedom. But it also had meant that *Fury*

19

e again a fugitive ship, fair game for any man-of-war
_ _ _ _ed to take her as a prize. The snow had no proper cre-
dentials now, no flag to fly and few enough friends to turn to.
With a crew of fifteen — barely enough men to handle her sails,
much less to work stations in an engagement of any sort — the
snow had gone to ground in a manner of speaking. For a time at
least, Dalton had no option but to run and hide, to stay far out
to sea and scavenge for provisions where they could be found,
to avoid contact with anyone. Because anyone — for a small,
undermanned warship with scant supplies and no flag — could
be the enemy.

Striding the foredeck for a moment, Dalton spied the morning. He would have course reports from Charley Duncan at the
turn of watch; but he knew where they were, and he knew —
from the feel of the ship, the sounds of its high sails and the song
of the sea — their direction and speed. *Fury* was, as mariners in
these waters termed it, "in the trough." South of the great Atlantic lanes, north a bit of the slave lanes, and making four or five
knots on a steady starboard tack. Somewhere ahead were islands — some part of that great chain of countless land masses
that were the Baja Mars . . . or Bahamas . . . the Antilles and
the Indies. Somewhere ahead were a thousand opportunities to
make landfall.

It would soon be time to make a decision. *Fury* had avoided
social contact as long as was practical. Dalton had need of men,
provisions, stores, tackle . . . he needed everything, and that
meant he needed a place to put in, a place to do business one
way or another.

At the stem of the snow's towering foremast, he looked aloft
and called, "Report your sighting, Mister Fisk!"

From high above the voice came. "Aye, sir. It's a ship, sir. Still
hull down, but I see sails. May be a four-master, sir. Like a bark
or such, though it's hard to make out."

"What is it doing, Mister Fisk?"

"It's just . . . there, sir. Not doin' anything as I can see. It's
heeled a bit on the wind, but its sails are askew. I think it's just
driftin', sir."

Dalton walked the fifteen paces aft to the base of the snow's
doubled mainmast — actually two masts rigged in tandem, the

big mainmast towering aloft with its three spanning yards, and just aft of it a smaller upright called a trysail standard or jackmast, which carried the gaff for the ship's big fore-and-aft drive sail, the spanker.

Again Dalton called aloft, "Maintop ahoy!"

Pliny Quarterstone's voice came down. "Maintop aye, sir!"

"Report, maintop."

"Aye, sir. Nothin' in sight on any quarter, except Mister Fisk's bark, sir. A fine clear mornin', an' except for that one we have the ocean all to ourselves . . . sir."

Dalton growled slightly, then shook his head. Now was not the time to berate a man for flippancy. Not a man aboard had managed more than two hours' sleep at a stretch in months, and they were all a bit vague from fatigue. Still, as one who had come up amidships on vessels of the king, it was ingrained in Patrick Dalton that discipline was essential to the handling of a ship. He made a point — had always made a point, when he thought of it — of not tolerating laxity aboard his ship.

Or so he was fond of saying, at any rate.

He shrugged it off. "You're fresh in the tops, Mister Quarterstone. Do you have anything to add to Mister Fisk's report?"

"Ah . . . no, sir. It's just as he said. A square-sailer, looks to be bark-rigged, still hull down, though her courses are in sight. Sails a'shamble an' just driftin' on the tide. I wager she's derelict, sir. Nobody yonder is handlin' sail or rudder."

Dalton turned away, thoughtful. Derelict? Maybe abandoned? A ship of that nature adrift out here with no hand at her helm? It was possible. For three years, the waters of the north Atlantic had been alive with conflict — His Majesty's Royal Navy trying to contain the myriad privateers and letters-of-marque set loose by the rebellious American colonies, colonial against Crown, privateer against whoever got in the way, and more than a few outright pirates feeding off the chaos.

There might be a lost ship adrift in these waters. Or it could be a decoy — bait for someone's trap.

He ran thoughtful fingers along the varnished surface of the jack-mast, admiring its architecture. An American innovation, and one the British had yet to understand. In many respects, the snow resembled an armed brig — a smallish

21

warship, a cruiser and seeker. But the snow was no brig. The Americans had improved upon the brig design — given it a new mast configuration and a deeper, stronger hull to balance increased weight of sail. With long legs and sharp teeth, American-built snows had repeatedly surprised the planners of British strategy.

Though less than a full frigate, *Fury* was far more than a brig — and *Fury* was his. By right of salvage, by right of recovery, by right of prize or right of possession . . . by whatever right it took, *Fury* was Patrick Dalton's ship. His honor and the ship's honor were intact, and she was *his*.

The bane of the Irish, he thought sardonically. The sheer, hard-headed, arrogant Gaelic pride of the black Irish, that when a man won a thing of value it was his. Not the king's, not the Admiralty's, not some colonial claimant's, but his. *I am black Irish, God help me,* he thought. *I acquired this ship fairly and fully, and nothing means more to me than my ship, at my command.*

Well, almost nothing, he corrected himself, thinking — as he always did, it seemed — of Constance Ramsey. *Fury* was not, he admitted, more important to him than John Singleton Ramsey's auburn-haired daughter.

But in the way of the black Irish, he balanced the two devotions and found no need for choices. And with Gaelic honesty he admitted to himself that what he intended — though what the goal might require was yet a mystery — was to have both.

"Keep a sharp eye about us, lads," he called aloft. "For in this time and this place we surely have no friends."

He started aft, hesitating as the companionway hatch banged open and Billy Caster hurled himself up the ladder to the deck, his eyes wide and his hair tousled. Panting, the youth peered at the quarterdeck, then turned. Dalton stifled a grin and said, "At ease, Mister Caster. If it's me you seek, I'm right here."

The youth sighed his relief. "Aye, Captain. Beg pardon, but I thought I'd overslept again, and . . ."

"I'd hardly call two hours of sleep 'oversleeping,' Billy." Dalton shook his head. "Yes, I know you were afoot through the night doing inventory and logs. Have you had your breakfast?"

"No, sir." Billy cleared his throat, trying to control a voice that had an embarrassing tendency to break into adolescent falsetto. "I was in a hurry, sir."

"Obviously. Very well, Mister Caster, I am about to relieve Mister Duncan. You can stand reports with me, then go below and get some of Mister Wise's smoked goat and biscuit. There has been a sighting ahead, but nothing interesting is likely to occur for at least two hours."

"Aye, sir."

At five bells of the morning watch — with only fifteen souls on board, *Fury* had given up all semblance of civilized eight-bell duties, and every man aboard was doing watch and watch — Patrick Dalton assumed the quarterdeck, relieved Charley Duncan and set Claude Mallory to the helm. *Fury* was on course due south, making a sedate four knots on jib, jigger and topsails, and there were no sightings except for the drifting vessel eleven miles out and now dead ahead.

"I believe we must have a look at the stranger," Dalton decided. "Mister Mallory, steer two points to port if you please. The lads coming up from galley can trim sail accordingly. Mister Duncan, your watch can rest, but rest wary. Should this seem a trap or a decoy, we may need to make all sail smartly."

"Aye, sir."

"Mister Caster, have you noted course and intercept orders?"

"Aye, sir."

"How do you read the day, Mister Caster?"

It was an old game that the captain played with his clerk, and Billy had long since grown accustomed to it. Irish or not, navy or not, Patrick Dalton was a British officer to the bone in many ways. And having no complement of midshipmen to instruct, it fell to Billy to be instructed in the ways of navigation and the ways of the sea.

He looked at the sky, and at the few sails braced to the wind. "Wind is westerly and a bit north, sir, at eighteen to twenty knots. A clear day with high clouds on the west quarter, and the sea is running nor'easterly at two knots."

"Very good." Dalton nodded. "And how shall the day make?"

"Rising wind by midday, sir, and clouds overhead. The sea will run more then, because we shall be farther into the stream."

"If the vessel ahead of us is truly adrift on shrift sail, and we

23

steer two degrees east of south, then when will we intercept it?"

Billy hesitated, calculating, then said, "Seven bells of the watch, sir, though we'll be looking at her escutcheons half a glass shy of that."

Dalton nodded again. "Go below and have breakfast, Mister Caster. And try not to think of it as smoked goat. Perhaps roast pork with applesauce would be a helpful fiction."

"Is Mister Wise still in the galley, sir?"

"He is."

"Then, fiction or not, it is still smoked goat."

At just past six bells of the watch *Fury* crept to within a mile of the derelict — for derelict it seemed to be.

A four-master, bark-rigged with a few flapping and luffing sails open upon its yards and no hand at the rudder, the ship drifted askew on the current and leaned astarboard with its wales on that side barely four feet above the cresting waters.

From *Fury*'s little quarterdeck, Patrick Dalton studied the vessel through a telescoping glass, puzzled. Not a hole or a tear showed in hull or sail, not a sign of combat anywhere, but there she drifted. An abandoned ship slowly taking the sea into her holds, she crept sideways across endless ocean, and not a man could be seen anywhere aboard her.

"Odd," he mused. "She has her boats and her tiers, and nothing seems missing from her deck. Her bow anchors hang a-cock-bill, but they are there, at the catheads." He lowered the glass. "Hands a'deck," he ordered. "Tops keep a weather eye about, and let us have the fore portside guns at the ready. We shall approach for boarding."

At three cable lengths the merchantman's escutcheons were clearly visible, and Dalton's memory tugged at him. *Fury* carried no ship's registry, but the vessel there was one he had seen before, somewhere.

Her name was *Pride of Falworth.*

Three

The merchantman had been hull-scuttled, though sloppily in the opinion of Ishmael Bean, who seemed to know more than the average able seaman about such larcenies.

"Had it been me set to scuttle this bucket, sir," Bean assured Patrick Dalton, "she'd have been awash to the scuppers before a man could say 'God save the king,' an' I'd have put her down by the bow or stern, whichever pleased them as gave the orders. From th' looks of things below, though, I'd say what these blokes did was just to prize up a brace of bilge stringers an' drive a splittin' maul between some hull timbers in the keel. Amateur work, sir, as I sees it."

"Still, she would have sunk, eventually, it seems," Dalton pointed out.

"Oh, aye, sir, eventually. As it is, she's shipped water up to her knees, so we can't see very much down there. But Mister Locke, he tripped over a bit of flotsam below deck an' kind of fell in, so we had him feel around a bit down there before we hoisted him out. He says he believes the parting of the timbers has been punched full of cotton, as though someone tried to patch her, sir."

"Patched?"

"Aye, sir. What he said."

"Where is Mister Locke, Mister Bean?"

"Forward, sir. Mister Hoop is danglin' him by the heels to drain bilgewater out of him."

Dismissing the tar, Dalton continued his tour of the merchantman's deck. *Pride of Falworth* was in excellent condition, considering that she had been obviously abandoned, hull-vented and left to sink. Her decks and fixtures were in service-able order, masts and rigging seemed sound and all the accouterments of a working vessel — at least all those visible from the deck, hold hatches and companionway — were present and stowed in orderly fashion. And there was considerable cargo below, bales of cotton visible through the hatches, with no apparent sign of having been vandalized.

The ship obviously had not been looted, and there were no signs of a fight. *Pride* was in every respect a taut and ready sailing vessel, from her varnished sternpost and fresh-painted jib to her suit of sails aloft. Yet here she was, far from the shipping lanes, adrift in mid-ocean, and someone had opened her seams below.

Mutiny? He wondered. Such was not uncommon aboard the long-haul merchantmen of the time. Crewmen driven by too harsh a master or kept for too long on short rations had been known to stage mutiny in retaliation. A crew with a leader and a plan might well overpower the officers of a vessel and take charge. But what then? Why scuttle a good ship with valuable cargo aboard?

To destroy the evidence? Possible, he thought. Possible, but unlikely. Much more likely that the culprits would set sail for a barter port where they might find a buyer for an unregistered vessel and its cargo . . . or for an island somewhere, or at least for a shore where they could land and vanish.

Piracy, then? He looked around him, doubting. The ship had been neither shelled nor boarded in force. There had been no battle here. There were no signs of attack and defense. And *had* a pirate somehow taken the ship without violence, then why was it not now headed for some trading lair? Why scuttle and abandon?

He walked to *Pride's* starboard bulwark, swung over to her mainstay channel and leapt across to *Fury's* portside shrouds. With light seas, the ships were lashed alongside, separated only by dangling coils of heavy cable to serve as fenders. Snugged together so, the big four-master towering over the small warship, the two vessels might have appeared almost as a mother and child, but the appearance was deceiving.

Though by far the smaller of the two, the snow was a warship, built and equipped for the chase and the kill, while the bark was only a bark—a vessel with holds for goods and sails to carry them from place to place.

Charley Duncan came to meet him, and Dalton glanced toward the snow's tops. "All clear, Mister Duncan?"

"Not a sight nor a sign, sir. We've this part of the world all to ourselves for a time, it seems."

"Very well." Dalton nodded. "Go across, Mister Duncan. The bark has a hole in its hull, but it can be fothered for a time with sailcloth and tar. I've set Mister Caster to an inventory of stores, beginning with the galley. If we find some decent provisions there, possibly Mister Wise can prepare something tastier than goat for us, to fortify us in our labors. You shall want the bark's pumps rigged, and eight men to man them—four on and four off—until we can inspect the holds. Once we raise the merchantman's main wales above sea level, I believe we can set some of her sails and be under way."

Duncan stared at him, stunned. "Sails? Sir, do you intend to take the bark with us, to . . . to man it and sail it?"

"I do, Mister Duncan. Right of salvage. I believe providence has handed us an answer to some of our problems."

"Aye, sir. Some of them. But who's going to sail the ship, sir? I mean, there are only fifteen of us, and we can barely manage *Fury,* not to mention a second ship . . . and a four-master at that."

"I believe we shall devise a way, Mister Duncan."

"Aye, sir. But . . . well, I don't see how you are going to—"

"Oh, I'm not going to sail the bark, Mister Duncan. You are."

Through the hours of a waning day they labored, pumping seawater from the bark's hull, locating and transferring stores, and perfecting the "fothering" on *Pride's* hull—an awkward but serviceable bandage over her hidden wound, fashioned by lashing a spare topsail to her hull with lines running beneath her keel and secured to the chain plates on each side. Drawn tight with handclamps, these lines secured the sail to the wide hull as though it were a bit of the ship's skin. And when the water level was down to the bilges within, a ring wall of coiled

27

hemp was secured on the inner surfaces around the hole, and the cavity pumped dry so that hot tar could be packed into the broken seams.

The westering sun was low on the horizon by the time this was finished, and Dalton crossed over again to the bark to inspect.

"It isn't a pretty repair," he decided. "But it will hold for a time until we find a place to do it better."

"I still don't see how —" Charley Duncan began, then stopped as a muffled clamor erupted belowdeck, sounds of shouting, scuffling and a pair of screams coming from the bark's forward hold. The men on deck turned to look, and Billy Caster hurried past, his ever-present inventory list clutched in his hand. Victory Locke's head popped from the open hatch, and he waved for attention.

"Hoy!" the tar shouted. "We can use some hands down here, lively-like. Mister Hoop's found somethin' new!"

Billy Caster arrived at the transom just ahead of Dalton and — Duncan, and squinted at his list, then down at Victory Locke. "We've inspected every compartment, Mister Locke. What else did he find?"

"In the chain locker," Locke said as further commotion erupted below. "Mister Hoop was — well, it just occurred to him to have a look there, an' sure enough . . ."

Sounds of a struggle floated up from the cargo hatch, and Locke looked around, then ducked out of sight.

"Mister Locke!" Dalton roared.

The tar appeared again, looking abashed. "Aye, sir?"

"What has Mister Hoop found?"

"Well, sir, so far I believe there's a pot of boiled peas, some biscuit, a keg or two that might be rum, an' two frogs."

"Frogs?"

"Aye, sir, a pair of 'em, an' frisky, too, though . . . ah —" The noise below suddenly stilled, and Locke ducked away, then reappeared. "All under control, sir. Mister Hoop has got the frogs quieted down."

Locke looked around again, then eased aside, and Mister Hoop appeared in his place, head and shoulders almost filling the near end of the forward cargo hatch. If Mister Hoop had a first name, none aboard knew what it was. Mister Hoop was twice the size of most sailors and, though generally docile, was not one that anyone—short of Dalton himself and possibly Duncan—cared to take a chance of riling.

The big man was laden now, by the grin on his homely face and the inert men slung one over each of his massive shoulders. At sight of the captain, he hesitated, then said apologetically, "Hope you don't mind, sir, but I had to rap these gentlemen on their heads. Otherwise it didn't seem like they was willing to come out of the chain locker."

Having spoken his piece, Hoop flipped the unconscious men up and out of the hold, depositing them more or less gently upon the deck.

Locke reappeared then, beside the giant. "I'm certain they're frogs, sir. I don't know what they was hollerin' about, but I know French when I hear it."

Dalton nodded, and squatted beside the two unconscious men, looking them over. Both were dishevelled and rank, dressed in filthy clothing, both unshaven and both obviously sailors by the horny calluses on their hands, the corded muscles of their forearms and the buckle shoes on their feet.

"What were they doing in the chain locker?" Dalton asked.

Hoop shrugged massive shoulders. "From the looks of it, sir, I'd say they've been livin' there, though the good Lord knows a chain locker's no fit place for man nor beast. Why, supposin' you'd decided to drop anchor, sir, these two would have been—"

"I know what occurs in a chain locker, Mister Hoop."

"Aye, sir. I took it on myself to remove them, sir, but I'll be glad to put them back if the cap'n says . . ."

"Never mind, Mister Hoop. You did the right thing."

Hoop blushed with huge pleasure. "Aye, sir. Thank ye, sir." He stepped down into the hold again, then started passing up other items as Victory Locke handed them to him below: a stained pot partially filled with what appeared to be boiled peas, a pair of rum kegs followed by another keg with its bung knocked out—he sniffed at this one, then handed it up. "Rum, sir," he said.

Dalton leaned to smell the breaths of the two unconscious

men, then straightened and shook his head. "It's a wonder these two were conscious when you rapped them, Mister Hoop."

The big man tossed a pile of filthy blankets out of the hold, then a pair of empty kegs and another partially filled one, and finally several tins of sealed biscuit and some empty tins. "Looks like they been there for a while, sir. An' they've had candles, too. Lucky they didn't burn the ship, the shape they're in."

Dalton stood and turned away. "Lay out a bit of bedding amidships and put these men there for now," he said. "We'll sort this out later. Mister Caster, is your inventory complete?"

"Aye, sir. I think it is now."

"You may log the entries 'in fine' at another time, then. For now, simply state in *Fury*'s log that as of this date and this time we have found, secured, inventoried and taken into our possession one four-masted bark and its cargoes and stores, as claimants under Article the Ninth of the Standards for International Commerce."

"Aye, sir. Ah . . . that means salvage, doesn't it, sir?"

"It does. Do you have a question of propriety, Mister Caster?"

The boy frowned, then nodded. "Yes, sir. I believe you instructed me once, sir, that 'salvage' applies to a vessel or contents found sunken or aground and having neither claimants aboard nor a claim flag or keg attached."

"I see no claim flags or floating kegs, Mister Caster."

"No, sir. But the vessel is neither sunken nor aground."

"No, it is neither." Dalton cocked a brow at the youngster. "Therefore, Mister Caster, what would *you* say is our justification for claiming right of salvage?"

Billy thought it over for a moment, then asked, "Because it has been scuttled, sir?"

"Very shaky justification, Mister Caster. Can you elaborate a bit?"

The boy screwed up his face in furious thought, then grinned. "Scuttled and adrift . . . we assume it has been sunken or aground, and was abandoned, then either raised itself or floated off due to natural causes."

30

"Very good," Dalton nodded. "Excellent. List it so, please."

"Aye, sir." Billy wrote one word on his notations: flotsam.

With the clerk padding along behind him, Dalton strode aft to the bark's sterncastle and called for assembly. When the dozen *Furies* aboard were gathered before him, he said, "Gentlemen, we have claimed this vessel as our rightful prize under the standards of salvage. Now we need to take it to a place where we can do something with it. Mister Duncan will be in command of the prize crew."

"Aye, sir," Duncan agreed, looking worried. "Ah, pardon, sir, but how many men can you spare for a prize crew? We're a bit short-handed, it seems to me."

"We are indeed. Therefore your crew will be limited."

"Aye, sir. Who will they be?"

"They will be Mister Hoop. He and yourself will have to manage, by the helm on set sails, and we must hope the wind doesn't change for the next two days."

"Two of us, sir?"

"You have permission to sign those French gentlemen on as crew when they are able. That will make four. We shall cast loose *Fury* on a hawser, long enough for the setting of sails on the bark. I think forward courses and jibs will be sail enough, with the spanker at mizzen to assist the rudder. The rest of us will return to *Fury* then and follow along for a day or two. We should sight land in that time."

"Aye, sir." Duncan continued to look dubious; but he squared his shoulders in readiness, and Dalton nodded. The sandy-haired sailor was a scoundrel, a known thief and a practicing ne'er-do-well; but he was a first-rate seaman for all that, and Dalton was proud of him.

In the assembly, a tenuous hand was raised, and Dalton turned to its owner. "Yes, Mister Mallory?"

"Might I ask where we're bound, sir?"

"Landward, Mister Mallory. Due south or as nearly so as we can manage with two undermanned vessels. Two days of fair sailing with the wind we presently have should bring us within sight of some of the islands. It's a bit hard to say which islands, exactly, but there are quite a number of them."

They all stared at him blankly, astounded to hear such im-

31

precision from the man they had all come to realize seldom made mistakes and almost never left his reckoning to chance. Of the thirteen able seamen and one clerk at Patrick Dalton's command, seven had sailed with him from the moment of that now-legendary escape from New York Harbor aboard a requisitioned trade schooner named *Faith*. . . . now no more than a shattered hulk lying in shipyards at South Point on the Delaware. Of the remaining seven, four had been with him when he turned almost certain defeat at the hands of Spanish pirates into a victory, and captured the jaunty snow, *Fury*. And all of them had seen him tack the snow into a black squall to evade the guns of a seventy-four-gun man-of-war . . . and then escape once again, this time from the very heart of a flotilla of king's vessels. They knew Patrick Dalton as a fighting seaman, a crafty strategist and as a master mariner.

But then, as every man of them realized, precision navigation was unlikely in the circumstances. They would do their best to trim the bark's forecourses for a southward course on a westering wind, but once trimmed the only corrections possible for those left aboard—even if Duncan could get the Frenchies to help—would be by shifting the spanker and by sheer brawn at the helm.

As the final trim was sheeted in on the *Pride's* forward courses, Charley Duncan and Mister Hoop watched from the bark's sternrail as Dalton and the rest put out by launch to return to *Fury*.

"Bedammed if I don't miss those Americans we had with us before," Duncan muttered. "Bless his colonial heart, even Michael Romart would be a comfort about now—though I've sworn at times that his devilin' tongue would drive me past all tolerance."

"Aye," Hoop rumbled, setting his great shoulders to the tug of the helm. "But Cap'n had to put them off when he did, you know. Otherwise they'd have been took as rebels when we had our court-martial."

"It was *his* court-martial, Mister Hoop. Captain Dalton's. Not ours. He saw we were cleared before ever he went before the magistrates."

"But I testified, I did," Hoop pointed out, proud as a peacock of having stood before senior officers of the Royal Navy, in the great gallery of a ship of the line.

"I just wish we had those Americans back." Duncan sighed.

The helm bucked on a wave, and Hoop's big hands fought the spokes. "I wish we had just about *anybody,* right now, sir."

Four

As fair light of evening colored the great sails of a mismatched pair of ships bound southward beyond the Gulf currents, an entirely different scene was unfolding twelve hundred miles away, above Baltimore at an estate called Eagle's Head. A great coach with four matched bays came to a noisy halt in the curve of the gravel drive, and its right side door swung open. Without waiting for his footman to place a stepping bench, the merchant-patriot Ian McCall sprang to the ground and strode away across tended lawns. At the main house he took the wide porch steps two at a time, brushed past a bowing gardener and pounded at the wide doors, scowling mightily.

After a moment he pounded again, then dropped his arm when the door swung inward and a dark face above a starched collar peered at him. The servant blinked; then his eyes widened. "Why, Mist' Ian! Squire didn' say you was comin' to—"

"Never mind, Colly," McCall growled. He stepped past the old man and went in. "I shall announce myself. Where is he?"

"He . . . uh . . . why, he in the study, Mist'—"

An interior door opened, and a ruddy face appeared, squinting over wire-rimmed spectacles. "Here now! What's all this? Ah! Ian! By heaven, I hadn't expected you, sir, but welcome! Come in and—but you already are in, aren't you? Well, come and sit with me in the study, then. Colly, take Squire McCall's—"

"Where is your daughter, John?" McCall snapped, brush-

34

ing aside the civilities.

John Singleton Ramsey blinked at him, surprised. "Constance?"

"Of course, Constance!" McCall's voice was a growl. "How many daughters have you, sir? Where the devil is she?"

"Only one, mercifully," Ramsey assured his guest, taking the questions in order. "And as to her whereabouts . . ." He shrugged, then glanced past McCall. "Colly, do you know where Miss Constance might have gone?"

"Not exac'ly, sah." Colly shrugged, closing the main door. "Maybe out to visit somebody. She had that Dora send a boy for her carriage; then they gone off."

"Well, I'm certain she won't be gone long, then," Ramsey assured McCall. "Come in and tell me what's —"

"When did they leave?" McCall asked the servant.

Colly frowned, thinking, then raised his eyes. "I b'lieve that was Tuesday, sah."

Ramsey gaped at Colly. "Tuesday? Do you mean to tell me my daughter has been gone for three days?"

"Yes, sah. I b'lieve that's right."

"Aha!" McCall snorted. Hands on hips, he glared at Ramsey. "I suppose it is unlikely, then, that you know where she might have taken my construction crew."

Ramsey stared at him. "Your . . . construction crew?"

"Precisely. Six carpenters, several riggers and a hoist designer. The crew I set to build my new warehouse and loading docks, at South Point. Damn it, man, I have schedules to keep, you know!"

"Schedules . . ."

"Of course, schedules! Within the month, Clinton will withdraw his bedammed redcoats and hessians from Philadelphia, and the last fleet tenders will be off the Delaware. I'm moving all my commodity operations up from Chesapeake — I already told you that — and I count on having facilities to handle my cargoes when they arrive. And now this!"

"This?" Ramsey looked blank. "What?"

"Devil take it, John, I just told you! I came up from Fairleah just this morning, expecting to find my crew putting finishing touches on my warehouse. But what did I find instead? Noth-

35

ing! Shingles lying about still in their bales and nobody at work. No one even *there* except my watchmen."

Ramsey adjusted his glasses. "And why is that, Ian?"

"Because my construction crew has been taken away," McCall growled. "Because your daughter, Miss Constance Ramsey, came to South Point and . . . and borrowed them."

"Why would she do that?" Ramsey wondered. "For that matter, *how* would she do that?"

"How does your daughter do anything she does? She just does it . . . did it . . . damn it, John, a person doesn't just borrow a man's construction crew . . . I mean, just walk in and *borrow* an entire crew, as casually as one might borrow dried apples from a neighbor! It's . . . well, one just doesn't."

"You're upset, Ian," Ramsey said sympathetically. Taking the taller man's arm, he urged him toward the study door. "Come in and sit down. We'll get to the bottom of this. Colly, bring us rum and well water, unless Squire McCall would prefer brandy to grog. Would you prefer brandy, Ian? Come, let me help you off with your coat. That's the way . . ."

One of the tastes that John Singleton Ramsey had acquired from the young man he sometimes referred to as "Constance's Irish fox," was a partiality to a beverage seldom found in the finer houses of the colonies. Commonly called "grog," the beverage was nothing more than a mix of rum and water. A specialty of low taverns and waterfront dens, it was largely unknown to the gentry . . . unless they had been associating with sailors.

Ramsey, though, had found that he enjoyed the heady drink, and was doing his part to educate his peers on the matter.

"Two-water grog," he said, carefully mixing a second round for himself and McCall. "A bit of this sometimes can cut through the confusions of life and give a man better insight with which to resolve his riddles. Drink this down, Ian. It will clear your head."

"My head is perfectly clear," McCall snorted. "It's my finances I worry about . . . and the nature of my friends. Thank you, I will have another. Do you realize, John, that having you as a friend — and your daughter, of course — has so

36

far cost me in excess of eight thousand pounds sterling, not to—"

"I thought you swore off British standards, Ian."

"I did, except when I become rattled. Your friendship has cost me a good forty thousand dollars, in less than two years. Ever since your daughter took up with that wild Irishman . . ."

"Dalton," Ramsey said mildly. "Patrick X. Dalton. He has a name, and it should be used."

"Many's the time I've heard you call him 'that wild Irishman,' John."

"That's beside the point. You were saying . . . ?"

"Yes. Just the value of that armed snow that he took from me . . ."

"We've been over that before, Ian." Ramsey shrugged, shaking his head. "You did not lose *Fury* to Patrick Dalton. You lost *Fury* to Spanish pirates. Young Dalton acquired the ship that he has by taking it away from Spanish pirates. All perfectly respectable, you know."

"But it's the same ship!" McCall's stubborn jaws clenched. "I owned that ship! I paid to build it and outfit it as a privateer! Now he has it, and he refuses to return it to me."

"Why should he, Ian? It *is* his ship, by rights."

"There's more than one would dispute that, sir. From the talk coming out of New York, there are some Royal Navy folk who'd sail a long way off course for the chance to bring Patrick Dalton under their guns. Nor can I say I blame them, considering what he did."

Ramsey pursed his lips. "The way I hear it, the young man did nothing more than arrange a court-martial for himself to clear his name of that ridiculous charge of treason."

"Oh, aye," McCall agreed. "Reclaimed his honor, he did. Then went sailing off with a ship that wore a custody flag."

"He did no such thing! That custody flag was delivered to Fleet Headquarters along with all the reports. My best spies saw it there with their own eyes."

"But the ship wasn't delivered! Dalton escaped with it!"

"Of course he did." Ramsey smiled. "Quite a piece of doing, that must have been, getting off with an undermanned snow right under the guns of five or six of the Royal Navy's best . . . and at least two of them were seventy-fours, by God! *Cornwall* and *Royal Lineage*—two of the Admiralty's finest! But I am assured he wore no custody flag when he escaped. That would hardly have been the honorable thing to do."

"Honorable!" McCall snorted. "Right this minute your *honorable* Irishman is sailing about somewhere in *my ship!*"

"His ship," Ramsey corrected, mixing more grog.

Distantly, they heard the knocker of the main door, but Ramsey ignored it. Colly would attend to it. "And as to your missing constructors, Ian, I'm sure they haven't gone far."

"They are with your daughter," McCall growled. "They could be anywhere. Patrick Henry was right, by God! 'Let us look to our domiciles for the fruits of our actions,' he said. 'Like ourselves who seek self-determination, the ladies, too, have minds of their own.' "

"I never heard him say that."

"Well, he did. *I* heard him."

"Be that as it may, Constance may be a bit of a firebrand, but she isn't likely to lead your men far astray."

"Oh? And how many of *your* men went with her when she sailed off to New York Harbor to bomb British ships?"

"That was a different matter entirely. She went there to bring back my schooner, *Faith,* that some blaggard Georgie stole from the very docks at South Point."

"Oh, of course. And did you get your schooner back, then, sir?"

"You know very well I did not! That bedammed Dalton refurbished it as a bloody warship, and beat it to death sinking a frigate. Now nothing will do for Constance but that I build another one just like it."

"Yes, I've seen your pet project on the ways at South Point. Imagine, fighting tops on a schooner! Quite unusual, I must say."

"It's Constance's doing. She insists that the new *Faith* be identical to the old one. Lot of bother and extra expense, but I expect I can find a way to turn a profit with it."

"Smuggling?" McCall cast a knowing glance at Ramsey.

"Privateering, rather. Smuggling's . . . ah, that is, *free cargo-*

ing is a flat business these days. The war and all, you know. Little enough profit to be had from an enterprise that every man jack with a jolly boat has got into. Far better fortunes to be made in privateering . . . as you of all people have demonstrated, Ian."

The expression on McCall's face changed from skepticism to a sardonic grin. "Privateering. So we may finally see the great — and uncommitted — John Singleton Ramsey . . ."

The study door opened, and Colly came in, carrying a sheaf of papers. Ramsey beckoned him to approach and glanced at the documents. "What's this?"

"Requisitions, sah. Gent'man from South Point say he needs for you to sign them."

"Very well," Ramsey sighed. He uncapped his inkwell, found a fresh quill and scrawled his signature on the requisition lists: John Singleton Ramsey, Esq.

He blotted and dusted the fresh ink, and handed the papers back to Colly, who left the study, closing the door behind him. Ramsey reached for the grog. "Now, Ian. You were saying . . . ?"

"To commission a privateer, John, you must first decide whose side of this blasted war you're on. I have never seen a man so adept at avoiding commitment."

"I'm as committed as any man!" Ramsey snapped.

"You are?" McCall's voice was bland. "One foot on either side of every fence. Do you call that committed?"

"It isn't a question of commitment, Ian, and you very well know it. It isn't always politic to go blithering about shouting 'Down with the king,' you know. I do my bit for the cause, just as you do. It's only that I dislike making a public issue of my private leanings. I — "

Abruptly, Ramsey stopped talking, turned away and stared at his inkwell. "Wait a moment, now," he said.

It was McCall's turn to look blank. "What's the matter?"

"Those documents I just signed. Those were requisitions for marine outfitting and stores. What vessel am I outfitting in this season?"

"You have your schooner, John. The new *Faith*. We were only now discussing it."

"But that schooner isn't ready for outfitting. I don't even have a finishing crew on that job . . ." he paused, then turned to look sheepishly at Ian McCall. "Something tells me," he said, "that I know where my daughter has gone . . . and where your carpenters and riggers are, as well."

Several miles away, at South Point, a brawny young man hopped down from the rear of a trundling wood-cart, tipped his tricorn hat to the driver and said, "Blessings on you for the ride, sir!" The wood-cart went on its way, and the young man replaced his hat atop a brown mane tied back in an unkempt queue, straightened his worn coat and glanced around in the evening light. In the near distance were shipyards, some backed by mould lofts, sheds, cooperages, smithies and all the other appurtenances of a place where stout ships were assembled for the sea. Beyond, the Delaware River flowed wide and dark.

It took only a moment for his eyes to lock on the sight he had come to see. In the largest of the shipyards there, a sleek, deep-keeled hull stood tall on stanchions, two towering masts rising above its silhouette—masts with wide spars cleated into position aloft, seeming to be slim wings above the tapering traceries of shrouds and ratlines, stays and tackle.

He took a deep breath which caught in his throat for a moment, then whispered, *"Faith."*

It wasn't really *Faith*, of course. Not the *Faith* he had known—the *Faith* aboard which he and a handful of other Virginians had joined with a fugitive British officer and a flock of escaped English tars on a wild night in New York Harbor . . . joined forces in a common cause, to escape from the very heart of His Majesty's White Fleet.

He shifted his gaze to the right. No, there was that *Faith* . . . or what was left of her. A shattered, broken hulk lying on the flats, mostly dismantled now and seeming only a montage of wreckage. All that was left of a proud, jaunty lady of a ship that had bested the best that was thrown against her.

And yet . . . he looked again at the proud new schooner alongside, and saw *Faith* again as he had seen her. As though the old hulk in death had given birth to her own likeness. The new schooner was every inch the ship that *Faith* had been, right down to her odd, shingled deckhouse and the startling fighting tops at her mastheads — broad platforms from which men could fire muskets . . . or American rifles.

Most of the yards and ways were still now. Though Admiral Lord Richard Howe had withdrawn his flotillas from the Delaware after General Sir William Howe — his brother — had secured the occupation of Philadelphia, there still were armed vessels that flew the Union Jack on the river, and would be as long as British troops were garrisoned in Philadelphia. And though months had passed since the last shelling of shore installations by Crown warships, there still was the chance that some vessel's captain, suspicious of colonial activity along the river, might lay down a barrage for effect.

More and more now, in this springtime of 1778, the American colonists were pledging themselves to the effort for independence. The scattered flames of uprising that Lord North and the king's ministers had thought to squelch quickly two years ago had not been stopped, but instead had become a full-scale, organized revolution — thirteen embattled colonies waging full-scale war. The embers that "Black Dick" Howe, with his brother and an expeditionary force, had thought to extinguish with a balance of force and diplomacy had become a roaring conflagration.

The colonies now had the Continental Congress, and that congress had an army and a navy. The little navy even now was at sea, carrying the war to the home islands, and the army had wintered and was yet intact at Valley Forge. Few colonists now admitted to Royalist sentiments.

Still, whether Whig or Tory, business was business, and the war was only a war. Most of the commerce of the region had been transferred across to the Chesapeake, and had gone right on being commerce.

The man grinned at the thought, wondering whether that was a sign of how *American* the English colonists had become, or of how English the Americans remained.

American. It still seemed a strange word to him. Yet he accepted it as a second definition of his own status, though he

41

still thought of himself mostly as a Virginian.

There were people aboard the new schooner, and around it. Lanterns glowed in the dusk, and the sounds of men working came clear across the vacated yards between. He headed that way.

At his approach, a lantern was raised to show him clearly, and a small, great-coated figure appeared at the railing overhead. He waved, recognizing the auburn hair which escaped around her bonnet.

"Mr. Romart?" she called down. "Is that you?"

"Aye, Miss Constance," he hailed her. "You sent word you'd need of me, so here I am. How can I be of service, miss?"

"Come aboard," she said. "There's a ladder amidships somewhere. Not a one of these men ever saw how *Faith* was rigged after Patrick modified her, and I don't know enough of ship talk to explain it to them."

Five

The winds held true for the time, and through a day and a night *Fury* herded her prize southward on a vacant sea while Dalton kept a reckoning of their course as best he could on charts that could tell him little until there were landmarks. Even for a master mariner, the reckoning of longitude required certain knowledge of where one had been the day before, and the day before that. He could judge his latitude with some certainty, and did. Twenty-three degrees north latitude, he reckoned. Very near to the Tropic of Cancer. But what lay ahead—two or three days' sail—could be most anything from Hispaniola to the Leeward Islands of the Lesser Antilles.

Holding *Fury* close by to *Pride of Falworth*, he fared the winds and reckoned currents and drift while Billy Caster stayed near at hand to note positions. Twice during the daylight hours, when the seas allowed it, *Fury* hove alongside the bark at a cable's length, and the snow's launch raised mast and sail to carry cooked food across to those manning *Pride*.

With the bark standing pace on fore courses and jibs, and making little more than three knots against a flowing current, the launch with its stubby lateen sail had no difficulty keeping pace and shuttling between the ships. Dalton watched the first transfers and a smile tugged at his cheeks. *Enjoy your dinner, Mister Duncan,* he thought. *It is being delivered by your own means.*

Just a few short weeks before, the big launch had rested

in its davits on the boat deck of His Majesty's Capital Ship *Royal Lineage*. How Charley Duncan had managed to spirit away something the size of a whaleboat, from the busy and ordered midships of a seventy-four-gun Royal Navy battler, was one of those mysteries that would endure. But then, when it came to appropriating things, Charley Duncan was indeed a resourceful young man.

On the second ferrying, Dalton turned the deck over to Cadman Wise and went across with the launch. The cargo was a feast of far-better stuff than they had been eating in recent weeks, thanks to the stores they had found in *Pride's* larders—boiled beef with onions, oat pudding with a bit of honey and a flask of sweetened lemon juice from *Pride's* stores—though with Mister Wise's ministrations in the snow's little galley, it *did* still resemble goat-and-porridge.

Snugging the launch to *Pride's* shroud stays, Dalton climbed to the gunwale of the big bark and leaned over to receive the packets as Pliny Quarterstone handed them up. When he had them all, he called, "Stay with the launch, Mister Quarterstone. We shall be returning shortly." Then he carried the feast aft to where Mister Hoop was lashing the helm.

"Something to tide you lads over until breakfast," he told the big man, setting the packets on the sterncastle coaming. He looked around. "Where is Mister Duncan?"

"Below, sir." Hoop nodded. "He's got the frogs to give him a tour, lookin' for hidey-holes an' such. Shall I fetch him?"

"Not necessary, Mister Hoop. I'll have a look, myself." He let himself down through the open hatch and into the spacious cockpit of the merchantman. The area was well-lit from skylights set in the quarterdeck, and he noticed two more kegs of rum sitting beside the ladder. Hidey-holes, he thought. Every ship had them and every sailor learned soon enough where they were . . . and what they were for.

Down another ladder, and he was in the sterncastle with its cabins and its lockers, flanking a commodious galley. Little details here and there—the bright trim on cabin hatches, polished gleam of the bulkheads, the neat logic of the galley's arrangement—told him this was a ship that had been well-mastered and tightly run . . . until it was abandoned and left to sink. It was a puzzle.

Voices ahead led him forward, and he found them amidships in the low, crowded space between pump wells and holds. The two Frenchmen were prying back paneling from a short inner bulkhead while Duncan kept up a running chatter.

"Two more here, you say?" the sandy-haired tar was asking. "Uh . . . oughtry duh, uh, ay tee-see?

"Oui. M'sieur le Capitain." one of the Frenchmen muttered. *"Autre deux. C'est le dernier."* They peeled away planking, and one of the Frenchmen reached in and lifted out a keg, panting and sweating as he worked. *"Voila, monsieur,"* he said. The other was hauling out a second keg.

"Exploring the ship, Mister Duncan?" Dalton asked casually.

Duncan turned, surprised, then grinned. "Aye, sir. These lads has got their wits about them after a nice sleep, so I had them show me around a bit."

"So I see. Have you learned anything from them?"

"Aye, sir. So far we've discovered four fresh kegs of good contraband and—"

"I mean about this ship, Mister Duncan. How it comes to be adrift in these waters, or what became of its crew?"

"Ah, no, sir, nothing like that. I don't speak French, you see, and these good lads haven't but a word or two of English. Good hands they are, though, in spite of being French. Able seamen, the both of them. They can hand, reef or steer. I had them splicing line this morning while their heads deflated, and I expect I can set them to the sheets shortly so that Mister Hoop can have a rest while I'm at helm." He motioned with a hand, and the two Frenchmen set down their burdens. "This is Francois, sir, and the one with the pigtail is Rene. They're both from Calais, originally, though they've spent time with the French navy. They signed aboard this ship at Martinique, after they were beached there by, ah, unfortunate circumstances. Rene has

45

two sisters at home, and Francois can play a dulcimer . . . except he doesn't have one right now. Lads," — he waved a hand in presentation — "this is Captain Dalton, master of *Fury*."

The Frenchmen bowed formally. *"Bonjour, M'sieur le Capitain."* Rene said. *"Comment allez-vous?"*

"Tres bien, merci." Dalton nodded. To Duncan he said, "You never cease to amaze me, Mister Duncan. You speak no French, yet you have the life history of these two, it seems."

"Sailors understand sailors, sir." Duncan shrugged.

"But nothing about this ship."

"Well, no, sir. I didn't really try to ask."

"Then ask, Mister Duncan, if you please."

"Aye, sir." He rounded on the two sailors and raised his voice. *"Attendez-vous, s'il vous plait, q'uel* . . . ah . . . ship is this?" He rapped his knuckles against a handy upright and waved his arms, indicating the entire ship. The sailors looked at each other in puzzlement, then muttered together, and Rene shrugged. *"Quel bon bateau, M'sieur le Capitain. C'est bon."*

Francois frowned, then corrected, *"Quel bateau, Rene. Quel bateau!"* To Duncan he said, *"Pri'e of Falwort', m'sieur. Il c'est un grand bateau du commerce."*

Duncan glanced around. "Nothing yet that we don't already know, sir, but we're working on it."

Dalton shrugged. "Carry on, Mister Duncan. In the meantime, please see if you can have these gentlemen carry all the rum you have found topside and hand it down to Mister Quarterstone in the launch. We'll put it with the rest, aboard *Fury.*

"Aye, sir." Duncan looked disappointed. "Exactly what I had intended, sir."

Dalton climbed to the deck and nodded at Hoop, then strolled forward, his eyes and ears testing the rigging and trim of the bark. The color of the sky on the horizon said there would be a change in the weather, but until it came, *Pride* would cruise steadily southward at three knots, with no need for sail handling. He hoped they would not need

46

more time than that to reach a shelter of some sort.

When the four kegs were aboard the launch, Dalton clapped Duncan on the shoulder. "Keep your heading, Mister Duncan. God willing, we'll find the time and place to test those casks. We are in weird waters here, and need our wits about us. But we shall find a way."

"Aye, sir. I'll count on it."

As Dalton swung over the rail, one of the Frenchmen waved. *"Au revoir, M'sieur Capitain. A bientot."*

With its stubby spar holding to the wind and Quarterstone at the tiller, the launch scudded off toward *Fury* hovering astarboard. Dalton glanced back. "Do you speak any French, Mister Quarterstone?"

"No, sir . . . well, a few words, maybe, but they wouldn't do in polite company."

"Do any of the other lads, do you think?"

"Speak French, sir? I wouldn't think so. We was mostly all raised good Englishmen, I expect, and a man's judged by the company he keeps, y'know. Myself, I wouldn't want to have anyone back home think I'd hobnobbed with frogs. It's notions like that can get a man's head busted in any decent pub."

As the launch pulled alongside *Fury* and Dalton swung up to the boarding port, Cadman Wise raised his bosun's whistle, hesitated, then let it drop on its thong, looking disappointed. Since reducing the snow's crew to the impossible few she now carried, Dalton had attempted to lighten the work load on all hands by eliminating as many of the frivolous practices as he could—including the traditional ceremony of piping the captain aboard when he had been off ship. Along with a half-hundred other niceties of maritime tradition, this was in abeyance. But the captain wondered at times whether his judgment had been sound. Rather than being relieved of nonessential duties, and appreciating it, the tars seemed almost to mourn the loss of such practices.

I need to find more seamen, he told himself for the hundredth time as Quarterstone eased the launch astern and cast a line for tow. *A few good, able seamen the like of these I have . . . and of*

47

those I have lost.

He went aft and took command of his deck, set Hannibal Leaf at the helm and sent Billy Caster to ask about as to whether anyone aboard spoke any French.

Stifling a sigh, Dalton set a night watch schedule and settled in to the dreary task of playing shepherd to a creeping bark across trackless open sea. There had been no sightings, no sign that anyone other than their own company even existed in the far, lonely reaches of water and wind that had been *Fury's* world since her escape from Admiralty custody.

Leaning against the snow's after rail as stars came out overhead, he sighed audibly, and started as a voice at his elbow said, "Sir?" He hadn't realized that Billy Caster was there beside him.

"Nothing, Mister Caster," he said. "Just thinking."

There was a pause; then the boy asked, "About Miss Constance, sir?"

In a thin voice, not looking around, Dalton said, "Yes, blast it, about Miss Constance! And about a great many other things as well."

The boy's response was apologetic. "Beg pardon, sir."

"Oh, I wasn't criticizing your inquiry, Mister Caster. Just giving vent to . . . never mind. I fear I have been moody of late, and that won't do. Make note of this, Mister Caster, for the day when you are master of your own vessel. The captain of a ship can neither afford nor tolerate distraction of any sort, and must forever guard against profitless revery. It is laxity, sir. Laxity of the worst kind, because it rests in the seat of command. It is not to be condoned or tolerated."

"Yes, sir."

"Did you find anyone who understands the French language?"

"No, sir. Not really. Mister Fisk can say a few words like 'parlie-voo grog' and 'conbienes say la june filly,' but he isn't sure what they mean. And Mister Bean can recite a verse in French, but he cautioned me never to repeat it in the presence of armed Frenchmen. A few others have heard a word

48

or two, but that's all."

Dalton sighed again. "Go and get your rest, Mister Caster. I shall just have to leave it to Mister Duncan to interrogate our Frenchmen."

"Does Mister Duncan speak French, sir?"

"Hardly a word of it. A few pleasantries, no more than I speak, myself. Good night now, Billy."

"Aye, sir."

It was in the dark of morning that Claude Mallory, in *Fury's* foretops, sighted light low on the horizon, off the starboard bow. And with first light, those high in the tops could see land—in two places. Hard astarboard, windward and abeam, a low green line stood clear in the westward distance. And dead ahead, hard down, a fainter line on the horizon stretched beyond sight off both bows. Puzzled, Dalton scanned the coastlines and decided it was time to refer to the charts. Assuming where he thought he was, what he was seeing shouldn't be here. Frowning, he stepped to *Fury's* gunwale, swung outboard on the main shrouds and swarmed aloft, his booted feet as sure on the ratlines as any tar's buckle shoes or bare toes. At the head of the lower mainmast he nodded to Ishmael Bean squatting on the trestles, and looked where the man pointed. Then he swung outward again and climbed higher, agile as a monkey on the narrow maintop stays that dwindled to nothing more than a pair of wrapped cables at the topsail spar blocks. Clinging there, more than a hundred feet above dark water rolling away from the snow's portside wales, he peered into the distance and had a suspicion of where they were. As first officer aboard His Majesty's Brig of War *Herret*—such a long time ago now, that seemed—he had seen similar coastlines before. Clinging to the spar's bullblock, his boots planted on ratlines, he scanned the horizons and the nearer waters. The waters were not as dark as they had been, and seemed clearer. A half mile away, ahead and a bit to starboard, the bark *Pride of Falworth* eased along, with no eyes in her tops. Dalton cupped his hand to shout, leaning down, "Mister Bean!"

Twenty feet below, the maintop lookout peered upward. "Aye, sir?"

"We have come upon shallows, Mister Bean. From the look of those islands we may be in the Bahamas. That could be the Caicos Banks ahead, or something very like it. Please hail the deck and have them signal Mister Duncan to ease sail and stand where he is, before he runs afoul of a reef."

"Aye, sir." As Bean hailed the deck to relay his orders, Dalton scanned the horizons once more, alert for any sign of sails. He found nothing, but paused for a moment, gazing at the low line of the nearer island, to the west. Something there had caught his eye for an instant, it seemed, but now there was nothing to see except the bright thread of beaches capped by greenery. Low haze above the land mass was just catching its first morning sunlight.

What island? A fair-sized one, it seemed, but there were hundreds of such in this part of the world. Was the place inhabited? He didn't know, but he had the impression that it was not. What he could see of the east portion of it seemed a wilderness. This had not the look of the northwest islands, but more like those to the east, fronting the Windward Passage. If so, this was far from the main islands of the group once named Baja Mar by the Spanish but now commonly called Bahama by the British subjects who had colonized them. Yet something had caught his eye off there, and there had been a light sighted hours earlier.

He shook his head, feeling the steady wind in his face, knowing that there was no way to go and explore. The island was directly to windward, miles away, and it would be a day's task to tack across the intervening distance—even if he had all of his men aboard and no second vessel to worry about.

With a final look around, he eased down from his perch and began the descent to *Fury's* deck. Far below, a man was at the snow's cathead, waving a pair of attention banners, while nearer at hand buntings climbed their halyards. He paused to gaze across at the creeping bark and saw no sign of response. Voices rose from below, and Ishmael Bean was waiting for him at the maintop.

"Deck says they don't answer our signal, sir," the tar said. "Mister Locke wonders if it would be all right if we saluted them with the bow chasers."

Dalton squinted, trying to make out figures on the bark's deck. Were they asleep over there? Duncan should have shown a response by now.

"Tell Mister Locke to salute them," he said. "Then lower and repeat the stand-to signal."

"Aye, sir." As Dalton started down the mainshrouds, Bean's voice directly above him was almost deafening. "Captain says salute them, deck! Bow chasers, then lower and repeat th' stand-to! Captain's on his way down!"

"Aye, tops!" the answer drifted up from below, and men scurried forward along *Fury*'s fighting deck to man the pair of long cannons in her nose. Ethan Crosby and Floyd Pugh were followed by others to lend a hand with the run-in and run-out of the guns.

Crosby arrived at his gun first and knelt to the quoins.

"Don't become overly enthusiastic and try to hole him, Mister Crosby," Dalton muttered to himself. "We simply want to get his attention."

Almost as though he had heard the thought, Crosby stood away from the chaser's elevating mechanism and bent to the lines.

As Dalton swung to the gunwale and stepped down to the deck, the first of the nose guns thundered, and a cloud of white smoke drifted off eastward, hanging above the water like a small thunderhead. A moment later the second gun fired, and Dalton paused to watch as a pair of iron balls threw geysers of water a few cable lengths out from the snow's climbing bowsprit.

Rings rattled above as the signal buntings dropped, then rose again on their halyards.

From aloft came a call, "On deck!"

Dalton cupped his hands. "Aye, tops?"

"We have his attention now, sir. He's showing color at his sternpost."

Dalton headed for the quarterdeck. "Mister Locke, add to our signal, please. Tell him to drop anchor and stand where he is. We'll hull that bark on a reef if we try to take it through these passes without top lookouts."

Six

"My apologies again, sir." Charley Duncan scuffed his foot on *Fury*'s decking as the snow got under way with all hands at station. He glanced beyond the stern features of his captain, at the big bark resting at anchor, receding now behind the rejuvenated snow. No longer burdened — for the moment — with playing shepherd for an under-sailed prize, *Fury* had put on more sail and was lifting her jaunty nose now as she cut spray, heading for the thread of coastline to the south.

"I was having a chat with the Frenchies," Duncan explained, "tryin' to find out about their ship and all, as you asked. But it turned out that Mister Hoop had got himself a'dangle between the helm's kingpin and the footrope on the spanker boom, and didn't have the time to keep an eye out astern. I take full responsibility, sir."

A'dangle between the helm and the spanker boom? Dalton considered it and decided he would like to have seen that. Of all the seamen he had known, only Mister Hoop might have had the brute strength to steer a bark by manhandling both the spanker and the wheel . . . but even for him, keeping his feet on the deck would have been difficult should a gust of wind take the spanker while its sheet lines were loose. "Consider it forgotten, Mister Duncan," he said now, his eyes roving the workings of his ship where a dozen men were doing the work of twenty. "Did you learn anything?"

"Aye, sir. I learned to keep a better eye on my escort when I —"

"I mean about the bark, Mister Duncan. Did you learn anything from the Frenchmen?"

"Oh. Aye, sir, I think so, though it seems a bit garbled. I take it they were crew on the bark, sir. Them and a baker's dozen-odd others—I can't get at whether there was eighteen or sixteen all together—was beached at Martinique and this ship come along and signed them on. The mate as took their marks was a M'sieur . . . ah, a *Mister* Leech. I haven't found out who the captain was, but it seems like he was a cold, gray man. Y'know, sir, I believe that Francois has the soul of a poet, the way he can describe things so you don't even have to know what he's sayin' to kind of understand. Did I tell you that he can play the dulcimer . . . ?"

"Mister Duncan!"

"Aye, sir?"

"About the ship, please. What happened?"

"Oh. Well, that's an odd thing, sir. They were chased by pirates, and run to ground at a little island somewhere; then the pirates attacked, and a lot of men in boats put out from the little island—*petite ile,* they called it, but they sort of like drew me a picture, y'see—and boarded the ship . . ."

"I saw no signs of a struggle aboard that bark."

"It wasn't the bark that was boarded, sir. It was the pirates' ship that was boarded. There was a lot of fighting; then they started knocking people in the head and throwing them over . . ."

"On the pirate ship?"

"Aye, sir, I think so. At first, it seems like that's what was going on. But then everybody came back to the bark and rounded up all the new marks and started braining them, just the way they had done on the pirate ship."

"Who was doing that?" Dalton scowled, trying to make sense of it. "The pirates?"

"Doesn't seem that way, sir. Seems like it was the bark's crew—the regular crew, and some others that the French gentlemen hadn't had the honor of meeting—that was doing the head knocking. It all gets a little confusing in French, don't you see."

54

"I can certainly see how it might." Dalton nodded. "What happened then?"

"Well, sir, our two—Francois and Rene—they managed to slip off and hide in the chain locker; and when they finally came out there wasn't anybody on board except them, and no island or other vessel in sight, and the bark was beginning to list from being scuttled. They cut open a cotton bale and plugged the leak the best way they could; then they went and found some rum and got drunk."

"And how long was the ship adrift before we came across it?"

"They don't seem to have any idea, sir. From the amount of rum they put away, my guess would be at least a week . . . though that's assuming they were God-fearing Englishmen, sir. I don't rightly know the capacities of Frenchmen, where rum's concerned."

Dalton turned to look back at the bark growing distant now astern. He had left it manned by Mister Hoop, Abel Ball in the tops, and the cheerful Frenchmen—who now, it seemed, considered themselves to be part of his crew. Every empty water cask from both ships now rested on the snow's decks, and it was Dalton's intention to have a look at the coastline southward. If he could manage a close look at it, he might find it on his charts and verify where they were. In any event, he wanted to try to get his bearings, take on water if there was water to be had, then return to the bark's anchorage to consider his next course. He estimated twelve miles to the shore ahead. If the weather held, he could be there and back before sundown, and the anchored bark would never be entirely out of sight.

In waters that ran to shoals and shallows, and sported reefs that could tear the guts from an unwary ship, Dalton was navigating by what Senior Captain Peter Selkirk of His Majesty's Royal Navy—the man who was Patrick Dalton's teacher in his days as midshipman—called "thump and pray passage." It meant make good sail, put spotters in the tops and at the spreaders where the jib boom thrust forward of the bowsprit, "thump" constantly for depth changes and pray that the ship did not run into anything in the process of passage.

Selkirk had made it very clear to all of his charges that he did not approve — not in the slightest — of such use of a vessel.

In essence, Dalton agreed. If a man must put a ship at jeopardy, there were far more honorable ways of doing it. But at times, such as now in strange waters with a defenseless prize vessel waiting *Fury's* return and barely enough hours of daylight remaining for the task at hand, there wasn't much choice.

"Keep a sharp eye on Mister Wise yonder, Mister Locke," he reminded his helmsman. "Steer by his signal."

Cadman Wise, relieved again from galley duty for need of a bosun, stood amidships forward of *Fury's* mainmast, his arms spread like soaring wings, ready to relay steering orders to the quarterdeck as he listened to the chant of Purdy Fisk sounding depths, and to the calls of Ishmael Bean on the crosstrees and Claude Mallory in the foretop, both of them peering into the waters ahead for signs of shoaling. All the rest aboard except Dalton and his clerk stood by sheet lines ready to handle sail at the captain's command.

They had sailed in this manner before — at least some of them had — and Dalton had learned to trust their competence just as they trusted his judgment in choosing to navigate so in such waters. Still, there were worried looks each time they saw — or the foretop lookout saw — wreckage of some unfortunate vessel broken on the shallow reefs that bounded the narrow fairway of their course. By the time the shoreline ahead was in clear view, they had passed three such wrecks, and Dalton wondered how many more such there were that they didn't see.

Billy Caster voiced the same thought. "So many," the boy breathed, peering over the portside rail at the broken hulk of an old ship, clearly visible a hundred yards away, bits of its hull protruding from the water like black fangs.

"Rocks and reefs, Mister Caster." Dalton glanced at the wreckage and turned back toward the land ahead. "And more than bad luck, I'd warrant. These were trade lanes before the recent hostilities, and in waters like these I'm certain there were wreckers at work. Wreckers and who knows what else. These are weird waters. Weird waters indeed."

"Wreckers, sir?"

"The oldest form of piracy at sea." Dalton nodded. "Find a treacherous sea like this, then set fires or signal flares to lure passing ships onto the rocks. Many a good ship has fallen to wreckers."

The boy looked at him, wide-eyed. "Do they still do that, sir?"

Dalton shrugged. "Given the opportunity for a fast profit, there are always some willing to act on it. Trade lanes may shift from time to time, but not human nature."

From the foretop, Claude Mallory's voice called, "On deck!" Amidships, Cadman Wise responded, "Aye, tops!"

"Shoaling, deck! Dead ahead! The reefs close in there!"

"Whereaway?"

"Six cables or about!"

At the port bow, Purdy Fisk's soundings increased their cadence as he flung and read his sounding line. "An' a quarter, four! . . . An' a quarter, four! . . . By the mark, four! . . . By the mark, four! . . . An' three quarters, three! . . ."

"Shoaling," Dalton muttered, striding to the quarterrail. He stood spread-legged beside the bell-arch, his hands clasped behind him.

Far ahead, out on the spreader stays, Ishmael Bean raised his right arm. He had the reefs in sight. Immediately Cadman Wise relayed the signal, turning his right arm up at the elbow as though pointing to the sky. Behind Dalton, Victory Locke eased the wheel to port . . . a point, and then another when Wise held the signal position.

Out on the spreaders, Bean raised his left arm and touched his hands above his head. Instantly Cadman Wise lowered his arms and turned. "Sir," he shouted, "no clear passage!"

At the bow, the sounding chant went on. "An' a half, three! . . . An' a half, three! . . . An' a quarter . . ."

Dalton cupped his hands. "Luff the sheets, please, Mister Wise!"

"Aye, sir! Hands a'sheet, loose your lines!"

"Ease the spanker!" Dalton said, realizing even as he shouted that the only one available on the quarterdeck to cast loose and ease off big boom's sheet lines was Charley Duncan. As Duncan reached the starboard blocks, Dalton hurried to those aport. Two pairs of strong hands working in unison hove the big drive sail aport, easing it slowly alee. *Fury* settled into the swells and stood, dead in the water except for drift.

Duncan secured his sheet line and glanced across. "Chancy, that," he noted.

Dalton cupped his hands and raised his head. "Foretop ahoy!"

From more than two hundred feet ahead and above, Claude Mallory's voice drifted down. "Aye, sir?"

"Read our drift, Mister Mallory, if you please! What's aport?"

There was a pause, then, "Clear for a bit, sir, then we'll hit shoals!"

"Can you see a break in the reef ahead?"

"No, sir! From here it looks as though we're in a pocket!"

Dalton swore under his breath. So much for running along the shoreline yonder and having a look at it from the ship. The island—if such it was—was still nearly three miles away. He turned. "Mister Duncan, take four hands and man the launch, please. Take as many casks as you can, and go have a look at that land yonder. Observe what you can of it, quickly, and bring back water if you can find some. I shall drop a kedge and hold here as long as I can."

"Aye, sir." Duncan hurried to the quarterrail. "Misters Fisk, Quarterstone, Nelson and . . . ah . . . Leaf! Aft for shore patrol! Haul the launch alongside!"

Dalton turned to Billy Caster. "Break out five of the American rifles, if you please, Mister Caster. With powder and ball."

"Aye, sir." The clerk headed below.

"On deck!"

Amidships, Cadman Wise took the call. "Aye, tops?"

"We seem to be in a current, deck! We're drifting at a good clip, an' those shoals are comin' up!"

Dalton turned to the port rail and peered over. The water beneath *Fury's* keel, though still some twenty feet deep, was as clear as morning sky, and each detail of the bottom stood clear. Schools of bright fish played here and there above a bottom that looked like craggy peaks and valleys, with great stands of coral spread among them. Eerie fans and feathers waved in the current. The school of fish just below exploded off in all directions as something large and dark disturbed them.

"I may not be able to stand here, Mister Duncan," he said. "Yon is no bottom for a kedge. I'll need way."

"Aye, sir." Duncan squared his shoulders and tried a grin that failed to show much cheer. "You'll be somewhere about, though, I warrant."

"We shall do our best, Mister Duncan. Good luck to you."

"Aye, sir."

At the starboard gunwales, casks were being lowered overside to the launch. Duncan headed that way, pausing to relieve Billy Caster of an armload of rifles as the boy struggled through the companion hatch with them.

British sailors, Dalton thought. *And American rifles. We are what we are and we use what we have.* He cupped his hands. "Mister Wise, stand by to make sail. Jib and jigger, and keep your lookouts in place. When the launch casts off, bring us through the wind for a port tack, please."

"Aye, sir. Are we going back to deep water?"

"We are looking for a place where we can wait without the seabed rising up to scuttle us, Mister Wise."

"Aye, sir. Hands a'deck, stand by th' sheets, jib an' jigger! Spotters look alive!"

Dalton removed his coat, rolled up his sleeves and headed for the waist pinrails where the spencer sail's sheets were secured. He saw Billy Caster rolling up his own sleeves and nodded. "Mister Caster!"

"Aye, sir?"

"Can you ride a jibtop, Mister Caster?"

"Aye, sir," the boy called. "I can try."

"Then, go forward please, Mister Caster, and relieve Mister Bean for sail handling."

"Aye, sir!" Tense with excitement, the boy hurried off toward *Fury's* jutting stem. Never before had he ridden the spars thirty feet ahead of a ship's bow, but he had watched others read the waters from there and was sure he could manage it.

"Pray don't fall, Mister Caster," Dalton muttered under his breath. "I'm not sure I could ever forgive myself."

Fury's entire complement now was eight. With one at the helm, one out on spreaders and one in the foretop, that left five to handle the sails and the working deck. *Fury* now could not afford the luxury of captains and clerks. It would be all that all of them could do just to keep the ship in the narrows between shoals.

"On deck!"

Dalton peered upward. "Aye, tops?"

"That island, sir . . . the one to the west, that we saw . . . there is something going on over there, sir."

"What do you see, Mister Mallory?"

"Can't rightly say, sir! Too far away! But I think I see boats in the water there. Some of them have sails!"

"Very well, Mister Mallory. Keep a sharp eye out."

Dalton shook his head, setting his shoulders to the controlling of sheet lines. Whatever was occurring at the island to windward would just have to occur. There was absolutely nothing that *Fury* could do about it now, whatever it was.

Looking like a little barge from the ranked water casks lining its length, moving cautiously on four sweeps while Charley Duncan hung over the bow and peered into the teeth of reefs just below, the launch made its way south and then west, seeking an opening for its five feet of keel. *More than a clear fathom,* Duncan kept telling himself, *for when we come back we shall be carrying water . . . I hope.* They had skirted three hundred yards of reefline before he found the opening he wanted, and he marked it with a float—a rope with a twelve-pound cannon ball at one end and an empty rum keg at the other.

Carefully, then, he guided the launch through surging breakers and into clear water beyond. Satisfied, he had his shore party rest the sweeps and raise the boat's lateen sail. With Purdy Fisk at the tiller, the launch took fair wind and headed for shore.

Duncan wiped sweat from his forehead. "Break out the rifles, lads," he said. "Let's have proper loads and dry pans when we set foot on that beach, for we have no idea who might be there to welcome us."

He glanced back the way they had come. In the sunny distance, *Fury* crept northward, away from them, unsheeted sails dangling from her high yards and only her jibs, spencer and spanker taking wind.

Purdy Fisk was looking back, too. "By my count," he said, "there's not but eight souls on the snow's deck now. I wonder that they can handle her at all."

Duncan didn't respond, but he was thinking the same thing. Off there, creeping on minimal canvas, was a proud, fighting warship . . . or a ship that should have been such. Eighteen guns she carried. Eighteen guns, and all the sail a ship of her size might want. Thirteen standard sails — four square sails on each of her two great masts, plus three staysails at her stem, the fore-and-aft spencer in her waist and the big spanker on its own jack-mast. And sails beyond that, should she need them. With a proper crew, and the need to fly, the snow could increase her sails by fifteen and her total canvas by two-thirds . . . studding sails, a gafftop amidships and a ring-tail on the driver, and *Fury* could baffle most pursuit.

But only with proper crew. Seven men and a boy could do no more than make her creep.

Duncan turned away. There was something very melancholy in the sight of the proud, jaunty ship reduced to a scow by lack of manpower.

With clear water under her keel, the launch cut a nice vee of wake as it headed for the land that they could now see was a tight-packed group of islands presenting a long, sand-beach coastline from east to west with only narrow breaks where channels separated the lands.

Closer at hand, the shoreline was a vision of white beaches backed by lush, green forest rising slightly into the distance. As they neared the beach, Duncan had Fisk steer aport. Before making landfall, he wanted to see at least a mile or so of the place. For a time the launch sailed eastward, running parallel to the sandy beach a hundred yards away. A haze lying on the wind beyond the low rise of the forest puzzled Duncan. Smoke? Or simply a mist rising into the wind to be swept away?

"I believe we can go ashore now, Mister Fisk," he decided.

"Observe as much as you can," he told those with him, turning. "Captain Dalton will want a thorough report."

Finian Nelson was shading his eyes, peering almost directly ahead as the launch veered toward the beach. "What I'm observing right now, Mister Duncan," he said, "is those people who are observing us. I wouldn't say they look too friendly, would you?"

"What people?" Duncan jerked around, squinting. Directly ahead, a dozen or so men had appeared among the nearer trees. They were working at something, and as they turned, Duncan could see what it was. A brass cannon stood there, mounted on carriage wheels.

Duncan raised his arm, started to wave a cheery greeting, and one of the men ashore lowered a smoking fuse to the old weapon's vent. A thick cloud of white smoke billowed outward, and the gun's roar was accompanied by a resounding splash as an iron ball sheeted water across the launch, dousing everyone aboard.

"What th' bloody 'ell!" Duncan sputtered, his cheeks going livid. "Out sweeps!" he roared. "Rifles and cutlasses at the ready . . . row!"

Above the beach, the men were working furiously to reload the old cannon. They were a ragged and motley bunch, some wearing no more than stained shreds here and there. The launch arrowed toward them, driven by its lateen sail and four sets of powerful shoulders. In its bow, Charley Duncan stood upright, rifle in one hand and cutlass in the other. Dripping wet, outraged and ready for a fight, he stood poised, waiting for the scrape of sand on the launch's keel.

Seven

More than two miles away, aboard *Fury,* Claude Mallory glanced aft in time to see the smoke on the shore behind them. "On deck!" he shouted.

"Aye, tops?"

"Sir, there's been a cannon fired yonder where the launch went. I see the smoke!"

"Can you see who fired it?"

"Not rightly, sir. Maybe there are people ashore there."

Fury slid past a wreck, Victory Locke spinning the helm grimly as he read channel signals from amidships. He reversed the spin, and the snow slithered to the starboard, edging within a cable's length of a submerged reef that rippled the waves above it. "Like tryin' to thread a needle in th' blinkin' dark," he muttered.

"How far to blue water, tops?" Dalton called from the port sheets.

"Channel widens a bit just ahead, sir! Maybe another mile to the clear!"

"Let's get some decent water around us," Dalton called to Cadman Wise, "then we'll lay to and have a look."

"Aye, sir."

Fury crept past another wrecked hulk, and Billy Caster, perched forward on the jib cap, his knees gripping the spreader yards, turned to shout over his shoulder, "The channel is widening, sir! Clear water both sides and ahead."

"Tops?" Dalton called.

Mallory scanned, then shouted, "Th' lad is right, sir. We're comin' up clear in just a bit."

With a sigh, Dalton tightened the trim on the sheeting line, securing it to a belaying pin at the fife rail. "Trim and secure, please, Mister Wise," he said. "When we have open water, stand to the wind for reckoning. I'm going aloft."

"Aye, sir."

Going aft, Dalton ducked through the companion hatch and reappeared a moment later with his telescoping spyglass. He pulled on his coat and dropped the glass into a tail pocket. He strode to the gunwales, swung into the shrouds, then hesitated, turning toward the helm. "Did you hear the order, Mister Locke?"

"Aye, sir, that I did."

"At Mister Wise's signal, then."

"Aye, sir. Stand down at the signal."

Dalton headed aloft. At the mainmast's head he swung over the balustrade onto the snow's wide trestletrees. Capping both the lower mainmast and the spanker's jack-mast, the trestletrees here were a substantial platform of heavy timbers secured with iron collars and framing. Nearly thirty feet ahead of him, and a trifle below, Claude Mallory grinned and waved in the foretop. "Come up for a look aft, sir? There was *something* goin' on back there, but I can't see much now."

"I brought up a glass," Dalton said. He pulled the telescope from his tail pocket, extended it and leaned against the base of the main topmast to brace himself. Even with the glass, the shoreline aft was a long way off. He scanned along it slowly, then found the launch in its view. The boat stood empty, drawn partway up a sand beach. He searched around it, and saw no one. Just above the launch, though, at the edge of the forest, something bright glinted in the sun.

A cannon? He couldn't be sure, but if Mallory said he had seen gunsmoke, then that was what he saw.

He turned. "Did you see the people who fired the cannon, Mister Mallory?"

"I might have, sir. Too far to be sure, but there was movement yonder, like people just where th' green starts. Then

Mister Duncan put the launch ashore, and everybody just sort of disappeared into the woods."

Dalton started to lower the glass, then squinted through it. Just atop the distant beach, where brass glinted in the sunlight, he saw something else. A tiny figure separated itself from the dark forest and stepped into sun . . . and waved.

It was Duncan. Even at this distance, he knew the sandy-haired sailor. The figure continued to wave, now with both arms, as though signalling. But what? Dalton squinted, peered through the glass, and gave up. Duncan was trying to tell him something, but he had no idea what it was.

The maintop seemed to shiver and lean, and Dalton clung to a line as the mast below him pitched to starboard . . . not a severe lean, but enough so that the deck far below seemed to slide aside and what was directly beneath him was water. Sedately, *Fury* eased her prow to port, coming into the wind, and he heard the slap of slacking canvas as the ship came dead in the water. He looked down and cupped a hand to his mouth. "Ahoy the helm!"

Victory Locke straightened from lashing the helm and looked up. "Aye, sir?"

"Are you secured now, Mister Locke?"

"Aye, sir. Rudder's amidships."

"Then, break out the buntings, please, and run up a signal. Say, 'Message not understood.' "

"Aye, sir. Comin' up."

Moments passed; then the signal lanyard rattled in its blocks, and buntings rose from the deck, fluttering in the wind. Dalton raised his glass again. Duncan was still visible on the beach, not waving now. For a moment he stood; then he disappeared into the brush. Several minutes crept by before he reappeared, with others trailing behind him. Dalton counted them idly. Three . . . four . . . five . . . six. He caught his breath and squinted. A dozen tiny figures were there now, and more coming behind them . . . carrying things, pulling things. . . . Dalton swore under his breath. What was going on over there?

"Captain . . ."

Dalton steadied himself and tried to see details.

65

"Ah, Captain, sir . . ."

He waved his free hand in dismissal, trying to make sense of the view in his glass.

"Captain Dalton! Sir!"

He lowered the glass and turned. "Mister Mallory, I am trying to—"

"Aye, sir, but you'd best have a look the other direction, as well."

Frowning, Dalton shaded his eyes and looked northward. In the distance stood the bark *Pride of Falworth*, resting at anchor as he had left it. Then something else caught his eye, and he looked to the left, then raised his glass to peer through it. Coming out from the windward island, the one to the west, were boats. Boats of all sorts, it seemed, and all making for *Pride*.

Dalton's roar of exasperation brought the foretopman to abrupt and vertical attention on his crosstrees. "Sir?"

"Never mind, Mister Mallory. I was just—Mister Mallory, please don't stand unsupported at the foretop. You could fall."

"Aye, sir." Mallory grabbed a tops'l shroud and swung there for a moment, regaining the balance he had just lost. "I'm sorry, sir, but I didn't catch exactly what you said."

"I swore an oath, Mister Mallory. It was a very profound oath, one of the best I know. I swore it because I have left that prize vessel helpless out there, assuming the island yonder to be uninhabited; and now it seems it is not, and I am as helpless to defend those lads at the moment as they are to defend themselves."

Mallory gazed across at him, real admiration on his homely face. "You swore all that, sir?"

"In a word, yes." He hitched himself around the maintop couplings and raised his glass again, staring southward. There seemed a truly remarkable number of people over there now. Thirty—forty—perhaps even more. They were too far away to count, but what they were doing was even more amazing. Charley Duncan stood apart from the rest, again waving his arms enthusiastically. A few others—those would be the launch crew—were bunched to one side, and beyond them stretched a long, single-file line of men, all—he

66

could think of no other explanation — all *dancing.*

Dalton stared through his glass, entranced. Like players on a stage, the figures on the beach moved this way and that in perfect synchronization. They stepped to the right, then bent and backed leftward, their arms out in exaggerated pantomime. Like clockwork figures performing on a music box, he thought. Or like — his brow lifted — like a pantomime of deck hands playing anchor line to the pawls of a capstan. Blinking, he shifted the glass, and saw what he had expected to see. To one side of the miming line, a smaller group walked around and around in a tight circle, their arms held stiffly out ahead of them.

There on the distant beach, under a tropical sun, men gestured in pantomime as though on a theater stage. And what they mimed was the raising of an anchor.

They were sailors!

Dalton almost dropped his glass getting it closed and into his tail pocket. He swung down from the trestletrees, planted his boots in ratlines and shouted, "Mister Wise!"

"Aye, sir?"

"Back to the sheets, Mister Wise! Mister Locke to the helm, please! Let's have some way for the rudder, then smart about for starboard tack by spanker, jigger and jib. Spotters in place, and look alive. We are going back for Mister Duncan."

Fury made better time now, with experience of the shoals at helm and lookout, and the lateened launch drove out to meet her well outside the reef pocket.

Without waiting for the boat to be snugged alongside, Charley Duncan scrambled over the gunwales and snapped a grinning salute at his captain. "Sir, I've complemented the crew, by your leave," he said.

Dalton returned the salute, hardly realizing that he had done so. "Complemented, Mister Duncan? Do you mean you have signed on additional hands?"

"Not exactly 'signed on,' sir. I told the lads you'd have to approve, but I did sort of promise as many berths as we could ship. They're a fine, raw bunch of lads, sir. Full of spirit. They tried to sink us at first sight, then set up fortification abaft the beach and held us off for the better part of an hour before we managed to thump a number of them into havin' better sense. We do need sailors, sir, and these lads can hand, reef and steer to a man, all except Mister Claremore who hasn't but one arm . . . and he can cook."

Dalton raised a speculative brow, peering at the beach beyond the reef-ringed shallows. There were quite a few people over there, loading casks and packets aboard several makeshift rafts.

Duncan pressed on, excitedly. "Those are our water casks, sir. Once the hostilities were ended, the lads on the island were happy to haul and fill them for us, just on the chance of a berth and passage to civilization."

"I see," Dalton said. "Well, it may be our good fortune at that. We could use a few more hands, of course. Ah, how many did you recruit, Mister Duncan?"

"Sixty-seven, sir."

"Sixty-seven?"

"Aye, sir. It might have been more, but the rest decided to stay on where they are. They've taken a liking to the place, you might say. One way or another."

"Mister Duncan, who are those people and how do they come to be here?"

"Crew of the trader *Tyber*, sir. British registry, general cargo. They were wrecked on rocks, then marooned when their officers took all the boats and set out for Hispaniola. They never came back. That was more than a year ago, as best these lads can tell. Since then, they've been livin' off the land and standin' off pirates and Whigs and Frenchmen. At least, that's who they expect the people on the island northwest probably are."

"Remarkable." Dalton shook his head.

"Aye, sir. We all had a nice chat after we'd finished fighting one another. Can we sign them on, sir?"

"I'll approve the cook if he can cook," Dalton decided. "I shall inspect the rest after they have delivered our water casks."

"Aye, sir." Duncan grinned, snapped another salute and headed for the launch to lead the rafts through the reefwall.

"Sixty-seven?" Dalton muttered. "Mister Caster!"

68

"Aye, sir?" the boy responded, almost at his elbow.

"Oh, there you are, Mister Caster. You heard all that, I presume?"

"Aye, sir. Sixty-seven recruits, sir. Shall I bring up the roster and log for swearing them aboard?"

"In a bit, Mister Caster. Have you identified these islands on the chart?"

"I think so, sir. There is a grouping like this north of Hispaniola, though I'm confused at the names. In one reference they're called the Caicos Islands, but elsewhere they seem to be called Providenciales. I imagine that's Spanish."

"I'll have a look when there's time." Dalton nodded. "Have you identified the island northwest, that we passed coming in?"

"I think so, sir. There is such an island on the charts. It's called Mayaguana. It is listed as uninhabited, the same as these."

"Listings can be confusing, Mister Caster. Especially in troubled times."

"Aye, sir."

"Sixty-seven," Dalton muttered. "And fifteen is eighty-two. Famine to feast, it seems. Bring up the company roster and logs, Mister Caster. We likely will be expanding our company presently."

"Aye, sir. Ah, what articles will you read them, sir? We have no flag, do we?"

Dalton thought it over. A ship's company was bound by the vessel's articles to the law of a land, but at present *Fury* had no allegiance. He shrugged. "The Articles of War, Mister Caster, the one same discipline as remains to all the rest of us, from our own various swearings-in. I have no doubt of the men who have sailed with me heretofore. The loyalty of our *Furies* is beyond question. But our new hands will have had no such experience. A code of behavior must be required, and the Articles of War require no nationality."

It was a strange-looking complement that came aboard *Fury*, following the water casks and such other stores as Charley Duncan's shore party had liberated. By fives and tens as they boarded, Dalton questioned them and noted the motley,

69

threadbare attire, the unkempt hair and beards, the sun-dark features of men long marooned in the tropics. They were a mix of seafarers of their time, though a fair number looked to have sailed at one time or another on king's ships.

Some among them admitted readily to past sins, crimes and breaches of conduct, and Dalton could find little fault with their admissions. Few indeed were the sailors of the time who had not committed such, and worse — mayhem, thievery, fornication and cheerful disrespect for authority were more the rule than the exception. Yet he noticed an absence of guilt — or at least admitted guilt — of a number of more serious breaches of conduct. Not a man of them, it seemed, had ever so much as carried a lighted candle into a ship's hold, much less assaulted an officer, been party to a mutiny or participated in sabotage or the keeping of secrets.

After several group interviews, he took Duncan aside and mentioned this phenomenon.

Duncan shrugged and grinned. "Well, sir, we did a bit of inquiring when we were ashore. You might say we sort of shook out the chaff, as it were."

"I see. Then, those who decided to remain here and not join us . . . ?"

"Aye, sir. Rummy lot, mostly. Several had done mutiny, or simple murder. And then, there were a few that may have been stranded a bit too long. They had some funny habits, sir."

"How did you ascertain such guilts, Mister Duncan?"

"How did we what, sir?"

"How did you persuade them to tell you what their crimes were?"

"Oh. Well, sir, since we had the honor of *Fury* to consider, and yourself not available to guide us, we just made do."

"Obviously," Dalton said. "But how?"

"We picked out a dozen of 'em and had them kneel down. Then one by one we stuck a rifle barrel in their mouths and offered them a choice between swearing allegiance to us or sampling the grace of God. Naturally, they all decided to be on our side. After that, it was just a matter of them telling us all there was to know about each of the rest. There aren't many secrets when men have been marooned for a year in hostile waters."

"Selection by sworn jury," Dalton said. "Mister Duncan, sometimes I wonder if the Admiralty itself might not benefit by seeking out your wisdoms."

"I don't know, sir," Duncan admitted. "They never asked me for any of those."

Dalton continued his interviews. When he had finished he assembled the entire enlistment on *Fury's* gundeck and read them the Articles of War as the Articles of Service aboard *Fury*. Some of them—those with Royal Navy service—had heard the articles before. Most of them, he guessed, had not, judging by the frightened eyes and creeping pallor of many among them as he recited the dread document with its ominous words, its strict and thorough listing of acceptable and unacceptable behaviors, and its blunt and dreadful descriptions of the dire punishments that were sure to befall any transgressor.

He recited the articles in full, made certain that every man understood them, then accepted their solemn oaths to abide by them and by his orders as captain. With the entire group duly sworn, he set Billy Caster to enter their names into ship's records and get their marks.

A dozen or so that he judged to be capable sailors he took aside from the line and set to deck and top duties. Among these were two or three that he made mental note to watch closely, as possible troublemakers. The rest he gave over to the charge of his first officer.

"Drill them to this deck and these riggings," he ordered Charley Duncan. "Before we recontact our prize bark, I shall require an assessment of each man, as able seaman or ordinary seaman, and a brief of any certain skills each might have. As an example, see whether any of them speak French."

"Aye, sir," Duncan said happily. He turned to his charges and bellowed, " 'Oy now, you beggars! Form up in companies amidships fore an' main! Count off by sixes for going aloft, manning the capstan, stowing the casks, sheeting and trimming, cable-tiers drill and batten-down drill! To places by the count! Look lively and keep yourselves out of the way of the sailing crew, for the captain's got a ship to handle while you lubbers learn the ropes!"

Like a marine drill sergeant with recruits, he marched them off amidships while the others on deck gazed after them.

"Mister Duncan might have made an officer had he mended his ways," Cadman Wise muttered to Victory Locke. "He has the very soul of a tyrant."

"Brings to mind a bosun's mate aboard the old *Clemency* that I sailed on my first up." Abel Ball nodded. "Sad case, that. Some of the fo'c'sle lads knocked the bastard in the head and fed him to the fishes."

Dalton strode to the quarterdeck and turned at the rail. "Stand by helm," he ordered. "Mister Wise, hands a'deck to stations, stand by to make sail. Tops aloft, please. Mister Fisk, do the honors at the jibcap. Stand by to make sail and trim for port tack. At my order, please, Mister Wise."

He looked around him, satisfaction in his dark eyes. Where before had been a scant handful to do the work of many, now *Fury* was crowded with men. The decks that had seemed so forlorn now teemed with bustling humanity.

"Have you learned the channel, Mister Locke?"

"Aye, sir. By signal, sir, I can steer it."

"Very well, then. Steer it we shall. Make sail, please, Mister Wise. Jibs alee. Courses and tops. Sheet home!"

The bosun's pipe wailed, and *Fury* seemed to sprout sails even as her nose came across the wind. More sails than she had worn since her escape from custody in the north Atlantic. Powerfully, gracefully she turned and leaned, trimming to the wind while rippling waters along her hull rose in pitch to the thrum of a rigged vessel taking the wind.

"By the signal and by the mark, helm," Dalton said. "Take us to where there's good water, and we'll see how it feels to have wings again."

Fury gained way and headed for the open sea while aromas of cooking drifted up the companionway from the galley and larders where one-armed Nathan Claremore, once second-watch cook for the merchantman *Tyber*, banged and rattled about, converting stores from the bark *Pride of Falworth* into a meal for ninety or so aboard the snow *Fury*.

Eight

Pride of Falworth had old, nine-pound stem and stern guns, and a brace of small carronades at each beam. The bark had not been designed or intended to fight, but no vessel of her time put to sea without at least a bit of a sting for the occasional social encounter. From a masthead, Pliny Quarterstone watched the flotilla of boats put out from the large island to windward, and when it became clear that the boats were heading for *Pride,* he called down, "Mister Hoop, we will have callers! Do you think we should load some guns?"

Hoop considered this, his big face writhing at his efforts of thought, then shouted, "I expect that's what Captain would want done if he was here."

"Can you manage that, Mister Hoop, or do you want me to come down?"

"You'd best stay aloft and keep an eye on those people," Hoop decided. "I've got these frogs here; maybe they can help." He strode forward to where the two Frenchmen sat cross-legged, patching canvas. "I'll need you lads to help me run in some guns for loading," he said.

They looked up blankly. *"Excuses-moi, nous ne parlez pas bien anglais, M'sieur 'Oop."* one of them explained. *"Parlez-vous francais? Peut-etre un petit?"*

Hoop scowled at them, raised his voice and said, slowly, "You pair is to lend a hand at loadin' the guns!"

Still they only stared at him.

With a rumbling curse, he strode to the nearest beam gun and pointed at it. "Gun!" he explained.

73

"Gun," they repeated in unison.

"Aye, now we're makin' progress," Hoop beamed. "Gun . . . you see?"

They got to their feet and came closer, listening intently. "Gun . . . hew see?" they repeated.

"Gun!" he shouted.

"Gun!" they shouted in unison.

Quarterstone's jeering voice came from above. "You lads sound like true repentance at a Calvinist town meeting!"

"Shut your bleedin' mouth, Mister Quarterstone!" Hoop roared.

"Shu' 'er bleetin' mout', Mees'ehr Cortehrstone!" the Frenchmen echoed.

"Load th' friggin' cannon, ye blighters!" Hoop thundered at them.

"Loa' th' frickin' cannon, 'e blotters!" they sang, getting into the spirit of it.

"Blast!" Hoop roared, turning away and ignoring the chorus of "Blest!" and the cackle of Quarterstone laughing aloft. With a heave, he rolled the gun inboard on its carriage and grabbed a swab. "I'll charge th' blinkin' things myself," he grumbled.

Behind him, the Frenchmen chatted together for a moment; then one of them tapped him on the shoulder. He turned, scowling, and the man said something incomprehensible to him.

"I don't know what the bleedin' 'ell you're talkin' about, frog," he snapped.

From aloft came Quarterstone's suggestion. "I expect they're saying that if you want the cannon loaded, Mister Hoop, they'd be glad to help out."

"Oui, M'sieur," a Frenchman said, reaching for the loading swab. *"Mais c'est un plaisir."*

"Mother of God," Hoop muttered as they bent to the loading of the gun.

Francois grinned up at him. *"N'est-ce pas, m'sieur."*

With charges and balls in both of the starboard beam pieces, Hoop led his Frenchmen to the fore and set them to the chasers. They were willing but awkward with the longer weapons, and Hoop decided that whatever they had been before, they were not gunners.

"Some of those boats are getting close, Mister Hoop!" Quarterstone shouted from aloft. "Maybe you'd better hail them!"

"And say what?" Hoop shouted back.

"I don't know! What would Captain Dalton say if he were here?"

"How would I know that? I'm no blinkin' ship's master!"

"Well, you ought to do something!"

The Frenchmen rammed a ball home, primed the vent and straightened, gazing over the bark's lofting bowsprit at the approaching flotilla. Rene pointed. *"Alons, M'sieur 'Oop! Les bateaus!"*

"Boats," he corrected them. "Those are boats."

"Boats," they said in unison. " 'Ose ehr boats."

"Right. Boats."

"Rot. Boats." Rene glanced at Francois. *"Ou'est-ce que c'est* 'boats'?"

Francois shrugged. *"Les bateaus."* He gazed at them, counting. *". . . dix-huit, dix-neuf, vingt, vingt et un . . . formidable!"*

With a grunt, Hoop hauled them aside and started them aft. "Stop yer chatterin' now and go get me a linstock with fuse."

"M'sieur?"

"Oh, blast!" He gritted his teeth and mimed the firing of a cannon, leaning down as though touching fuse to vent.

Francois brightened. *"Ah, mais oui! Le few! Oui, M'sieur 'Oop!"* With a grin he grabbed Rene and both of them hurried away amidships.

From aloft came Quarterstone's shout. "Mister Hoop, are you going to have a talk with those people or not?"

Hoop strode to the rail. There seemed to be nearly thirty boats bearing down on the bark, boats of all descriptions from masted launches to gigs and jolly boats. And in the distance, rafts. All full of people. The nearest ones were barely a hundred yards out now.

At the gunwale he cupped his hands. "Ahoy the boats! Stand off and identify yourselves!"

75

In the bow of a whaleboat, one of the nearest, a man stood and cupped his hands to shout, "Ahoy yourself! What ship is this?"

It seemed a reasonable question, and one that Dalton might answer. "Prize bark *Pride of Falworth!*" he shouted.

For a moment there was silence; then the man called, "Prize, you say? Whose prize is it?"

"Prize of the snow *Fury,* Captain Patrick Dalton commanding! What do you people want?"

The boats continued to approach. "We don't see any snow, nor any sort of prize escort!" the man shouted. "Are you Captain Dalton?"

"Of course not," Hoop shouted, aghast. "I'm nobody but Hoop! Stand off, now, blast you! I'm warning you!"

"Warning?" The man's voice took on a jeering tone. "I see you well, sir, and I think that's a drift ship. Not a soul on quarterdeck or at helm. We are refugees, in desperate need of a ship, you see, and maybe yours is for us."

"Be damned if it is!" Hoop roared. "We're tendin' this ship for Captain Dalton. Now stand off!"

"Three or four men. So few of you aboard and you warn us away, sir? I think not . . ."

Hoop's temper had reached its limit. "Few!" he bellowed. "Why . . ."

Six feet to Hoop's right a cannon roared, almost deafening him and blinding him with thick, sour smoke that rolled back over the gunwales. He choked, turned and gaped. There in the haze were his Frenchmen, grinning like idiots as a gun recoiled in its lashings.

Francois raised a smoking linstock, showing him. *"Le feu."* he said proudly.

Pliny Quarterstone scrambled down the shrouds and thumped to the deck, breathless. "I hope your intentions were to make those people angry, Mister Hoop, because I believe you just did."

Hoop spun to the rail. On the sea to starboard and fore, boats were pulling in all directions, but mostly toward *Pride.* "Did we hit anything?"

"Not unless it was a fish," Quarterstone said. "Why did you commence firing?"

"I didn't! The frogs did that. With *le feu.*"

"Le what?"

"Feu!"

The second cannon roared, and this time there were answering sounds beyond the smoke—a crash, shouts and the hard reports of several muskets. A ball sang past Hoop's ear, and he ducked, pulling Quarterstone down with him. The Frenchmen pounded past them, heading for the bow.

Cautiously, the two *Furies* peered over the rail. Beyond was a boat slowly capsizing while men dived from it in all directions. As the boat rolled, it exposed a gaping hole in its bilges, cutting across its keel.

Ignoring musket balls and shouted curses, Hoop came upright and sprinted after the Frenchmen. "No!" he shouted. "Stop that! Cease fire!"

Pliny Quarterstone peered wide-eyed at what Hoop had just seen. In many of the approaching boats, those farther out, were women and children.

And even as the sight registered with him, boats thumped alongside *Pride* and angry men came over the rails.

Ringed around by cocked muskets and angry faces, Hoop and Quarterstone stood sweating amidships while the pair of French sailors with them gawked about, trying to understand. The leader of the boarding party was a stocky, brown-faced man with the high boots and fringed hat of a planter. His name was Aaron Fairfield, Esquire, and he had made it clear — at least to the two who spoke English — that he was within a whit of braining the lot of them and throwing them into the sea.

"It's God's pure mercy that no one was killed," he snapped at Hoop. "What manner of man opens fire on helpless refugees without at least hearing them out?"

"It was accident, sir," Pliny Quarterstone intervened. "You see, these frogs here don't speak barely a word of English, and we don't speak frog; and I believe they misapprehended something· Mister Hoop may have said in passing, was why they touched off the guns."

"Accident or not," Fairfield said, "Mister Hoop is responsible for the conduct of his men, and I hold him accountable·. . ."

"But they aren't his men, sir, beggin' your pardon. Mister Hoop is a simple sailor, like my own self. We can't be held responsible for what we've no authority to control, you see."

Fairfield pinned the topman with a glare. "If he wasn't in charge on the gundeck, then why would these French blighters have taken orders from him, if as you say that's what they thought they were doing?"

"It might be that they may have thought I was in charge, sir," Hoop suggested.

"And why would they think you are if you are not?"

"I expect they haven't got the vaguest idea of who's in charge here." Hoop shrugged. "They aren't rightly ours."

"Then, whose are they?"

"We don't know, sir. They just sort of come with the vessel when Captain Dalton claimed it for salvage. We found them in the chain locker, which is no fit place for even a Frenchman to be."

Some of Fairfield's men came from below. "Nobody else aboard, Squire," one of them said. "These four is it."

At both rails now, boats were snugged in, and more and more people were coming aboard. Landsmen, by the looks of them. Planters and merchants, craftsmen with their kits, clerks and potters and smiths . . . and a large number of women and children, being helped aboard over the wide gunwales.

"I don't know what Captain is going to have to say about this," Quarterstone muttered to Hoop. "He said we should —"

"Quiet!" Fairfield snapped. "I'm trying to decide what to do with you four. Salvage ship, I believe you said? A prize?"

"Yes, sir," Hoop assured him. "Claimed all proper by Captain Dalton. It's his vessel, an' we're his crew."

Fairfield turned, looking around. "I see no sign of this being a prize vessel, mister. For all I know it could be a mutiny ship and the four of you mutineers and murderers."

Hoop's big face went dark, and his muscles bulged. "I don't take to bein' called things like that," he started, then subsided slightly as several musket-muzzles prodded him. "What I mean is, sir, we're no such a thing as that, an' we'll swear by it. All we are is honest sailors."

"What's your flag, then?"

"Our flag?" Hoop blinked at him, then nudged his companion. "What's our flag, Mister Quarterstone?"

"I don't know," Quarterstone admitted. "I guess you'd best ask Captain about that."

"I see no captain here, though."

"He'll be along directly," Hoop assured the man. "Maybe if you'd all like to get back in your boats and wait a bit . . ."

"Get back in our . . ." Fairfield stared at him. "Why would we do that? We have this ship, mister! We are in control here, and if you aren't daft, you can bloody well see that."

"Yes, sir," Hoop admitted readily. "But what I mean is, well, Captain Dalton is one for the proprieties, sir, an' he hasn't given you permission to come aboard."

At Fairfield's shoulder a man with a musket snorted. "Why listen to any more of this, Squire? Let's throw them overboard and be on our way. Governor Dobbs could have ships on the way right now to —"

"Do you know how to sail a ship like this, Claude?" Fairfield asked.

"Well, no, but . . ."

"Do any of us, do you think?"

"No, but how hard can it be to sail a ship? You simply unfurl those canvases up there so they hang from those timbers, and let the wind do the rest."

Some among them nodded their agreement, but others shook their heads.

"You've been on ships, Claude," one said. "Did you watch the sailors, to see what they did . . . or how they did it?"

"Of course not," the man snorted. "I'm a tailor, not a sailor."

"And how about navigation?" another put in. "Do we have anybody who can guide a ship to where we're going?"

"Where is it you gentlemen want to go?" Hoop asked, curious despite himself.

"Virginia," someone said.

"The Carolinas," another chimed in.

"Grand Bahama," another suggested. "My wife has kin there."

"It's our business where we go, mister," Fairfield said, glaring around at the rest, silencing them. "But the lads may be right about one thing. We've little enough of the nautical skills among us. Now you four, though—"

"We're swore to *Fury*," Hoop cut him off. "At least two of us are. We don't know how to swear frogs. Might be you could work out something with Captain Dalton, though. For fee passage, he might . . ." he paused and glanced upward. High aloft, on *Pride*'s foremast, spars rattled and creaked in their mounts. Hoop spun around, staring over the heads of the landsmen ringing him, and roared, "Here! You there, stop that! God's name, do you mean to dismast us?"

Shoving aside men and muskets, he plunged forward through a scattering crowd of people. The decks seemed packed with people everywhere. In the fore, a dozen or more men had discovered the bark's forward capstan and were trying to use it, hauling a heavy line that shivered from capstan to the portside deadeyes, then downward out of sight.

Hoop reached them and pointed a large, shaking finger. "Back that off, you blighters! Now! Steady and easy . . . just back it down to slack!"

Wide-eyed and surprised, the men complied. The capstan creaked in reverse, the spars overhead complained, and then the line went slack.

Hoop breathed a great sigh of relief, then rounded on the culprits, seeming to tower over them. "Are you all daft? That's no kind of use for a capstan. Worse yet, you nearly cost us our shrouds!"

"Sh-shrouds?" one of them stammered.

The big man pointed. "Those! Like big cables that goes aloft? That's shrouds! It's them that keeps the mast from fallin' down an' takin' the ship with it most likely."

At his side, Pliny Quarterstone looked on in amazement. "Would you look at that?" He pointed. "What kind of way is that to clew a capstan? Like windin' wool on a spindle . . . you

80

can't use even a windlass that way, ye bedammed fools, much less a capstan."

Aaron Fairfield was with them then, pushing through the crowds on the deck. "What's wrong here?"

"You tell your people to unhand the workin' decks!" Hoop demanded. "Or there won't be a ship here to talk to Captain Dalton about. Jesus have mercy!"

Quarterstone went to the rail and looked over. Below were several large rafts with railed sides. "Mister Hoop, come here," he called.

Hoop hurried to join him, and Quarterstone pointed overside. "Cows," he said. "They was trying to hoist cows aboard, by God."

"I concede a point, gentlemen," Fairfield said. "We don't know how to operate a sailing ship. Therefore, I believe I must talk with your captain Dalton."

"Well, you'll have your chance to do that, right enough." Hoop pointed southward.

Just out there, closing on a thousand yards of distance, stacked sails taking the wind like a falcon to the kill, came *Fury*. The people crowding *Pride's* deck stared for a long moment at the lithe, compact, predatory grace of the warship; then one after another, without a word, the armed men aboard laid down their muskets and backed away from them to await the return of the prize ship's master.

Nine

With seven men in its close confines, the little starboard cabin in *Fury's* sterncastle was as packed as biscuits in a tin. Patrick Dalton sat at the ward table, gazing across at the three landsmen who stood before him, flanked by Charley Duncan on one side and Cadman Wise on the other. Billy Caster crouched in the shuttered gallery behind his captain, quill and ink at hand, ready to write any orders or comments Dalton might require.

"Refugees, Mister Fairfield?" Dalton raised a brow. "Refugees from what?"

"Squire," Fairfield said. "It is *Squire* Fairfield, Captain."

"Squire, then. You are all from that island yonder, I take it?"

"We are. The island is called Mayaguana, one of four under the governorship of Sir Edward Dobbs. And it's Dobbs who's the cause of our evacuation. The blaggard has brought in troops against us because we — those of us here, at least — refused to pay taxes on our taxes. He's declared us rebels, is what he's done. So we — those of us here — we all moved across to the east end of the island hoping we might find a ship, and here we are."

"I see. And are you indeed rebels, Squire Fairfield?"

"Who is asking, Captain Dalton?"

"I claim no flag, sir. Circumstances have dictated that *Fury* and her company are — for the moment at least — ah, independent."

Fairfield arched a brow. "Does that mean that you are rebels, Captain?"

"We have joined no cause, Squire."

"Nor have we, Captain. We simply desire passage to some decent place beyond the jurisdiction of Edward Dobbs, where we might seek justice by whatever means presents itself. We are willing to pay for passage, in some reasonable amount."

"Misters Hoop and Quarterstone report that you boarded my prize vessel without permission, and at gunpoint."

"We had little choice in the matter. Your men were firing cannons at us."

"Yes." Dalton made a steeple of his fingers and frowned. "It may be that an apology is due on that account. It was a misunderstanding, I'm told, having to do with the oddities of the French language." He looked up. "Do any of your people happen to speak French?"

Fairfield looked at the two with him. They shrugged. "Not that I know of, sir," he said. "Possibly we could ask about . . . in the course of our journey."

Dalton sighed. The care of a band of refugee colonials was not something he coveted, but he knew already that he was not going to send them back to their island. There were innocents among them, and it was wartime. "How many of you are there?"

Fairfield glanced at Claude Dunstan, beside him.

"Two hundred and twelve, sir," the man said. "Forty-nine men, thirty-one married women and twenty-six children . . . and the servants, of course. About forty indentures and the rest black Africans."

"And you propose to take your slaves along, as well?"

"Well, of course we do! They're most of what Dobbs is after us for. To take them for himself. He plans to build a fort and needs the manpower."

Dalton glanced around. "Mister Caster, what would you expect a trade vessel to charge for passengers?"

"In Provincial coin, sir? Ah, fourteen dollars a head . . . I believe that's what Mister Romart said Squire Ramsey's ships charge for Indies passage. And a fourth that for servants, he said, if their masters provision them." He had been noting the count as Claude Dunstan recited. Now he tallied it and showed the page to Dalton. It was a fair amount of money.

"Can you pay this amount, Squire?" Dalton asked.

Fairfield turned to the second man with him, a wiry, gray-whiskered gentleman named Prosper McPherson.

"We might pay half that," McPherson admitted. "The rest would have to be in barter or in kind — or paid when we have arrived where we want to go and had a chance to sell some wares."

"Half now, half when we land you," Dalton decided. "You have your funds with you?"

"On the other ship, sir," McPherson said. "All our money is in a chest that we set on the deck. Mister Keith Darling is sitting on it."

"Keith Darling?"

"One of our group," Fairfield said. "A trustworthy and sturdy lad, nigh a match for your Mister Hoop in size."

"It should be safe enough, then," Dalton observed. "Very well, gentlemen, I might accommodate you, depending upon where you want to go."

"Virginia," Fairfield said.

"The Carolinas," Dunstan said.

"Grand Bahama," McPherson said, then added, "although there's several as believe we should make for Rhode Island."

"We are not going to Rhode Island," Fairfield stated.

"If you do, it will not be aboard my ship," Dalton agreed. "Nor do I intend to sail for Grand Bahama, for reasons of my own."

"The Carolinas, then?" Dunstan suggested.

"Virginia," Fairfield insisted.

Dalton shook his head and stood, careful not to crack his head on the low timbers of the little cabin. "I am willing to set a course generally west by north, and hold to it for as long as seems prudent, and to do my best to put you and your party ashore at some Christian port away from the immediacies of the war," he said. "But whether that will be on the Chesapeake, the Delaware or somewhere farther south will depend upon what we encounter along the way. If that satisfies you . . ."

Fairfield squinted at the tall young man. "I took you for British," he said. "Those are not likely British ports, are they?"

"If any are, then we will not land there," Dalton assured

84

him. "I have reasons for avoiding the exchange of pleasantries with His Majesty's navy right now."

"You are American, then? Colonial?"

"As I said, Squire, *Fury* is an independent party at the moment. Do we have a bargain?"

Fairfield shrugged. "I suppose we have no other choice. When do we make sail?"

"Immediately." Dalton addressed his first officer. "Mister Duncan, have you drilled our recruits?"

"Aye, sir. They know the workings of a snow now, sir."

"Then, take thirty of them and teach them the workings of a bark, if you please. I give you command of the prize vessel and its stores and passengers. You may have Misters Hoop, Nelson and Quarterstone with you, and you'll need a bosun . . ."

"One of the marooned lads is a bosun, sir," Duncan said. "His name's Jim Porter. He was bosun aboard *Tyber*."

"Then, take Mister Porter, and select your crew. But leave me any with experience aboard a warship. Mister Caster, go along and keep the rosters, if you please."

Fairfield raised his hand, interrupting. "Captain, we have a bit of livestock as well, and several rafts of hay and grain, but we shall need some help in getting them aboard the ship."

"Livestock," Dalton breathed. "Yes, so I heard. Mister Duncan, when you are assembled aboard *Pride,* have someone show the squire's men how to rig a hoist and the proper use of a capstan." He turned to Fairfield again. "Squire Fairfield, when Commander Duncan is ready to sail, we sail. Pray have your cattle, your hay and anything else of importance to you aboard ship at that time."

"And our boats, Captain? What of our boats?"

"Abandon them, Squire. My men will have a look at them. Any that might be of use, we shall keep and credit to you. The rest can go where God and the currents take them."

As Charley Duncan hustled the landsmen through the companionway to the ladder that led to *Fury*'s main deck, Fairfield glanced back and asked, "How can a man be uncertain of his nationality?"

"Who, sir?"

85

"Your captain. He doesn't seem at all sure what he is."

"Oh," Duncan grinned. "There's no question there, sir. Patrick Dalton is Irish. As true a black Irishman as ever was. But since an Irishman has to be something else as well, and since *Fury*'s not on the best of terms with His Majesty's Admiralty right now, it *is* just a bit uncertain what else we might be besides Irish."

It was six bells of the dogwatch when *Pride of Falworth* edged northward into deep water, with *Fury* flanking her as a herd dog flanks its sheep. The wind had come to south of west at a good eighteen knots that scudded wisps of pink cloud across the evening sky, and more than one soul aboard each ship breathed a happy sigh as hands in the tops unfurled great sails while hands a'deck heaved sheeting lines to the pinrails to trim for course.

It seemed like an age — to those who had come to these waters — since they had truly had the manpower to rig and run a jaunty ship so that she could sail the winds and sing the songs of passage.

Pride would set the course for now. With her massed stacks of square-rigged canvas, the big bark was designed for tail or quarter winds and was limited in tacking. She could angle no closer than sixty degrees to the wind, without losing way. So the snow, which could trim to fore-and-afts for a tighter tack, would follow her lead northward until they found more favorable winds for a westerly course.

On *Fury*'s quarterdeck, Patrick Dalton set himself to feel the little warship's song through her planking, and gazed westward. The last flush of evening played on dark eyes in a ruddy face, and the wind from that quarter tousled the dark hair that seemed always to be escaping from its bound queue.

"She sails again as she should," he said, addressing no one. "A sweet snow with canvas aloft and the hands to play her as she deserves." He turned to the helm. "Give us two points to port, please, Mister . . . ah . . ."

"Popkin, sir," the helmsman said. "Peter Popkin. Aye, sir. Two points it is."

"Strongly but gently on the helm, please, Mister Popkin. Have you steered a snow before?"

"No, sir, but I've helmed a brig, and this seems very like it to —" The wheel went over, and *Fury* seemed to surge, leaping gracefully and powerfully into the course correction. "Bleedin' 'ell!" Popkin gasped.

"This is not a brig, Mister Popkin," Dalton said. "This is a snow. Learn her helm, Mister Popkin, and make no mistake about what manner of vessel she is."

"Aye, sir."

Dalton turned. "Mister Caster, please note. When breakfast is finished in the morning, I shall want assembly. All hands on deck for maneuvers. I think it is time to put *Fury* through some paces for the benefit of our new gentlemen on board. We wouldn't want any of our lads to misapprehend the nature of their ship. There might be others who haven't learned the difference between a brig and a snow."

Below the quarterrail, Cadman Wise grinned a devilish grin. Nearly fifty men were aboard *Fury* now, thirty-seven of them new hands. A dozen or so had sailed warships, and all had sailed something. But not one of them, he warranted, had ever seen a snow shaken out — and certainly not by Patrick Dalton.

They had an experience in store. By the time Dalton completed his "maneuvers," they would all be men to match their ship — all, except those who might have fallen overboard or something.

Lucas Peady was a pirate.

Through sixteen years of early life in Essex — first as a drayman's son and later as a fugitive from press-gangs — he had dreamed of becoming a pirate, of roving the trade lanes with a fast ship and great guns, taking what it pleased him to take. Three miserable years as a seaman aboard His Majesty's Escort Cutter *Sprite,* doing wartime patrol in the British Indies, had evolved for him first a plan and then actual opportunity to become what he had dreamed. Lucas Peady had bided his time, schemed his schemes and recruited his accomplices carefully and with fine craft. Then he had acted.

In the shoaling waters off San Salvador, following an abrupt and bloody mutiny, five Crown officers and eight loyal sailors had gone over *Sprite's* leeward rail to feed the fishes. By a simple replacing of escutcheons and a quick layover at the Island of San Rafael to recruit a few practiced cutthroats and a makeshift black flag, His Majesty's Cutter of War *Sprite* had ceased to exist. In her stead now sailed the venture cutter *Mako*, and she stood at sea in the trade lanes awaiting her prey.

Nearly thirty men were aboard her, men enough to man the wide sails and the eight ranging guns of the little predator. Though hardly longer than a large launch in her hull, *Mako* was deep-keeled and swift, with massive sails and trim lines. A proud cutter of her time, she was all legs and teeth, a killer boat rigged to rake and take much larger vessels — provided they were merchant vessels.

At six bells of a fine tropic morning, the spotter aloft on *Mako's* high mast made sails — a bare three miles away and slogging northward on a westerly wind. Lucas Peady himself climbed the shrouds for a look, and his grin glinted in the morning light. A bark she was. A four-master, riding heavy.

"Charge all guns," he ordered his mates. "There's easy prey yonder, and we've the advantage of the wind. Make all sail, lads. At this range we'll be on them before they can even come about."

Eyes a'glitter at sight of a prize that could make wealthy men of them all no matter what it carried, they spread *Mako's* wings, and the cutter sliced bright water as it shot forth to head off the bark. It had closed to a distance of two miles before the merchantman turned hard astarboard, getting the wind on its tail for a run.

Lucas Peady laughed aloud and slapped the nearest man on the back. "Outrun a cutter, would he? See how that ship slogs; there's cargo yonder an' plenty. Passengers as well, by the looks of it. Bless us, lads, I'd wager there's women aboard that ship. Rig for wing and wing, there! Look alive, now, for today we take our first ship!"

Within a bell, *Mako* had closed to less than a mile of distance, and the gunners stood by her cannons with smoking fuse. Through his glass, Peady could read the bark's escutcheon. *"Pride of Falworth,"* he gloated. "Bring us to range of the bow guns, Mister Skinner, and let's pierce her sterncastle with a pair of loads!"

At half a mile the bow gunners aligned their notches . . . and aligned them again as the big bark rounded into a change of course, coming sharply to port, losing way as its square sails took the quartering wind.

"He's giving us his broadside." Peady grinned. "Gunners, fire!"

Mako's bow chasers thundered, and smoke drifted on the wind. Peady squinted, then frowned. The first ball spumed just aft the bark's rudder. The second fell short.

"Blast!" Peady swore. "You there, reload an'—"

He didn't finish his order. Just beyond the turning bark, hidden until now by its larger silhouette, was a second ship—smaller by far than the four-master, but rigged as no merchantman was rigged.

"What th' devil is that?" a man nearby shouted. "A brig?"

Peady brought his tiller over sharply, then shaded his eyes, squinting into the sun-haze. A brig? Possibly . . . but within moments he knew it was not, for no brig ever could have moved the way that vessel moved. Like a fox after a chicken, the warship made way on tight tack, standing into the gap between *Mako* and the fleeing bark. Then it brought its stem directly into the wind, and even as it came about for the chase, its bow chasers thundered.

The two shots *Mako* had fired were all that she ever would. An iron ball threw spray thirty feet into the air ahead of her, then skipped like a thrown stone and crashed into her bow alongside the jutting sprit. Men screamed and wreckage flew as the ball travelled half the cutter's length, shearing away decking and timbers.

The second ball took out her portside shrouds and three guns—and their crews.

Again there was smoke and thunder, this time a drumroll that belched and rippled along the warship's gunwales, and seemed to go on and on. The last thing Lucas Peady saw in this world was a bow escutcheon, breasting through the smokes of hell as the warship turned to close.

The name on the escutcheon was *Fury*.

89

* * *

All along the portside rails of *Pride's* main deck, wide-eyed faces stared at the drifting smoke astern, the shower of blasted wreckage still pelting the waves . . . and at the small, jaunty warship just breasting through its own smokes several hundred yards beyond.

"He blasted the blighters to kingdom come," someone breathed.

Near the quarterrail, Charley Duncan leaned on a stanchion and grinned. "Bonny lads, those," he declared. "But they were in error not looking beyond their prize to see what else awaited."

"You led them right into a trap," Aaron Fairfield accused. "What sort of people are you, to do that? It was only a small boat."

"Boat?" Duncan blinked. "That was a cutter, Squire. An armed cutter that intended to sink or take this ship—and would have."

"Phaw! Bit extreme, if you want my opinion . . . blowing the little thing right out of the water like that."

Duncan shook his head. *Landsmen!* "Captain Dalton has no liking for pirates, Squire," he said. "No liking whatsoever." He glanced forward, then gawked and roared, "Mister Hoop! What are those cattle doing on the main deck?"

"Some of the ladies led them up for milking, sir!" Hoop shouted from ahead.

"Have them milked somewhere else! Not on my working deck!"

Pliny Quarterstone came hurrying aft. "We're having something of a problem with that, Commander," he explained. "Most of the passengers have taken up residence in the forward hold, you see, and that's where the cows are, too; but there's no room there for milking them, and the main hold is up to its timbers with cotton bales, so . . ."

Duncan gritted his teeth. "Sort it out, Mister Quarterstone. Just get those cattle off the handling deck."

"Aye, sir. We'll see what we can do."

Ten

Four hundred miles to the west, on the same day that Dalton exercised *Fury*'s gunners and Lucas Peady's fledgling pirates went the way of Davy Jones, another encounter was taking place. The cruiser *Valkyrie* was no darting cutter playing at piracy games, but a full-rigged and heavily armed vessel of frigate class, and her master was no ambitious deckhand, but a calculating and experienced mariner who knew the ways of sail and the habits of merchantmen as well as any captain of his time.

On this day *Valkyrie* stood to leeward of Hawksbill Cay, a stalker at rest and almost invisible against the background jumble of hundreds of little islands flanking the west expanse of Exuma Sound. For nearly a week the predator had lain in wait here while eyes in her tops scanned the northward horizon. There was no happenstance in her being just here, for the man who now called himself Jack Shelby left little to luck. He was here because he knew what he would find, and on this day his information proved correct.

"On deck!" the foretopman called.

Amidships the bosun, Caleb Strode, responded. "Deck aye, Mister Summers!"

"Sail off the starboard bow!" The shout drifted down through abruptly silent rigging. "Three ships hard down an' comin' on!"

Strode turned toward the stern of the ship, to carry the message, but Timothy Leech was there.

91

"I heard, Mister Strode," the big first said. "Let's have fresh eyes aloft to watch their progress. Stand by to weigh anchors and make sail, at the captain's order."

"Aye." Strode nodded. "Are they the ones, do you think?"

"We'll know that when Captain Jack tells us," Leech said. "Just stand ready."

Leech didn't bother going to the gunwales. If the sightings were hard down from the tops, there would be nothing to see from the deck for a while. Instead he strolled aft, pausing here and there to cast a critical eye on the positioning of gun carriages, the lashings of clewing lines, the general readiness of the vessel. The men who made up *Valkyrie*'s company were of a type, and it was a thing well to keep in mind. Ruthless and bloodthirsty, fighters without mercy when there was a fight to be had, they shared the tendency to become surly and lax if they weren't kept busy.

It was Leech's task—and his pleasure—to keep them busy and alert. His authority came from the captain. His right he had established himself, by personally beating to death the first among them to test him and by flogging into submission those few who had offered to interfere. The exercise had cost *Valkyrie* six crewmen—three of those he had flogged were dead now, and two others had gone overside in the night—but it was well worth the small loss. *Valkyrie* was a tight and well-disciplined vessel and would remain so.

Jack Shelby demanded no more, and would settle for no less. As a merchant captain he had learned the ways of pirates. He knew the strengths of the breed and the weaknesses, and Leech shared with him the belief that what befell most pirate ventures in the end—barring bad luck or an encounter with a ship of the line—was sloth. Sheer laxity and sloth.

They had vowed that such would not be the fate of *Valkyrie*.

When Jack Shelby came on deck, Leech gave him the sighting report and an evaluation of *Valkyrie*'s readiness for assault. Within the hour, top lookouts had descriptions of the three vessels coming down on the wind. Two merchantmen and an escort.

Shelby nodded. "It's them," he told Leech. "My man in Virginia has earned his commission. Two fine prizes. The Spaniard will pay well for what they carry."

With select hands reading winds and currents, Shelby studied his charts. "Here," he noted, pointing. "They sail southward as though to skirt Eleuthera to the east. As though they were making for Hispaniola. But they will turn into the northeast channel, out of sight of Hatchet Bay, and set new bearings on Hawksbill. Their destination is the Camaguey trade ports."

"Cunning," Leech said. "The merchant becomes elusive."

"Not so cunning, Mister Leech." Shelby gazed northward with cold gray eyes, pulling his coat about him. "Predictable, in fact. It's a trick I myself taught McCall's mariners . . . when I sailed for him."

"And the escort ship, Cap'n? Will it come, too?"

"Oh, aye. It will come, with a weather eye eastward, expecting a challenge from Crown ships at Governor's Harbour."

"But there are no Crown vessels in Governor's Harbour, Cap'n. They're all out looking for us, thanks to that evening's amusement we gave them."

"Aye, but McCall's agents don't know that, and neither do his captains."

"Then, we attack from the west . . ." Leech grinned.

"Aye, from the west." Shelby looked at his charts again and then at the sky. "With the wind at our stern to give us the advantage and the sun behind us to blind them until we are on them. I trust the men are prepared?"

"Blood in their eyes an' fire in their bellies, sir."

"I'll want to make short work of the escort, Mister Leech. Once we engage, you may direct fire from the gundecks. No flag, no dancing about, and no quarter. Sink the escort as you please, but quickly."

. "Aye, Cap'n. With pleasure."

As the three ships came in sight off Dunmore Point, skirting the shoals above Exuma Sound, Leech made the rounds of his gundecks to personally order his strategy. Bow chasers and the heavy guns in the fore would be charged with ball, and the gunners would sight for close-range waterline strikes. The portside batteries would be charged with chain and barbel to devastate rigging and clear the decks. Stern guns would fire heated balls.

Silent as a panther, *Valkyrie* waited, anchors up and sail ready, still hidden by the camouflage of the cays and by the glare of the lowering sun beyond her. By seven bells of the dog watch, just as Shelby had predicted, the little flotilla was abreast and sailing southward, bound for Cuba's coastal ports. The escort ship, a refurbished brig that had been some privateer's prize, had edged toward the east flank of the two square-riggers, alert for challenge from British sail.

Jack Shelby went to his quarterdeck. "To helm, Mister Trice," he ordered. "Mister Strode, hands a'deck to make sail. Gunnery to stations. Misters Boyd and Ames, you'll take your firing orders from Mister Leech. Mister Trahan, command the tops. Stations, if you please."

Men scurried to stations, and Caleb Strode's pipe shrilled amidships. "Hands to make sail! Hands a'sheet! Tops aloft! Make sail! Sheet home . . . sheet home . . . sheet home!"

"Trim for port reach," Shelby ordered. "Full and by." Sails drummed taut, and *Valkyrie* lifted her stem and took spray in her teeth, a predator beginning its charge.

"Steer to intercept that brig, Mister Trice," Shelby said. "Cut the wake of the two square-riggers if you can. A bit of panic there will do us no harm."

The helm came over, and *Valkyrie* threw sheets of bright spray into the wind as she homed on her kill.

"A fine, bloodthirsty ship," Leech noted. "She growls and keens for the fight."

"A ship for our purpose." Shelby nodded. "Thibaud was a fool to lose her so." He crossed his arms and judged the closing distance ahead. "To station now, Mister Leech. You know the maneuver. Fire as you will, and sink that brig."

"Aye, Cap'n." His eyes aglow, Timothy Leech headed amidships.

Shelby's tactic was sound. *Valkyrie* was within a thousand yards of the nearest merchantman when abrupt activity aboard that vessel said she had been seen. Buntings ran aloft, and the merchantman's yards hove about for a dodge, then rattled and leaned when her helm fought rudder to avoid colliding with the second vessel just beyond. A cannon belched smoke at the first vessel's stern as *Valkyrie* rammed across its wake barely two chains aft, but Shelby and his crew ignored it. Their first target was the private brig beyond the pair, the armed escort just now fighting its sails to come about, leaning as its captain tried to bring his nose — and his ranging guns — to windward. With perfect wind on her quarter, *Valkyrie* closed relentlessly.

Leech counted the seconds as the range between the two diminished to a thousand yards, to seven hundred, to five hundred and smoke billowed at the waist of the brig. Aloft, a ball ripped through the foretop, and screams sounded there. Bits of wreckage clattered down. Two flailing men, both screaming, plummeted from above, one to the foredeck, the other overside. Leech raised his arm, still counting, then lowered it. "Forward batteries, fire!"

Flares of hell spat from *Valkyrie's* stem and bows, and in the rolling smoke ahead there were the sounds of chaos.

As though dancing to a silent tune, *Valkyrie* came smartly to starboard, riding it seemed on the echoes of her cannons. Leech raised his arm again. "Portside batteries, rake their decks! Ready . . ." He lowered his arm. "Fire!"

This time he could see clearly the devastation of his guns — clearly and near, for the brig was a scant hundred yards away. Well within point-blank range. Chain shot and barbel, devilish whirling engines of death, smashed into the shrouds at deck level, taking with them everything in their way. Howling their banshee wails, the lengths of chain tore apart rigging, rails and the flesh beyond them while the whirling barbels gouged out great gaps in masts and uprights. For a moment it seemed that the entire midsection of the brig had exploded, leaving only its stem and its little quarterdeck intact. Then a delayed volley raked its stern and the quarterdeck, and those on it were carried away.

The effects of the first volley were there as well — gaping holes in the brig's hull just at waterline.

He had only a moment to admire his gunners' work. *Valkyrie* was continuing her turn, hard hands shifting spars and recleating sheets at orders from the command aft.

He has no doubt of our effect here, Leech thought, grinning. *He said to make short work of the brig, and that is what he expects. He has dismissed the brig entirely now, and is aligning to run down the merchantmen. Captain Jack Shelby has no thought of failure or delay, because neither is a thing that he will tolerate.*

There was no answering fire now from the brig. It sat asunder upon the waves, beginning even now to list as its bilges filled, and the only sounds that carried across were the shrill screaming of maimed men and the staccato rattle of falling rigging.

Leech hurried to the after command and raised his arm. "After batteries and chasers ready," he ordered. Along both quarters and below in the stern, sweating men used great double forks of heavy iron to lift heated balls from their flaming beds in sand tubs and set them into the muzzles of cannons. Gouts of steam erupted as loaders seated them in the breaches, with wet rams. The guns were trundled out and secured, and linstocks hovered over their vents.

Leech brought down his arm. "Fire!"

Cherry-red and trailing ropes of smoke darker than the clouds that billowed outward at their release, the heated balls smashed into the hull of the brig, and more screams echoed back.

"That should do it nicely," Timothy Leech said, speaking to no one in particular. *Valkyrie* was already gaining speed on a new course, away from the shattered brig, her feral stem pointing like death's finger at the pair of fleeing merchantmen amassing sail for a run down Exuma Sound. Leech gazed aft for a moment more, admiring his work, then raised a hand in casual salute. "Misters Boyd and Ames," he called. "Have all batteries reload with shot and stand by stations. You may give your gunners a 'well done,' but please admonish them that their next volleys will be at prize vessels and it's our loss, one and all, should anyone cause them to sink."

The brig in their wake was wreathed in smoke as Leech

joined Captain Shelby on the quarterdeck. Shelby didn't even look around as he asked, "I assume the escort is sunk, Mister Leech."

"Very soon she will sit on the bottom, Cap'n. She's —"

A roar like the thunders of hell echoed across widening waters. Leech looked back and grinned. The brig had exploded. From the looks of it, fire had reached her main magazines. The explosion seemed to go on and on, fire and thunder mounting ever higher where the ship had been. Myriad tiny things that might have been bits of wreckage, kegs of stores or human bodies — or some of each — tumbled and flew in all directions.

"Like to amend the report, Cap'n," Leech said. "There isn't any brig anymore."

Still, Shelby did not look back. Hard-eyed and intent, he focused on the prizes fleeing ahead. "I thought not," he said coldly. Then to his helmsman, "Port a point, Mister Trice. Bring us onto the flank of those two as they run — close enough to discourage them from making for land yonder, but hold back a bit. We'll let them have their run."

"It will be dark in an hour, Cap'n," Leech pointed out. "Shouldn't we . . ."

"There are people on that island over there, Mister Leech. A capture this close might tempt them to come out with boats or something and interfere. No, we shall let the prizes run for a time. There is no place for them to go once the light fails, except the way they are going, and we shall be right here behind them to hurry them on their way. By morning we should have open sea about us. We can take them then, one at a time, at our leisure."

In the brief dusk of a spring evening, boats were sent out from Governor's Harbour to search and salvage among the bits of flotsam that were all that remained of a private brig that had been escorting trade vessels. From floating wreckage the searchers identified the brig *Pliny*. Admiralty records would reveal that *Pliny* had been a Crown vessel, taken by colonial privateers off Hatteras the year before and sold to persons unknown in the Carolinas. Witnesses ashore, who had watched the Exuma Sound encounter through glasses, would confirm that the attack had been an act of piracy and not of war . . . the dark frigate had shown no colors and issued no challenge. It had simply appeared and attacked.

As long as there was light enough to see, and for an hour afterward with lanterns, the searchers gleaned the flotsam for survivors. They found none.

Long after the bronze bell in the little fort's tower had sounded midnight, a piece of shattered decking washed ashore a mile to the south, and something moved there in the misty starlight. For a time the man lay silent, struggling to get his wits about him. Finally he got to unsteady feet and looked around, remembering.

He would not forget that dark frigate. Its every line was engraved in his memory, as was the name his glass had picked out on its port bow just before the deck beneath his feet had erupted and flung him over the side.

Valkyrie.

And as he trudged northward along a starlit beach, a resolution grew in him. First, he must find a way back to Virginia, where his voyage had begun. He must personally report to Ian McCall on the loss of the cargo ships that it had been the brig's duty — and his own duty — to escort safely. Secondly, he must find employment. Another ship, perhaps? Another command? Would anyone again trust a former Royal Navy officer who now had had two ships shot out from beneath his feet?

Unlikely, that seemed. But he could only ask.

And finally, somehow, some day, he must go in search of that pirate.

Whatever it took, whatever the means, Lewis Farrington resolved that night to find *Valkyrie* and end her career.

Nearing Governor's Harbour, he paused. He could seek help in the little Crown settlement. It would not be difficult to seem a subject of the king. Until recent years he had in fact been a subject of the king. But much had happened since then . . . too much.

He skirted around the settlement and continued north-ward. Somewhere ahead was Gregory Town, and there— where the riots had occurred—he would find rebel sympathizers. *Once a man has changed coats,* he told himself, *the honorable thing is to abide by his own commitment.* Lewis Farrington had little interest in the rebellion in America, and less in the politics and causes of it. He had never been one for causes. British by birth, he was American now by circumstance and—he admitted—by choice. It was as simple as that, no matter of causes. Relieved of his commission by misfortune and Admiralty politics, stranded thus in the colonies with no-where to go, he had become Colonial.

But he had a cause now. Rogues with frigates had pushed him just too far. He clenched his jaws, remembering. That rogue commanding *Courtesan* had shelled his own flag and cost Lewis Farrington his sloop and his career. *Courtesan* was gone now, he had heard—sent to the bottom, unlikely as it seemed, by the very schooner her captain had been so bent upon re-capturing. But the pirate *Valkyrie* still sailed, and Lewis Far-rington made a resolve—to find and sink the *Valkyrie.*

Eleven

Morning sun and spring breezes kissed the ways at South Point. Warm zephyrs soft with the combined scents of salt water and new-plowed fields drifted across the shipyards there and became raucous airs heady with the smells of hot tar and new rope, loud with the sounds of enterprise. Clatter of tackle hoisted aloft for fitting, song of shrouds and stays being drawn to pitch like great strings on giant violins, the chants of teams of burly young men working windlass and capstan, whine of stressed spars coming about in their fittings to the cadence of fitters and riggers at their lofty tasks—all of these were the music of the ways, where vessels lay for careening and refitting, where new hulls sprouted the trappings of sailing ships to suit the needs of those whose fortunes required them.

Along the Delaware it seemed almost a time of peace. Few Crown vessels remained on the river, and those kept themselves well up the river—support for the impending evacuation of Philadelphia, official reports to the White Fleet's headquarters said, although it was surmised by many a Colonial that the captains of His Majesty's ships on the Delaware were either exceedingly nervous or secretly mortified after a winter of fighting what Squadron Commander Carlson had termed "UFO's." Unidentified Floating Objects. To many, the saga of David Bushnell's exploding kegs was a subject of glee. But not to the British Navy. How many thousands of cannon rounds, grapeshot charges and volleys of musketry had been expended on logs, bits of driftwood and—some said—even a pair of unfortunate muskrats, would never be known. But the "Battle of the Kegs" had made history. The only certain casualties of Bushnell's floating mines with their spring-lock detonators were a small dinghy and a barge, but for a time the Delaware had been a very noisy river.

The entire episode — British men-of-war doing battle against anything seen floating on the water — had lasted for weeks and had provided high entertainment for the residents of the area, few enough of whom now harbored any Royalist or Tory sentiments after three years of war.

But now the kegs were gone, and to all intents and purposes, so were the king's ships. Now it was back to business as usual. There were crops to be planted, barns to be mended, crafts to be practiced, trade goods to be traded and ships to be repaired . . . and built.

One such was the sleek, and oddly feral-looking, schooner nearing completion at the yard of John Singleton Ramsey below Wilmington. The schooner was a subject of local curiosity for a number of reasons. It was crafted as a cargo vessel might be; but it had the deckhouse and fighting tops of a warrior, and rumor had it that it would mount at least seven cannons. It was, some said, a near-exact duplicate of an earlier schooner, the wreckage of which lay alongside the ways where the new one was now being outfitted. Strange tales were told about the hulk, and about those who had sailed it. Some even whispered that it had bested a forty-four-gun frigate in head-to-head combat.

And, oddest of all, the work proceeding at those ways seemed not to be directed by Ramsey, nor by any of his usual overseers, but by a small, striking, auburn-haired young woman whom some said they recognized . . . Squire Ramsey's pretty daughter, Constance, they said.

In each tavern and grogshop from South Point to Wilmington there had been lively debates about what the schooner's use would be, who would command it and why an attractive and headstrong young woman seemed to be in charge of its equippage. Most of those actually working on the project were not locals at South Point, and close-mouthed about the matter. All the local gossips could glean was that the men rigging the schooner for sea either didn't know what use it would be put to or chose not to say.

Locals had singled out nine among them who seemed to be confidants of Mistress Ramsey — all sailors, it seemed. But only three of the nine even hailed from the southern colonies — one Michael Romart, who was obviously a Virginian, and a pair of red-haired brothers named O'Riley, who spoke as Carolinians did. The ship's master carpenter, some felt, might be a Maryland man, but the remaining five were from other parts entirely.

In all, the schooner and its readiers remained a mystery to most who were curious. Yet each day they were there, the lady, her maidservant and her motley assemblage, directing a swarm of workmen and purveyors, riggers and sailmakers, fitters and chandlers, none of whom learned much of substance beyond such facts as "The young lady, why, she trimmed the notches and fined the carriage of each great gun aboard yon ship. Aye, herself, personal. Skirt tied up an' sleeves rolled like a man's, and orderin' quoinin' same as any gunnery officer. Mates, ye've never seen th' like!"

The jaunty schooner would soon be ready for sea, and she wore proud escutcheons salvaged from her wrecked companion alongside.

Her name was *Faith*.

On a bright morning a polished carriage rolled into South Point and up to the head of the ways there. The footman swung down and set a step stool, then swung the lacquered door open, and a portly gentleman of middle years stepped out. Wide-shouldered and sturdy, he evidenced in his arms; his stout hands and the lines of his ruddy face, the signs of a man who has known hard work; and in his alert eyes and fine dress, the evidences of one who has profited from his ventures.

"Take the carriage around to Master Jack's, Colly," he instructed the immaculately garbed black servant who was with him. "Wait there and take your ease for a time. I shall send for you when I need you."

"Yes, sah." Colly sat back in the cushioned seat and rapped his stick on the carriage top. "Master Jack's livery, Wilson," he said.

The carriage made a smart turn and rolled away. The man watched it go, then strolled through the gate and into the ship-yard, nodding at a sentry. "Morning, Albert."

"Morning to you, Squire Ramsey," the sentry said. "Inspection this morning, sir?"

"No inspection, Albert. I've come to visit with my daughter. I assume she is aboard that schooner?"

"Expect so, sir. She usually is. Do you want escort for boarding, sir?"

"Why would I want escort?"

Albert swallowed, lowering his eyes. "Well, sir, since they started shipping stores aboard, them folks has been right choosy about who comes around."

Ramsey turned, his mouth dropping open. "Choosy? By God, I own this yard! I'll go where I please within it."

"I meant about folks comin' around th' schooner, Squire." Albert sounded as though he were forcing the words out. "They, ah . . . well, they mean for folks to stand off."

"I own that schooner, too! At least, I seem to be paying for it. *Choosy?* By the great . . ."

"Maybe you'd best talk to them that's aboard, sir. If that's what you've a mind to do. I was just sayin' how it seems that it is. To me, I mean . . . it seems so."

Ramsey squinted at the young man, wondering if he had come down with the vapors or something. Albert seemed to be making less and less sense.

"Let us hear no more about it, Albert," the great man said. "In my yards I go where I please." With that he turned away and headed for the schooner standing tall upon its slipways.

On the angling dray path, he stepped aside to allow an ox cart to pass. The ox driver glanced at him, scowling. "Mind w'at ye're about wi' them folk, guv'ner. They be touchy as ear fleas."

Approaching the bright new schooner, Ramsey heard a shout overhead and looked up. High above him, balancing on the ship's spreaders, a young man frowned down at him.

"I said, stand off!" the challenger repeated. "What's your business here, anyway?"

"My business is my own business!" Ramsey snapped. "Who are you?"

"Ives is the name," the man above said. "Phillip Ives. State your business and go away." He squinted, cocking his head. "Don't I recognize you from somewhere? I've seen you, I know."

"I am John Singleton Ramsey!" Ramsey announced.

The man peered down at him. "No, that doesn't seem right."

"What do you mean, 'that doesn't seem right'? You think I don't know who I am?"

"No, but I've seen you somewhere, for certain. I remember your hat." The young man grinned suddenly and snapped his fingers. "Aye, that's it. When I sailed for Cap'n Dalton, aboard *Fury*, you an' some others had dinner aboard with th' lady . . . blazes, I think you're right! You're Squire Ramsey!" He turned, as agile as a cat on the soaring structure of the schooner's stem, and trotted toward the high bow, his arms spread for balance. "Mister Romart! Gentleman below says he's Squire Ramsey! I believe he's right!"

Ramsey planted his fists on his hips, grunting in disbelief. After a moment a head appeared above the vessel's trim gunwale, peering downward.

Ramsey blinked. "Romart? Is that you? Where have you been?"

"Why it *is* you!" Michael Romart declared. "Morning to you, Squire. Where have I what?"

"Been!"

"Lately, sir? Right here, sir, giving the lady a hand with her schooner. Lovely sight, isn't she, sir? Spitting image of her mother."

"Mister Romart, what do you know of my daughter's mother?"

"Not a thing, sir. I meant the schooner. Just as the lady ordered, we've made her the very image of *Faith*. Right down to the rooftree bolsters at her knees and the barn shingles on her deckhouse. Have you noticed the tops? Mister Tower is special proud of those tops, sir. Why are you standing down there, sir? Wouldn't you like to come aboard?"

"I have every intention of it! Where is the gangway?"

"We don't have a gangway, sir. We've been shipping by hoist. Keeps the curious from sneaking aboard, you see."

"Then, where is a ladder?"

"No ladders, either, sir. Same reason. Would you like a hoist?"

Cursing under his breath, clinging to tar-dark cables and trying to balance his dignity in a swaying, turning mesh of rope net, John Singleton Ramsey was hoisted aboard the new *Faith* like so much kegged salt pork destined for the galley.

Finally on deck, he gazed around, remembering. The spanking-new vessel was, indeed, very much as the old one had been—not as she had been when first he'd had her, but as she had been when Constance and her wild Irishman brought her back from that improbable adventure in the northern colonies. Not a harmless, pretty cargo schooner, but something quite else—something that fugitives by dint of luck, skill and desperation had wrought upon the semblance of that.

"It's like before," he muttered, almost expecting to see the bloodstain on the deck that the other schooner had worn. "It is a jolly-be-damned warship, and no less."

Michael Romart hovered beside him, so pleased with the vessel that the sparkle of his grin was matched by proud moisture in his eyes. "Aye," he said. "She's Cap'n Dalton's *Faith* as ever was."

"The devil she is," Ramsey snapped. "I've paid through the very teeth for this folly, though no one has yet explained to me just why I should. Where is my daughter?"

"Miss Constance? Why, she's gone to the chandler's to order out some special stores, sir. She'll be back in a bit. Would you care for tea, sir?"

"I would indeed, Mister Romart, thank you."

Romart turned. "Mister O'Riley!"

Aloft at the mainmast's binding and below at the fife rail, similar carrot-topped heads turned. "Aye, Mister Romart?" they asked in unison. Then the lower one added, "Which Mister O'Riley did you have in mind, then?"

"It doesn't matter." Romart shrugged. "You'll do, Gerald. Go below and get Squire Ramsey some tea, please."

"I'm not Gerald," the indicated one said. "I'm Donald. That's Gerald aloft." But he went, hurrying aft to disappear below the companionway's coaming.

"They're our cook," Romart explained.

105

"Which one?"

"Whichever one is handy." The Virginian shrugged. "Hardly anybody can tell them apart. They're from the Carolinas."

Ramsey gazed around, noticing faces. "All these men look familiar," he said.

"Aye, sir, I expect they do. They all sailed with us — with Cap'n Dalton an' the rest of us — aboard *Fury*. Of course, I'm the only one here who sailed with him aboard *Faith*. That's why Miss Constance needed me here, sir. These are all good lads, but none of them ever saw *Faith* . . . I mean the first *Faith*, of course, as she was when we went to kill the frigate. She was like this. And some of her . . . as much as could be salvaged . . . is in this *Faith*."

Ramsey studied him, trying to understand what he was getting at. There was just no understanding sailors, he thought.

"What I mean is, sir" — Romart wiped his eyes — "is . . . well, this schooner here may not be quite exactly that schooner yonder, but she's the blessed same schooner for all that, seems to me, for in her beats the same true heart."

"Poppycock!" Ramsey snorted. "A ship is a ship, man. That's all it is. A ship."

"Aye." Romart dropped his gaze and shrugged. "Aye, there was a time — I suppose — when every one of us thought the same."

A man came from below, carrying tools in a wooden kit, and Ramsey recognized him both from Dalton's escapades and, more recently, as an employee of Ian McCall. Joseph Tower, a carpenter. Without glancing around, Tower set his kit on the coaming and said grumpily, "She's sealed to the bilges, Mister Romart, though why a decent ship should have such a thing is beyond—" He turned then, saw Ramsey and clamped his mouth shut.

"This is Mister Tower, Squire." Romart waved a casual hand. "He was ship's carpenter of *Fury* before Cap'n Dalton beached all of us colonials. Mister Tower, do you recollect . . . ?"

"Aye," Tower said sheepishly. "Th' lady's father. How do, Squire Ramsey?"

"What sort of thing?" Ramsey's eyes narrowed, pinning him. "Sir?"

"What sort of thing is it that you don't know why a decent ship should have, that this one does?"

"Nothing whatever, sir. I tend to talk to myself at times."

"Mister Tower is from Maryland," Romart observed.

"That should have no bearing on anything," Ramsey declared. "Please answer my question, Mister Tower."

"It's really nothing of note, sir. I . . ."

From the masthead a voice rang down. "On deck!"

Seeming generally relieved, Michael Romart lifted his eyes. "Aye, Mister O'Riley?"

"Th' lady's approachin', Mister Romart. Two points on the port bow."

"Thank you, Mister O'Riley." Romart favored Ramsey with a reassuring smile. "Here comes your daughter now, Squire. I'm sure you can ask her anything you want to know about *Faith.*" He turned to call, "Mister Ives! Hands to the scaffold, please. Miss Constance is back."

"Aye! You men, lend a hand on this scaffold now!"

Ramsey watched open-mouthed as a neat scaffold was lifted over the bow rail and lowered on block and tackle. He strode to the fore, saw Constance, Dora and a pair of cutlass-wielding sailors step out of a coach, and glared at Phillip Ives. "Why didn't you tell me you had a boarding scaffold?"

"You didn't ask, sir. You asked about a gangway or a ladder, but not a scaffold."

When Constance arrived on *Faith's* deck, she hugged her father, fended off his questions and took his hand. "Come with me," she ordered. "I have a surprise for you."

Down the companionway she led him, to a tiny sterncastle that seemed an exact duplicate of that in the original *Faith.* But when he paused to look around, she urged him on, into a tight little galley where one of the O'Riley's offered tea, then stepped aside so that they could pass. At the galley's fore bulkhead Constance smiled, raised her hand and slapped the sheer surface sharply.

"Well," she asked, "what do you think?"

Ramsey blinked. "About what?"

"About this! Honestly, Father. You yourself specified how the first *Faith* should be. Don't you remember?"

He looked again, and remembered. "Ah," he said. "Aha!"

Constance nodded. "Exactly. A false hold, just as before. It was the rum in it that paid you a handsome profit on *Faith*, even though you lost her. So what do you think?"

"Think?" he asked blankly.

"Of course. If I am to take this schooner to sea, I shall require —"

"*You?* You . . . take this to sea?"

"Certainly. Why did you think I was having it outfitted? But there are yet some items I'll need. First, a reliable captain . . ."

"You shall do no such thing! Constance, you are a woman. Women of my acquaintance do not put out to sea with —"

"Oh, poo! We've been over all that before. I have been to sea. And as to going again, I certainly can and I certainly shall. All you need worry about is . . ."

"I absolutely forbid it!"

". . . is a cargo worthy of *Faith II.* You know the kind of cargo I mean, Father."

"I take it you are referring to contraband of some sort . . ."

"Of course. Last time, it was rum. I suppose rum would do nicely again, but I leave that to you, as you certainly know far more about such things than I do."

"I forbid it! I absolutely forbid it! My daughter is . . . well, my daughter is no smuggler!"

"Nonsense!" She stood straight and determined, her eyes ablaze. "I expect I am a very good smuggler. After all, I learned the business from you, didn't I?"

Ramsey lowered his head, gritting his teeth. "So that's what all this has been about? This schooner and all? You want to smuggle contraband?"

"Poo! That's simply a means to make a venture profitable. It isn't the venture itself. My intention is to go and find Patrick Dalton. Now, do you find me a captain and a cargo, or must I find them myself?"

Twelve

As Dalton had fully expected, the wind had come southerly. Now *Pride of Falworth* rode strong on easy seas, her stacked squares driving on the sort of wind that commodity vessels cherish — a steady twenty-five knots abaft her port quarter. For three days no sail or land had been seen, and the two ships drove steadily onward, holding a northwestward course that required no sail handling beyond an occasional trim.

At least for *Pride*, there was no such fuss. Charley Duncan's mission as commander aboard the prize vessel was simply to take her where Dalton — whenever he saw fit to decide upon a destination — ordered, in as efficient and timely a manner as possible.

Aboard *Fury* it was another matter.

For the first time since he acquired the snow, Patrick Dalton had a full complement of hands to man her, and he wasted no time in — as he put it — "taking the measure of her limits."

It was a puzzle to some of those who had sailed with him before. A ship that had fought xebecs, had escaped a pursuing seventy-four, had played hopscotch through the very heart of a Royal Navy troop convoy and had weathered a black squall under tack sail, they supposed, had already had her limits fairly well measured. But it was the captain's way. Given a ship at his command, and a chance to truly sail it, he would play it to its limit as delightedly as a child putting a stick horse through its paces. Those who had sailed with him knew this, and while they might see fit to comment, still they shrugged and bore with him.

It fell, then, to the new hands aboard to stagger about in wide-eyed awe as *Fury* cavorted on the winds, trying first this and then that sail configuration, ranging far out from her larger charge, darting here and there in rushes and passes that most of them would never have believed a vessel of her size could accomplish and — simply as a matter of crew and sail drill — now and then sailing tight circles around the straight-running bark.

"Captain's got the bit in his teeth and the spray in his face," Cadman Wise remarked to Billy Caster as *Fury,* hands aloft and all stations fully manned, did a smart come-about through the wind a half mile ahead of *Pride,* then sheeted home on a starboard tack and shot off on a new course that made her timbers groan and her stays whine. "Puts me in mind of when we first boarded that schooner, up at Long Island, and managed to shake loose from the gunboats. Mercy, how he did shake the sleep out of that *Faith.* Like he had decided a ship can fly and was out to prove it."

Purdy Fisk had wandered near, carrying an armload of chain for repairs on the foremast stays. "Aye," he muttered. "As I recollect, we wound up makin' hull patches while half the world was lookin' to shoot the devil out of us, too."

Aloft a shout rang out. "On deck!"

Wise cupped his hands. "Aye, Mister . . . ah — !" he turned to Fisk — "who is that in the maintop?"

"I believe that's Mister Livingston." Fisk squinted. "He's a good lad aloft, the cap'n said."

Wise cupped his hands again. "Aye, Mister Livingston?"

"Signals from the bark, Mister Wise. They want to know whether the captain's decided yet where we might be going."

Billy Caster frowned, perplexed. "They can't say that, can they, Mister Wise? With buntings, I mean . . . there is no such message in the manual of codes."

Wise grinned at the clerk. "Liberal translations, Mister Caster. Far more can be said with buntings than's in any Admiralty manual. I expect what they signal is 'request destination,' or some such thing." He turned aft. "Quarter ahoy!"

On the snow's little quarterdeck, Patrick Dalton waved. "I heard the report, thank you, Mister Wise."

Billy Caster deposited his load — two buckets of tar — at the fore starboard pinrail, and headed aft in time to see banners rising on *Fury*'s stern lanyards. The message was simple, as he read it. "Maintain course," it said.

As he passed the bosun he tilted his head. "What would be the 'liberal translation' of that, then, Mister Wise?"

Wise glanced around. "That? Why, lad, that says, 'Attend to your business, Mister Duncan, and I shall attend to mine.' "

"Oh."

Dalton called new sailing orders from astern and Wise shrilled his pipe. All along *Fury*'s rails and aloft, men scrambled to trim sails as the snow's rudder bit water and the ship slewed about in a hard turn, throwing sheets of spray alee.

"Is that madman out to capsize us and drown us all?" one of the new hands complained.

Billy called over his shoulder, "Mind your tongue, I'd advise, Mister Pleasant. The captain knows what he's doing."

"Then, what is it that he knows he's doing?" another sailor chided.

From behind him, Billy heard still another voice — one of the ex-Royal Navy sailors among the recruits — respond. "He's makin' a sailor of you, Henry. Of us all."

"By damn, I already *am* a sailor!"

"Well, when he's done, you'll be *his* kind of sailor. Now shut your mouth and lend a hand on this sheet."

On the quarterdeck, Billy Caster stalked toward the stern rail, then stopped when Dalton wagged a finger at him. "Sir?"

"Don't involve yourself in forecastle chatter, Mister Caster. As clerk, you rank amidships, and it might be taken amiss."

"Aye, sir," Billy fumed. "But, sir, some of them say —"

"I have a fair idea of what they say, Mister Caster. Pay it no mind."

"But, sir . . ."

"Mister Caster, at the moment fully two-thirds of *Fury*'s crew are new recruits. And half of those have not sailed aboard a fighting ship. There are drills and reactions that they must learn, and the sooner the better. They will complain, but they will learn, and be glad they did should we have need of fancy sailing against an enemy."

"Aye, sir." Still fuming, Billy turned away.

Dalton said, "Speak your mind, Mister Caster."

He turned back. "Aye, sir. Well, I realize the new men may not be accustomed to our . . . ah, to your standards, but can't they realize it may save their lives to drill? You said, 'sailing against an enemy,' sir. Isn't that all we have of late? Enemies, I mean?"

For an instant, Patrick Dalton looked as though he would smile. But he held his face in check. "Feeling lost and alone, Mister Caster?"

"It does seem that everyone's hand is against us, sir."

"Oh, I expect we have few enough seeking to do us harm. There likely was a search for us, after we parted company with the king's custodians. I expect Captains Selkirk and Watson may have been a bit miffed at our departure, and I'm certain those cruiser commanders, Fell and Smith, would give their pensions for a crack at us. It was necessary that we go to ground for a time. But I imagine those gentlemen have by now found other ways to amuse themselves, so I expect we can go about our business now. And fortune has attended to our other problem. We are no longer short-handed."

"No, we aren't short-handed, sir," Billy agreed, glancing at the teeming deck and yards.

"All that being the case, we no longer need to rest in seclusion. You have noted, I'm sure, that at present we are pursuing a course."

"I apologize, sir. I was only thinking . . ."

"It has been a long, tiresome time since any of us saw a snug harbor, eh? Well, you are right in that, Mister Caster. Long enough, I'd say."

"Do you know where we are going yet, sir? Where we will take the bark, and all those people from the islands?"

"We should know soon enough." Dalton gazed critically forward, along *Fury's* working deck, then cupped his hands. "Mister Wise! I should enjoy seeing another downwind come-about, if you please! Hands to sheets for trim!" He turned to the helm. "Come a quarter to starboard, please, Mister Locke. Smartly now."

"Aye, sir." The wheel spun, and *Fury* shook herself like a fox in the rain, then skidded into a hard turn as sails aloft were brought about to respond to the rudder.

"Ah," Dalton said. "I believe we are getting the hang of it. At the next drill, Mister Caster, I'd like all gunnery stations equipped for tutelage. Also please advise Misters Pugh and Crosby that I shall need them to instruct."

"Gun and sail, sir?"

"By all means. Directly after breakfast tomorrow."

"Aye, sir . . . sir?"

"Something else, Mister Caster?"

"Yes, sir. You said you will know shortly where we are going. Beg pardon, sir, but how will you know?"

"A fair enough question. We are coming into sea lanes now, and can expect traffic. At the first opportunity, I intend to make inquiries." He raised his head, listening to the sounds of *Fury's* rigging as the snow came trim on her new course. "She sings, Mister Caster. With practice she will sing better, but doesn't she have a lovely voice?"

Billy listened and kept his peace. He knew his captain well enough not to speculate on how much of the thought was admiration for a trim vessel and how much of it was loneliness . . . how much of the distance in Dalton's voice was the distance of open sea to that shore where Constance Ramsey waited for him.

Aboard *Pride of Falworth,* Aaron Fairfield leaned burly arms on the bark's quarterrail and frowned, gazing at the cavorting warship in the distance. "Where the blazes is he going now?" he grumped. "If he's to escort us to safety, then why isn't he here now, escorting?"

"Captain Dalton?" Charley Duncan looked where Fairfield was looking, and grinned. "He's shaking out his ship, sir. Putting it through its numbers, and breaking in new crew as well. Don't worry your head about it. He'll be here should we have need of him."

"Well, I wish he would stay closer at hand. And I wish to blazes he'd tell us where he intends to take us. I've had near rebellion on my hands for the past two days. My people want to know where we're going, and they aren't pleased that the matter is entirely up to a man who seems bent on sinking his own ship before we get there."

"Get where, sir?"

"To our destination, confound it . . . wherever that proves to be. Why won't he tell us?"

"Beggin' your pardon, Squire, but you folks haven't been very specific yourselves about where you want to go. I believe I've heard every port in the Americas mentioned at one time or another since we allowed you aboard — Mister Quarterstone! Look yonder, at the portside topyard . . . who is that up there running along the footropes?"

Quarterstone squinted. "One of the children, I fancy. Do you want him got down?"

"I certainly do! What lunatic let a child go aloft like that?" Duncan rounded on Fairfield. "Squire, I must insist that you keep a tight check on your people. This is a sailing ship, not a bloody nursery!"

Forward on the passenger deck a woman looked up, screamed and vaulted to the rail, trying to climb the shrouds. Sailors there caught her and set her back on the deck, then several of them started up the ratlines. High above them a small figure clambered about happily, oblivious to height and danger.

"That was Mistress Cabot," Fairfield said. "It must be her boy up there."

"Does Mistress Cabot have a whaling rod, I wonder?"

"The widow Cabot is a devout woman, Mister Duncan, and not one to lay on with the rod where her children are concerned."

"Possibly she doesn't know the correct procedure," Duncan decided. "Mister Nelson, take deck watch, please. I'll be back in a bit."

Forward, sailors had closed on the child overhead and made their capture. Now they were handing the lad down, hand to hand, toward the deck. Duncan strode from the quarterdeck to the promenade and headed forward, pausing for a moment at the mizzen skirts to select a bit of stiff, wiry clew rope, cut a two-foot length of it and swat it against the open palm of his hand. Satisfied then, he went forward to demonstrate ship's discipline in the best traditions of East London Town, where he himself had learned it not so many years before, as a sandy-haired tyke in the warrens of Picadilly.

The arrival of the vessel's commanding officer amidst the crowd on *Pride*'s forecastle deck caused a stir even beyond the stir already in progress there. Passengers and sailors stood back to let him pass, then closed behind him, curious. "Some of you men."

114

He scowled. "I have noticed the cattle are tending to drift aft. I'll have the working decks clear of livestock." He stepped forward then, separated the salvaged child from its frantic mother and stood over the lad, glaring downward. "Your name, boy?"

The offender looked up at him with wide eyes and swallowed noisily, then managed, "Henry, sir. Henry Cabot."

"And how old are you, Henry Cabot?"

"Ah . . . nine years, sir. Almost."

"Were you told not to climb into the rigging, Henry?"

"Sir, I only wanted to —"

"Answer my question! Were you told not to go up there?"

"Well, they said don't, but I just wanted to —"

"Hush!" Duncan turned to Henry's mother. "Mistress Cabot, do you intend to discipline Henry for disobedience?"

"I most certainly do," she said. "I'll give him such a talking to that —"

"Nonsense!" He held out the length of stiff rope. "This is fit discipline, mistress. Will you apply it?"

"Oh, no, sir!" She seemed shocked. "I don't hold with violence. Children should be raised in the —"

"Then, I will," he said. He turned, knelt and hoisted the struggling boy across his leg, pinioned him there and delivered five sharp whacks to his behind. Then he set him on his feet, stood over him and roared, "Silence!"

Henry Cabot's wail of outrage cut off instantly.

"That's better," Duncan said. "Now, Henry Cabot, what is it that you are not to do?"

"C-climb up where th' s-sails are, sir."

"Bright lad." Duncan grinned. He turned again to the miscreant's aghast mother. "I've not had children of my own, Mistress Cabot; but I was one once, and I know that a child is most impressionable in early years. This —" he indicated the rope — "is a fine impressor." He handed it to her, turned with all the dignity he could muster and stalked off aft, scattering passengers and several chickens as he went. At the taffrail, Mister Hoop and his Frenchmen — the big man seemed to have taken personal charge of the pair — were watching with interest.

"Nicely done, Mister Duncan," Hoop said.

115

"Tres formidable, M'sieur le Commandant," one of the Frenchmen agreed.

"Little something I learned from Patrick Dalton," he admitted, stepping aside to allow passage of a pair of goats. "On a well-run ship, laxity cannot be tolerated." He gazed at the Frenchmen. "Have you learned anything more from this pair, Mister Hoop?"

"Aye, I believe so. Francois there . . . ah, Mister Leblanc, that is, he once kept company with three sisters all at the same time, and not a one of them knowin' about the other two, least 'til they found out some way, and that's why he became a sailor."

"I mean about what the captain wants to know, Mister Hoop. Anything about this vessel and why somebody tried to scuttle her?"

"Oh, that. Well, it seems likely it was her own officers done it, sure enough, so they could become pirates and nobody know who they'd been before. The captain's name was Boodelair, though it seems odd he'd have a French name and him bein' colonial English."

"Bood-lair?"

"Oui. m'sieur." Francois nodded. *"Le Pri'e d' Falwort', M'sieur le Capitain Bootlair. Jean Chelvie Bootlair. Oui."*

"Odd indeed," Duncan agreed. "But I'll report it, and maybe Captain Dalton can make sense of it."

"On deck!"

Duncan glanced up. "Mister Hoop, there are chickens in the main shrouds. Please have them cleared. Who is that at top lookout?"

Hoop shaded his eyes. "Aye, sir. That would be Mister Singleterry, I think."

Duncan cupped his hands. "Aye, Mister Singleterry?"

A man passing beside him stopped and turned. "Aye, sir?"

"I was calling to Mister Singleterry," Duncan said.

"Aye, sir. That's who I am. John Singleterry."

"Then, who is that in the tops, at lookout?"

"That's Raymond Mudd, sir. It's his turn."

Duncan tried again. "Aye, Mister Mudd?"

"Sail ahead, deck! One ship, tops in view!"

All around him, passengers and deckmen turned to squint to

116

the rails, although there was nothing to be seen yet from the deck. Hoop and his Frenchmen collared a few landsmen and began collecting chickens.

Astern again, Duncan retrieved his deck from Finian Nelson. "Run up the buntings, please, Mister Quarterstone," he said. "Sail sighted, dead ahead."

"And might I ask who you're signalling to?" Aaron Fairfield sneered.

"To *Fury*, of course. We are an escorted vessel, Squire. When there's a sighting, it's up to our escort to deal with it."

"What escort? I haven't seen that gunship since you left the deck to insult Mistress Cabot. Where is he?"

"I imagine you've been looking the wrong direction, Squire." Duncan grinned and pointed aport. *Fury* was there, just a few hundred yards away, bearing down from astern as though the bark were standing still. As they watched, the snow — big guns abristle and sails full of wind — dashed past and shot out ahead, going to intercept.

"Belay the buntings, Mister Quarterstone." Duncan grinned. "Captain's seen it himself and is off to have a better look. Aye, and isn't she a bonny sight!" He glanced down, then turned. "Mister Nelson, why is there a cat on the quarterdeck?"

"I don't know, Commander. I expect it belongs to some of the passengers."

"Animals do not belong on the quarterdeck, Mister Nelson. Even on a bedammed bark. Take it below and give it to the cook."

Nelson was a newcomer, but he was ex-Royal Navy and only paled slightly at the command. "Aye, sir. Ah, how would you like it prepared, sir?"

"I don't want it cooked, Mister Nelson. A cat's place is the galley, where there may be rats to catch."

Odd, he thought as Finian Nelson headed below with the new ship's cat, only a moment before he had watched the trim snow bound past, and had mentioned what a thing of beauty she was. But he wasn't at all sure whether he had been thinking of *Fury* at that moment, or of the golden hair of the widow Cabot.

117

Thirteen

At three miles' distance the stranger was fully visible — a single vessel sailing a slow, methodical easterly course and making no attempt to elude interception by *Fury*, though the snow obviously had been seen. Dalton laid his glass on the stranger, then climbed aloft on the port shrouds for a better look.

The ship was not of a design usually seen in these lanes, but he knew its class. Some might call it a barkentine, from the set of its sails, but the vessel was more than a barkentine. Stubby and square-nosed, with the sloped deck of a cargo cruiser and a wide belly that somehow avoided the ambling-cow look of many freighters — rather it had the appearance of that breed of man who might seem fat at first impression but was in fact as broad and solid as a keg of drawn nails — the vessel was of the type called corrida.

Dalton had seen such ships before, in his service amidships in the Mediterranean, and now this one lofted its pennants in greeting.

Thirty feet above him, in the main trestletrees, Purdy Fisk also was watching the stranger. "He flies a trade crest, sir," he called. "Is it one you know?"

"I've seen it, Mister Fisk. The gull and shield of the Calderas."

"The Portuguese company? What would their ship be doing here?"

"Trading, I imagine. That is what Caldera ships do."

"But alone, sir? In these waters? He's just asking to be taken."

Despite himself, Dalton grinned. "I wouldn't want to be the pirate who tried it, Mister Fisk. More than one hound has burrowed for the hare and found the badger. And bled for his efforts. That ship may look like a stodgy cargo vessel, but it has skin six inches thick and most certainly as many guns as we do."

"Well, sir, he sees us now for what we are, though he hasn't a notion *who* we are, yet he hasn't so much as hove a spar to avoid us. So it stands to reason he's confident, right enough."

"Keep him well in view, Mister Fisk. And you and Mister — who is that forward? Mister Hemingway?"

"Aye, it's him, sir."

"You may both keep a wary eye for other sails as well, if you please."

"Aye, sir."

Dalton swung down to the deck and strode aft. "Mister Caster!"

"Aye, sir?"

"I believe we have an East India Company ensign in the flag locker, do we not?"

"Aye, sir. We have just about any flag you might want, sir."

"Bring it up, then. Mister Locke, stand by the lanyards please. We shall favor the gentleman ahead with colors."

"Aye, sir."

As the two ships closed to within a mile, *Fury* raised her colors with salute pennants at fore and main, and buntings aft requesting an interview. For long minutes there was no response, though Dalton knew the Caldera captain was glassing both him and the distant bark in the background, making up his mind whether this was, in fact, a friendly cruiser on peaceful escort, or possibly a trap.

"Badger he may be, as you said to Mister Fisk," Victory Locke allowed. "But he is cautious."

"Well he might be, Mister Locke." Dalton stood casually at *Fury*'s rail, waiting out the inspection. "These are weird waters in these parts, and many a ship that's sailed here was never seen again."

"Pirates, sir?"

"Pirates, aye. And war, and storms . . . and some say other things as well."

"On deck!" the call came from aloft. "He's running up signals."

"I see him, Mister Fisk." He raised his glass. The two ships now were close enough that he could read the name on the trader's bow escutcheons. She was the *Sao Molino*. At least a dozen guns he could count at fore and bows, and they were more than the popguns usually found on cargo vessels. These were ranging guns and fighting guns, and he had no doubt the men behind them knew the use of them. Above her port wales, buntings flew. "Approach and be recognized" was the signal.

"He says to come over and have a chat, but mind how we behave ourselves," Victory Locke read, helpfully.

"I read him, Mister Locke. Please respond that we will come about for him."

"Aye, sir."

"Two points astarboard, helm. Hands a'deck, stand by to come about and rig for starboard tack. Stand by to furl mains and tops."

"Aye, sir."

Amidships pipes shrilled as *Fury* lay over to her right, swept cleanly out away from the trader's path, then turned her jaunty nose through the wind to stride alongside at three chain lengths' distance, giving *Sao Molino* courtesy of the wind.

Across the intervening water, at the trader's poop, her captain grinned and raised his hat, then said something to a man beside him, and more buntings went aloft.

"He makes us for a brig, sir," Victory Locke said. "He wonders what sort of repairs we have made, that there is an extra mast aft our mainmast."

"Run up our request for interview again, please," Dalton ordered.

This time the request was granted, and the corrida lost way as her mains were reefed. *Fury* followed suit, edging closer in the process until the two vessels crept along side by side, not fifty yards apart.

Billy Caster was standing by with a speaking horn, and Dalton raised it. "Ahoy *Sao Molino!* Do you speak English?"

The trader captain's dark beard parted to reveal white teeth. He raised his own horn. "I speak English most good," he called.

"Pasco Santua at your service, senor! Who are you?"

"Patrick Dalton, captain of *Fury,* on civil escort. What can you tell me of lanes and conditions westward?"

"I can tell you more over a little Madeira in my cabin than I can with this idiotic cone, senor. Will you come across for a visit?"

"Delighted," Dalton called. "Myself and my clerk, by launch."

Billy Caster stared wide-eyed at the strange ship so close alongside. "Are you sure, sir? Do you see the guns he has pointed at us?"

"Aye, and he sees what we have aimed at him. At this range, we would both likely go to the bottom if anyone fired. Therefore, I believe we will behave ourselves as gentlemen. Mister Wise! Hands to davits to lower the jolly boat, please. And four rowers."

"Aye, sir."

"Mister Locke, please signal Mister Duncan to maintain course and keep his distance."

"Aye, sir."

Pasco Santua's private cabin in *Sao Molino's* wide sterncastle was as richly appointed as Dalton's own cabin aboard *Fury* was Spartan. And the Portuguese trader was totally at home in his surroundings. A short, burly man with a wide belly, thick arms and a pair of mischievous eyes above his full, dark beard, Santua was every inch the merchant trader as he offered ornate, cushioned chairs to Dalton and Billy, and poured scarlet wine into silver mugs from a crystal decanter.

"Saludes, senores!" He raised his goblet and tossed back a long sip, then perched on an elaborate tapestried divan with ornate silver scrollwork. "Now we can exchange information, eh? Where are you bound with your cargo vessel?"

"That depends a bit on conditions in the colonies," Dalton said. "I have passengers who are somewhat choosy about who they encounter."

"Ah." Santua grinned. "The Whigs and the Tories, eh? Things are most upset in the English colonies now. Royalists, loyalists, patriots, privateers, pirates. Here am I, simple Pasco Santua, a man of peace trying only to deliver a bit more than

121

my respected factors — the Family Caldera — require so that I, too, might share a bit of profit, and see! Two months at the American ports and still I sail with half a cargo." For a moment, it seemed the mischievous eyes above the dark beard might fill with tears. Then he shrugged. *"Hors d'combat,* as the French might say, *senores.* Victim of the misfortune of other peoples' wars. Tell me, which sort of colonial would your people prefer to encounter . . . those who presently favor the English king or those who do not?"

"You've seen my colors, Captain," Dalton said, watching him closely.

"The British Indies flag? Of course. It is what I myself would have chosen had I met me here and wanted to talk about the west. Tell me, Captain, why does a British brig such as your *Fury* have such odd masts . . . and such rigging as though for a great many more sails than it has shown?"

"Because it isn't a brig," Dalton said. "It is a snow. A design originated in the American British colonies. You used a French term, Captain. Do you also speak French?"

"A bit," Santua admitted. "In order for a Portuguese trader to trade, it is useful to have a number of languages. That is because hardly anyone outside of Portugal — and of course some of the South American colonies — ever seems to speak Portuguese."

"And you sail with short cargo? What cargo were you hoping to acquire, Captain?"

"Ah, any number of things make trade. Indigo, some spices, smelted copper, a little American rum, perhaps. What I most expected was a cargo of cotton to be transshipped. A neutral transporter is useful to people whose vessels are subject to seizure. But the ship from Virginia never arrived at the traders' port, so I go home half-empty. It is very sad."

"Many things can happen to a merchant ship these days." Dalton nodded.

"More than usual, lately." The Portuguese spread his hands. "The pirates, they multiply like rats it seems. At Governor's Harbour they tell of one who destroyed a warship almost in the fairway, then took two merchantmen the following day. Those. ashore could even see the villain's name. It was *Valkyrie.* That was Thibaud's ship, but they say it has a new master now. Jack Shelby, he calls himself."

Dalton shook his head in revulsion, then changed the subject. "Cotton, you said?" He glanced at Billy Caster, who was already assembling inventories atop his ledger case. "Captain Santua, we are well-met, I think. Perhaps we can do a bit of business."

Charley Duncan held *Pride* on a wide course and was abreast of *Fury* and the trader at a distance of two miles when his top lookouts read signals at the snow's high arms. Even at this distance there was no mistaking the message or its source. Patrick Dalton requested his presence.

"How do you know that is a true signal?" Aaron Fairfield protested as *Pride* came hard aport and hands went aloft to reef her mains and topsails while sheets were hauled a'deck to trim for the difficult sixty-degree tack.

"I know it's true because it is from Patrick Dalton." Duncan sighed, holding his patience between his teeth.

"You don't know what is going on over there," Fairfield argued. "That could be a bloody pirate ship. Likely the blaggard has gulled your captain into surrender and now waits to take us as a prize."

"Hard over, Mister Hoop," Duncan called. "You men! Let's haul about those yards in unison! This may be naught but a slogging square-rigger, but let's look alive and see if we can't make it go in the proper direction!" Turning, he almost collided with a goat that had cleared the portside ladder at a bound and now was nibbling at the stern sheets wound about their pins. With a curse he shooed it away and wagged an irritated finger under Fairfield's nose. "I have asked you politely, Squire, to have your people keep their bloody livestock forward of the stem, and preferably below. And while you're about it, if you don't care for the way I direct this vessel, you may leave the quarterdeck and good riddance."

Fairfield herded the errant creature down to the deck and wagged a finger at a large young landsman, who hurried aft to collect it.

"You have no call to address me in such manner, sir," Fairfield growled up at Duncan. "We are paying passengers aboard this ship."

"Then, act like it!" Duncan turned his back on the man, exasperated, and strode to the helm. Almost at his heels, young Henry Cabot trailed after him, copying his every move.

"If you deliver us into the hands of pirates, it's on your head!" Fairfield called.

Duncan didn't look back, but clenched his right fist and swatted it upward, slapping his arm with his left hand in a gesture he had learned in the Mediterranean. Behind him, Henry Cabot copied the motion.

At the helm, Mister Hoop's eyes widened. "Beg pardon, Mister Duncan, but I didn't know that ship's officers knew about things like that."

"I'm in command because Patrick Dalton put me here," Duncan seethed. "But you mind your tongue, Mister Hoop. I'm no more a bleedin' officer than you are, and well you know it."

"Oh, aye." Hoop lowered his eyes in apology. "I know that, Mister Duncan. But, well, *somebody* has to be an officer here. Otherwise how will any of us know what to do? You see?"

"You'll do what I say to do. Captain Dalton said so."

"Aye, that's what I mean. Folks is as folks does, I say, an' I never saw any officer make gestures like that."

Duncan took a deep breath, knowing the man was right. He had to set the example, or risk laxity aboard his ship. "What do you suppose a proper officer would do about a bloody nuisance like that squire, Mister Hoop?"

The big man scratched his head, thinking. "Hard to say for certain. Knock the bugger in the head, maybe, or throw him overboard. But he'd doubtless be polite about it."

Pride could manage no more than three knots on a hard tack, but she hadn't far to go. *Fury* and the trader came to meet her, sailing side by side on an easy reach, *Fury* with her greater press of sail holding the lee position as was customary between ships met at sea.

At three cables the pair went about and reefed their sails, and *Pride* crept between them at Dalton's order.

Nearly rail-to-rail, Duncan looked down at his captain on

124

the snow, and Dalton hailed him. "Snug your vessel to the trading ship, please, Mister Duncan, and rig your yards for cargo handling. Captain Santua has agreed to buy all of the cotton you have on board."

"Aye, sir. That's good news. We can well use the extra space below."

"I daresay you can. When you are snugged, Mister Duncan, please send your Frenchmen across to the *Sao Molino*. They speak French there, and have agreed to interrogate them."

"Aye, sir. May I send Mister Hoop to look after them, sir? They seem to trust him."

"As you please, Mister Duncan. Look alive, now."

"Aye, sir."

"Mister Duncan?"

"Aye, Captain?"

Dalton pointed. "What is that, standing beside you?"

Duncan glanced aside and down, then shrugged. "It's a child, sir. His name is Henry Cabot, and I whaled him for climbing aloft. Now he keeps following me about, sir."

"I see. And what are those, along your taffrail?"

"Those are chickens, sir. I've had them forward a dozen times, but . . . well, sir, chickens do seem to just go where they please when they wander."

While the sheered yardarms of *Pride*'s fore-and-aft mainmast courses were reinforced with cable from the topsail cleats and pressed into service as gantries for the transfer of heavy cotton bales, Dalton invited Pasco Santua to supper.

It was a fine occasion, around a hastily erected trestle table on the neutral ground of the bark's quarterdeck. Warm tropic breezes wafted from astern, muting the clatter amidships where winches whined and strong men sweated in transfer of cargo, carrying off the stench of livestock assembled at the forecastle taffrails and the chatter of passengers there trying to keep their families and their goods safely distant from the working arena.

Nathan Claremore proved himself a worthy cook by sending up from *Fury*'s little galley a four-course meal. Pea soup with onions was followed by a heaping platter of what might once have been smoked goat, though the one-armed cook had so laced it with salt and lemon juice that it might have been anything. And the main course brought applause from those at table — all except Aaron Fairfield, who frowned when he recognized it.

Baked chicken.

Dessert was oat cakes with honey, and Santua capped the meal with a bit of fine brandy, tobacco and pipes from his personal stores aboard *Sao Molino*.

As they settled back, as relaxed as men might be aboard a thin-skinned bark flanked by fighting ships with crews at their guns to keep things honest, the trader raised his goblet. "To war and fortune, senores," he said.

"At least to fortune," Dalton responded.

Fairfield, Duncan and Santua's first officer raised goblets in response.

"My sailing master has brought to date your charts," Santua said. "And your clerk has note of all the latest intelligences that I have heard. You will note that the English fleet seems to have withdrawn itself from the Chesapeake and the Delaware. They say the American general, Senor Washington, is on the move with his army now, and the English generals have gone to meet him in the north; so that is where King George's ships must be."

"I rely upon your assessment and your ears, sir," Dalton assured him. "And by the way, have we learned anything new from my Frenchmen?"

"The name of their captain, the one who scuttled his own ship."

"We already knew that, sir," Duncan reminded Dalton. "A Frenchy name. Boodelair or some such."

Santua grinned. "Not Boo'dlair, Mister Duncan. Butler. A good English name, I believe."

"Butler?" Dalton frowned in thought. Somewhere he had encountered the name. A Captain Butler.

"One other thing that might interest you," Santua said. "Not from the French sailors, but from the guild codes."

"Guild codes?"

"On the cotton I have just bought from you. Guild codes.

The cotton was consigned by a Virginia gentleman, Senor Ian McCall. Maybe this was his ship that I was waiting for at the islands."

Only one who knew him very well might have known that just at that moment, a puzzle came together in Patrick Dalton's mind.

Fourteen

Tropic dusk was on the sea when *Pride*'s crew secured from cargo-handling and swung the bark's yardarms back to sailing position. In the forecastle and forward holds, Aaron Fairfield's fugitives were hard at work fitting themselves into expanded accommodations. At the stern, Dalton and Santua stood at ease, watching the sun's last haloes recede beyond westward waters. The sunset had been spectacular, a brilliance of crimsons and golds that flared and danced aloft before muting down to a whisper of brilliant red just at horizon . . . red, then deep rose, then abruptly, just for an instant, a flash of bright green as final day bowed out.

"We take our amusements where we find them, eh, senor?" Santua puffed his pipe contentedly. "It is the way of the sea."

Dalton nodded, but a tracery of concern played at his brow. He tasted the breeze, read its messages in the whisper of rigging aloft and in the unruly dark hair teasing about his ears. "Weird waters," he muttered.

Santua glanced around at him. "Senor?"

"It was nothing, Captain Santua. Just an odd fancy."

"Ah? What means this word, 'weird'?"

"It is a Saxon word, I suppose. Or possibly Nordic. It means a thing is unusual, or seems unsettling somehow. Possibly it is just a change in the weather, as those cloud colors might indicate."

"You have sailed these latitudes before, Captain Dalton?"

"Only a very little, some years ago."

"Maybe it is the little ones . . . the little people . . . telling you their secrets." Santua grinned. "Yes, I know of the stories of the Irish. Some of them are very like the tales of the mountain folk in the north of my own land. Very odd."

"Children's tales." Dalton shrugged.

"You think so? Once I had a sailor on my ship — my first ship — who was from Toska. More than once he warned me of dangers that had not yet occurred. I learned to listen when he spoke. He was often right."

"Valuable man to have in your service. Is he still with you?"

"Alas, no. One evening off Pascobal he came to me and asked that I write for him a letter, to his family. He said he would not see them again. The very next morning he was in the forward hold, securing netting, and a wave caused some cargo to shift. He died instantly."

"Secured from off-loading, Captain," Charley Duncan called. "We are ready to make sail."

"Then, we shall leave you your deck, Commander." Dalton turned. "Mister Caster, are the accounts settled?"

"Aye, sir. Cargo shipped aboard *Sao Molino* and payment received, as agreed. I've fixed your seal to the lading for Mister . . . ah, Senor Letitho, Captain Santua's cargo officer, and he has given us receipt."

"Very well. Captain Santua, it has been a pleasant meeting. Possibly we shall meet again."

"My pleasure, senor." The trader's mischievous eyes twinkled in lantern light. "Possibly ashore next time, though? Even the best of meals is better enjoyed when one is not sitting between the muzzles of loaded cannons. Such nervous situations give rise to . . . ah . . . weird notions."

"I agree," Dalton said.

With great ceremony, two captains shook hands, descended to the bark's main deck and parted there, each bridging an opposite rail to return to his own command. *Sao Molino* cast off first, taking on way from her sails even as she cleared the bark's bow and signalled a goodbye with her stern buntings. When she was clear and away, Dalton looked at the sky, gauged the wind and said, "Mister Locke to helm, please. Mister Wise, hands a'deck to make sail. Stand by to cast off and come to the wind. Course north by west."

129

He paused when a commotion broke out yards away and above, on *Pride's* higher deck. After a moment, Charley Duncan appeared there with a lamp. "Moment, Captain," he called. He turned away, listening to someone out of sight, then reappeared. "Captain, I'm sorry to report, sir, but there are some aboard that Portugee vessel who are less than honorable people."

"What is the problem, Mister Duncan?"

"Our best cargo windlass seems to be missing, sir. It was secured at the port stanchions, but now it's gone. It looks as though the Portugees stole it." At Duncan's side a small head appeared at the rail, gazing eastward at the vanishing corrida. As though punctuating what Duncan had said, little Henry Cabot slapped his fisted arm upward in a gesture of derision.

Dalton sighed. It was far too late now to do anything about it, even if he had been tempted to confront an armed corrida over the loss of a windlass. "Never mind, Mister Duncan," he said. "When I am clear, you may make sail by the wind on course north by west."

"Aye, sir. Do we know where we're going yet, sir?"

"We are bound for Virginia, Mister Duncan."

"Aye, sir. I've some aboard who'll sleep better for knowin' where we're bound. I'll tell her straight away."

"Her?"

"I mean them, sir. The passengers. Ah, sir?"

"Yes, Mister Duncan?"

"Bit of a surprise for you below, sir. In your cabin. Something you might see fit to enjoy, and I couldn't very well keep it here aboard *Pride,* what with all them thievin' Portugees about."

"What is it, Mister Duncan?"

"Oh, just a bit of a comfort, sir. We're standin' by to loose lines whenever you want to cast off."

"Very well, Mister Duncan. Mister Wise, stand by lines fore and aft, please. Cast off and make sail to come about to course."

"Aye, sir." Pipes shrilled, and *Fury* shivered as pike poles thrust the two vessels apart and her jib sails rose to take the wind. In evening's last light the jaunty snow veered out from the bark, making a long, languid half circle while the larger vessel got the wind in its sails and picked up way. Only when *Pride*

130

was rigged and running on a course that aimed her at the distant American shore did *Fury* make her final trim, move in on the bark's windward flank and secure for the dark-hours watches.

When all was well, Dalton turned his deck over to Claude Mallory and went below.

And found Charley Duncan's "bit of a surprise" in his cabin. An elaborate, tapestried divan with ornate silver scrollwork. The very settee that had been in Pasco Santua's sumptuous cabin on *Sao Molino*.

As Billy Caster, on his way to his own quarters, paused to gawk past his captain, Dalton sighed and shook his head. "Mister Duncan, you are incorrigible," he muttered. "And you so righteously indignant over the loss of a windlass, too."

Distantly, through the open companion hatch overhead, he heard, "On deck!" and the reply, "Aye tops?"

He couldn't hear the report, but he heard rapid footsteps above the skylights and swung to the ladder just as a silhouette appeared at the hatch.

"I'm here, Mister Mallory," he said. "What is it?"

"Fog risin' ahead, sir. Tops says it looks deep."

"I am coming up, Mister Mallory. Please have a'standby lamps fore and aft."

"Aye, sir."

He buttoned his coat and hurried to the deck, turning to peer ahead. There rode *Pride,* three cables off the starboard bow, and beyond was the dark sea with starlight overhead. But there was another thing, as well. In the distance, the horizon had become thicker . . . an indistinct dark band between the bowl of sky and the distant star-glittered sea.

Behind him, Dalton heard Billy Caster arrive on deck. Without turning, he asked, "How do you fare the night, Mister Caster?"

"Wind at twenty and steady," the youth said. "Holding on the port quarter. Clear sky."

"Do you see what lies ahead, Mister Caster?"

"Aye, sir. I see the fog."

"And is this fog weather, would you say?"

"No, sir. I wouldn't have said so."

131

"Nor would I," Dalton admitted. "These are indeed weird waters." He went up the short quarterdeck ladder in two steps. "Have you a standby on bow lamps, Mister Mallory?"

"Aye, sir. Both bow and stern."

"Have you signalled the *Pride* yet?"

"No, sir. But he has seen the fog, sir. He signalled it."

"Very well, Mister Mallory. Signal *Pride* to display lanterns astern, port and starboard, and to tell spotters to keep a good eye on our lanterns. Visibility may be limited ahead."

"Aye, sir."

Dalton went to the quarterrail. "Mister Wise, open our bow lamps if you please. Spotters afore to keep the bark's stern lamps in sight, and we'll hold course and lay close back until the weather passes."

"Aye, sir."

Billy Caster was gazing ahead, where the fog bank seemed to grow like a rising wall, doubling its height minute by minute. "Pardon, Captain, but how can we approach so quickly? Is it coming toward us? Against the wind?"

"Not moving against the wind, Mister Caster. Rather, I'd say it is growing rapidly. Widening toward us."

Billy watched in fascination as the tenuous dark wall ahead began to tower into the night sky. Then his attention was caught by peculiar lights at the base of it — little shapeless glows of greenish hue that moved about here and there like the glow of lanterns carried by men obscured by heavy mist.

The foretop had seen it, too. "On deck! Lights ahead, in the fog!"

Everyone on deck was peering forward now, straining to make out what could be there.

Dalton studied the pattern of the lights — a random, running movement of glows within the fog, this way and that, with no obvious reason or order. The lights glowed and muted, moving from left to right to left again, low in the fog. They seemed to be floating about on the sea. And they were all of a color. A pale, pulsating green.

"Foxfire," he muttered.

"Sir?"

"Foxfire, Mister Caster. Or something like it. Vapors in the seaweed, possibly. Mister Wise, sounder afore please. Sound at intervals, report shoaling at mark eight."

"Aye, sir." The whistle shrilled. "Sound for depth at the bow! Hail at mark eight!"

"Weird waters," Dalton muttered. "Very well, we shall simply keep each other in sight and hold course."

"Sir?" Claude Mallory was at the compass stand, holding a hooded lantern high, tapping the glass face of the compass case.

"Mister Mallory?"

"You'd better have a look, sir. The compass has gone amok. It's spinning this way and that as though we were going in circles."

"On deck!"

"Aye, tops?"

"The bark has entered fog, sir!"

"Spotters afore! Keep an eye on those lamps!"

For a minute there was no answer; then Cadman Wise came scurrying aft. "Pardon, sir, but we can't find *Pride*'s lights. She must be dead ahead, sir. She was a bit ago. But there's nothing to be seen there now."

"Was he changing course?"

"Not that anybody could see, sir. True an' steady on he was . . . then he just wasn't there."

At the helm, Victory Locke held a steady trim to winds that sang aloft with no sound of change in them. Yet there was no sign of *Pride of Falworth*, which had been barely a hundred yards away off the starboard bow.

Then, abruptly, *Fury*'s stem penetrated fogs, and the warship slid into inky darkness. Dalton could not even see Cadman Wise, a few yards away on the working deck, almost under the cockpit. He turned. Claude Mallory's raised lamp was a fuzzy glow in darkness, and neither Victory Locke at the helm nor even Billy Caster, who had been just beside him, was visible.

"What is this?" he swore. "What the blazes is going on?"

Trawlers had been at work off Grand Bahama in recent days, whole fleets of stubby little boats with lateen sails and catwalk decks around teeming holds as capacious as their hulls would allow. The weather had been fine for trawling. Clear skies held above seas that rolled in a steady twenty-knot offshore wind, and the fishing had been better than any in months.

The waters were shallow here and teemed with fish, and the season was right for the netting. Flotillas of boats spread across the waters with each dawning, casting and hauling their nets. Some ranged as far out as Little Abaco, where onshore winds, if they came, could swell the sea into mighty rolling waves crashing shoreward from the nearby deeps — waves that could swamp a small craft. But when the winds were seaward, it was time for the taking of fish, and for many days the boats had ranged the banks, doing their work, returning home by moonlight to sort their catches.

On this evening, though, there was a feeling to the winds that raised the bristles on men's arms and sent the prudent among them homeward while there was yet a little light in the sky.

"*El Malo de Mar,*" some called it. Or "*La Obscuridad.*" The dark time. It was not wise to be on the sea at such times, the fishermen knew. Strange things occurred, and sometimes boats — even big ships — disappeared in the dark mists never to return. At first sign of a compass acting strangely, or the crackling of sparks along spray-soaked masts, or the ominous rising of fogs in the distance like great mushroom caps growing, swelling from the sea, the fisher-boats made for home or for the nearest shelter.

Too many stories were told of the *Malo de Mar* for anyone not to take heed.

On this evening there were the sparks, and to the east the domes of fog where green lights danced on the sea, and those who had magnetic compasses saw them gyrate wildly. A hundred boats put about in the fisheries above Little Abaco. A hundred lateens took the quartering wind and made for shore, and each man in each boat prayed for the feel of solid ground beneath his feet.

In a tiny pool of hazy light surrounded by blind darkness, Charley Duncan and Pliny Quarterstone huddled over *Pride's* useless compass, moisture beginning to drip from their chins.

"Blimey, I've not seen the like of this," Duncan admitted. "This stuff is as thick as storm rain, but it didn't come from clouds. It just rose right up out of the water, like."

"Well, we're not likely to be through it soon," Quarterstone frowned. "It's closed in behind, but it's ridin' with us, on the wind. Would you look at that, now? By this box, we're heading due south, not west by north as before."

Duncan turned. Behind him was only darkness. "Mister Nelson, have you . . . Mister Nelson? Are you still at helm?"

"Aye, I'm here," the darkness said.

"Have you altered course at all, then?"

"Not so much as a nudge, sir. Rudder's amidships just as it's been, steering by the wind."

"It's the blinkin' compass that's afoul, then," Duncan decided. "If there was a wind shift, we'd have heard it aloft right enough."

"I can't see hide nor hair of *Fury*." Quarterstone squinted into darkness. "She should be just there, a'flank on our port quarter."

A flicker of greenish light appeared suddenly, alongside the bark, and seemed to sweep across the ship's deck before vanishing beyond. Duncan felt the hair at his nape bristle and tug, as though trying to follow where the light had gone. "What th' bloody 'ell!" he snapped.

From the region of his belt, a small voice echoed him, "What th' bloody 'ell?"

He swung the lantern aside and downward. Henry Cabot stood close beside him, straining to see the erratic compass in its case. Duncan's jaw dropped for an instant; then he caught the boy by the arm. "Here now! What are you doin' aft? Didn't I tell you stop tagging me about, then?"

"Y-yes, sir."

"Then, why aren't you forward, boy? Your mother will be sore fretful."

"I just came aft to fetch the milk goat, sir; then it got to be awful dark, so I came here. Is it rainin', sir? It seems wet enough to be."

"It's only a mist, boy. Now, you get yourself forward where you . . ." He looked into the inky murk beyond the quarterrail.

135

"No, belay that. You'd likely get lost or fall overside. Just stay here for now, but keep out of the way."

"Yes, sir."

Pliny Quarterstone frowned at the youth. "Not *yes,* sir'," he scolded. "On the quarterdeck it's *'aye,* sir.' "

"Y-yes, sir. Aye, sir, sir."

Again there was an abrupt greenish glow that seemed to wash across the ship, and trailed eerie little balls of swirling light in its wake. Duncan felt the ship slew to the left, heeling slightly as its rudder went slack, and turned. "Mister Nelson . . . !"

Where there had been darkness, now there was light, and Finian Nelson crouched wide-eyed beyond the spinning helm, his arms spread at his sides. Just above the hub of the wheel floated a glowing orb, a sphere of light in the mist, and the spokes of the helm glistened as they danced through it. A faint hissing, crackling sound came each time a spoke touched the light.

"Mister Nelson, mind the helm!" Duncan roared, bounding toward the helm box. "It's only foxfire! Control the helm!"

Nelson hesitated for a second, then gritted his teeth and caught the spinning wheel. Dim radiances seemed to run up his arms, and the glowing ball of light diminished and shrunk, then disappeared with an audible pop.

In the darkness Duncan heard the helm being righted, and felt the rudder taking its bit below, but now the set of sails aloft had an unhappy sound. Canvas luffed and fluttered at high yards. *Pride* had lost her trim.

"Put to port a bit, Mister Nelson," he started, then raised an invisible hand and shook his head. "Belay that. Hold as she goes. Captain Dalton will expect us to hold fast to course, and if we come aport, we may collide with him."

"But we've altered course, Commander," Pliny Quarterstone said. "We're astarboard of where we ought to be."

"I know that, Mister Quarterstone!" Duncan snapped. "I just don't know how much or how far. Does the compass tell us anything yet?"

"Accordin' to this bloody thing, we might be going in a circle."

"Well, there's little enough we can do about it, except to try not to fall behind. Mister Hoop!"

"Aye, sir?" Hoop's voice came from just below the quarter-rail.

"Mister Hoop, hands to sheets, please, to trim to present course."

"Aye, sir." Feet scuffled below, and Mister Hoop's bellow echoed in the darkness: "Hands to sheets! Hands to sheets!"

Somewhere near, a voice complained, "I can't even find the blinkin' buttons on me bleedin' trousers, an' he wants me to find the blarsted pinrail?"

Somewhere else there was a thud, followed by cursing and scuffling sounds, and an angry voice. "Watch w'at ye're about there, mate!"

"You watch out, yourself, bloater! I'm tryin' to see what I — by God, it's a goat! Sails to make an' no bloody light to see by an' I've stumbled over a bedammed goat!"

Hoop's roar overrode the chaos on deck. "Look alive, there, blast your blind eyes! Get hands on those sheet lines and let's get the blinkin' sails to trim!"

Fifteen

"Steady ahead, Mister Locke," Patrick Dalton said, peering into a darkness that was complete except for the murky glow of nearby lanterns and the erratic, occasional rippling of what he had decided was either foxfire or some strange sort of lightning.

"On deck!" The hail came from the maintop, high above.

"Aye, tops?"

"It's closed in aloft, sir. No visibility at all."

"Have you had sight of *Pride of Falworth?*"

"No sight now, sir. But before we closed th' fogs, she was where she'd been, three cables off the starboard bow."

"Trust Mister Duncan to hold course until this passes, then," Dalton mused. "Steady on, please, Mister Locke. Mister Wise!"

"Aye, sir?" The voice was disembodied, somewhere afore.

"Mister Wise, do you think we could manage to ease sail just a bit on the courses? I should like to lose a knot of way."

"Aye, sir, we'll try. You lads! Whoever can, find your way to the brails! Captain wants a bit of sail taken in!"

Just astern, a faint glow of greenish light drifted across *Fury's* unseen wake, like a sad ghost searching for its grave. Near at hand, Billy Caster muttered, "Weird waters. It's as though we suddenly were somewhere else entirely."

"Weird, indeed, Mister Caster," Dalton agreed. "But yet sailing waters, and the same water. If we can't see it beneath our hull, we can hear it there, and the world remains as it was even in darkness."

"Sir?"

"It isn't a thing to worry about unduly," Dalton explained, letting his voice carry to any who might be listening. "We are in some sort of storm, nothing more. Beyond it you will see the same ocean we sailed before, and we shall be holding the same course. The seas shift and flow, Mister Caster, but they do not change their locations any more than the land does. All that moves here is ourselves, and we move by the winds, on the waters, just as we always did."

"Aye, sir. I'd feel better, though, if we could see the other ship over there."

"Precisely the reason we are standing back a bit. Without visibility, we need adequate distance so that there is no chance of an accidental collision. Mister Duncan will do his best to hold his course and speed, I imagine. We shall hold course and slack our speed by a knot."

Deck lanterns appeared forward of the quarterrail, a few muted glows increasingly dim with distance, and those astern knew that there were more there than they could see. The mist lay about them like a thick rain that didn't fall but just hung suspended in the air. Sound carried, though — the rattle of tackle blocks aloft as the snow's courses were loosed and reefed, the busy sounds of a deck at work. And *Fury* slacked her speed as the blocks rattled, the croon of waters along her hull diminishing in tone.

Several times during the next hour they tried to hail *Pride*, but with no response. Dalton realized that Charley Duncan might have added sail when visibility was lost, for the same reason that he himself had slacked his speed — to put a safe distance between the two until they again had eyes to see. He decided that likely was what he had done.

For a time the eerie lights in the mist seemed to subside; then abruptly they returned — eerie, dancing glows that moved about the ship and beyond, like things alive, glows that sometimes passed directly across the vessel, turning the inky mist to bright, silver-green cloud that still kept them blind but for moments seemed as bright as day. And each time a light touched the ship there were sounds — muted sizzling, crackling noises that seemed to run up and down the masts and along the yards, limning the structures aloft in hisses of sound. One such whispering light drifted across amidships, seemed to pause there, then turned and moved forward.

Excited shouts from the foredeck were relayed back. The weird light had found the portside cathead and clung there for moments, then had coalesced and "wrapped its blinkin' self about the anchor, hove there in its fish tackle." For a moment, they said, the anchor and all of its tackle had glowed like blue fire. Then it had popped, sizzled and extinguished itself.

With each light the errant compass swung wildly.

Long hours passed that seemed like days, and at each bell Billy Caster recorded the readings and soundings, writing on a tablet of stretched wet linen, with a sharpened bit of lead.

At eight bells Ishmael Bean and Purdy Fisk came from below to relieve Claude Mallory and Victory Locke. Dalton remained on deck, pacing and listening, noting every sound and feel of *Fury*'s course. What his eyes could not tell him of how the ship fared, his ears and the soles of his boots could — except for what lay beyond in the darkness.

At three bells of the midwatch there was a freshening of the wind, and the sound of sails aloft said it was shifting, coming more to the south.

"Accommodate the wind, please, Mister Fisk," he told the helmsman. "Bring us over to full and by. Mister Bean, whose stand is it amidships?"

"Mister Ball is there, sir. He relieved Mister Wise at change of watch."

Dalton stepped to the bell posts. "Mister Ball! Quarter please!"

A moment passed; then Abel Ball appeared in the murk below the rail. "Aye, sir?"

"The wind is veering a bit, Mister Ball. For the time, we shall adjust to it. But have your lads at station on the sheets, please. If we need sail handling, I'll want it done smartly."

"Aye, sir. Ah, sir, some of the new lads are being a bit grumbly. I expect this odd weather has got on their nerves."

"I see. Is it anything that you can't handle?"

"Not so far, sir. I've told them that I'm in something of a mood myself, and if they can't behave themselves as gentlemen, I might take it in mind to crack a few skulls. An' I've got Misters

140

Leaf and Ransom standin' by with belaying pins."

"Very good, Mister Ball. Carry on."

"Aye, sir."

"On deck!"

Dalton turned away, letting Ishmael Bean respond. The tar cupped hard hands and shouted, "Aye, tops?"

"I think it's raining up here, deck. The mist is moving."

"Moving? Moving where?"

"With the wind."

Bean stepped close enough to Dalton to see his features in the lamplight. "Would you say it is raining, sir? I can't really tell."

Dalton was staring at the glow of the nearest lamp. After a moment he nodded. "I believe it is, Mister Bean."

"Well, sir, at least that's something different."

"More than that is changing," Dalton said, raising his head to listen. "The wind is freshening, and seems cooler. Mister Fisk, how much have you corrected to accommodate the wind?"

"Four turns, sir. A point or so each, I'd make it. To starboard each time."

"Ah. Mister Caster, are you here?"

"Aye, sir. Right here, sir."

"Please make note of the hour, Mister Caster, and enter an estimation of northwest by north, fifteen knots on reefed courses and gaining way, wind freshening to . . . ah — Ahoy, tops! Can you read the gauge?"

"Sorry, sir." The voice drifted down from aloft. "I can't even see the blessed thing."

"Estimated wind near thirty and freshening," Dalton said. Striding to the bell rail, he called, "Mister Ball, do you have hands at station?"

"Aye, sir. I think so."

"Then, let's reef a third in the tops'ls, please. Lively now."

"Aye, sir."

The rain increased steadily, a drenching, soaking downpour that hammered at *Fury*'s flanks and sluiced along her decks, driven by a wind that rose and whined, changing the weird darkness of earlier hours to a whining, singing darkness. And now there was real lightning — brilliant flashes in the murk all around them, with thunderclaps that rolled and echoed like cannonfire.

A brilliant bolt exploded just off *Fury*'s portside, the crack of its thunder deafening, and as eyes turned to where it had been, a second bolt struck, farther away but still near enough to flare the murk like silver sunlight. And there, a black silhouette against the glare, was a ship. Three masts with high spars were ebon tapestry illuminated among glare-lighted sails, and in the echo of the thunder they could hear the booming of a great hull slamming through wave crests with the wind at its back.

The two vessels, *Fury* and the stranger, were barely a cable's length apart and angling toward each other on collision course.

"Helm astarboard!" Dalton shouted. "Hard over, Mister Fisk!" Billy Caster grabbed a rail and clung as the keening snow answered its rudder, rearing on a running wave and heeling hard aslant. Aloft, cables sang and whined, sails snapped in the wind and stressed timbers shrilled. Deep within her hull, *Fury* growled as massive knees and footings took the stresses transmitted from masts to keel. Darkness had followed the lightning's flare, and in the darkness was chaos on the snow's driving decks: shouts and scufflings, creak of cannons shifting in their slings, clatter of deadeyes and great blocks dancing at their cables. Forward somewhere, there was a shrilling of taut line and the loud report of something breaking apart. Someone screamed somewhere.

Then just beyond, surging alongside in the darkness, were other sounds that were undertone and counterpoint to *Fury*'s song — the thrumming, slapping roar of a heavy ship under sail and driving through tossed seas.

For a moment, the thunder alongside drowned out all other sounds, and a lightning flash glared on the towering flank of a big ship. A warship, larger than *Fury*, directly alongside the turning snow and crowding in . . . then passing.

As abruptly as it had come, the phantom was gone — vanished into the darkness and the sheeting rain.

"Rudder amidships, Mister Fisk," Dalton ordered. Shaking herself like a warhorse denied battle, *Fury* held footing on the churning sea for a moment, then slowly righted herself. In the diminishing whine of her rigging, there was a sound almost of regret.

142

Wide eyes staring into the darkness, Billy Caster got his feet under him and gasped, "What was that?"

"Mister Ball, report, please," Dalton called.

Ishmael Bean stooped to retrieve a fallen lantern. "Far too close a thing for my liking," he muttered.

At the helm, Purdy Fisk was considering Billy's question. "A warship, right enough," he said. "And big, too. Maybe a frigate, though its silhouette seemed a bit odd."

Beyond the quarterrail, Abel Ball called, "Something broke in the fore, Cap'n. We don't know yet what it was, but the shrouds seem secure and the sheets are responding."

"Anyone injured or swept over?"

"Don't know that, either, sir. Not just yet."

"Can we handle sail, Mister Ball?"

"Aye, sir. That we can."

"Stand by to trim to the rudder, then. Mister Fisk, bear off a point aport and steady us there. Mister Bean, can you see the compass?"

"Aye, but it's not—belay that, Cap'n. It seems to be working again. At least it stands steady and shifts with the helm."

"What is our heading by the compass?"

"Nearly due north now, sir, so it says."

"Direct the helm by the compass, please, Mister Bean. Bring us back to west by north, then have Mister Ball's crew trim to course and sheet home. And stand by to make or reef. God only knows what this weather is going to do."

"Aye, sir."

In the rain-drenched darkness behind the snow, something whined through the air and splashed somewhere astern. Distantly to the north, there was a report that was unlike a thunderclap, then another.

"Those were cannon shots," Ishmael Bean blurted. "That ship, sir? The one that skimmed us . . . do you think . . . ?"

"It could hardly be anyone else, Mister Bean. He fired blind, but at where we might have been had we held true."

"But why would he shoot, sir? We've passed and gone. We've no encounter. Blazes, we don't even know each other . . . do we?"

"I think not," Dalton said slowly, staring into the blind north.

"I can think of a few reasons why a vessel might shoot without acquaintance, but none of the reasons are honorable."

"Are we going after him, sir? Teach the blighter some manners, as they say?"

"Just steady on course, Mister Bean. We've more pressing business at the moment. Possibly we'll encounter that gentleman at another time. Then maybe we shall have cause to amuse him."

"I hope that vessel doesn't happen upon Mister Duncan," Billy Caster said. "All those people he's carrying . . ."

"I'm thinking the same thing, Mister Caster," Dalton admitted. "If Mister Duncan has held his course, though, he should be ahead of us somewhere and well out of range of that wing-top."

"That what, sir?"

"Wing-top, Mister Caster. Did you notice his silhouette in that moment when we had him in sight?"

"Well, yes, sir, I suppose I did. It was a ship-rigged vessel, big but less than a ship of the line. I took it for a frigate, or something."

"Very good, Mister Caster. Basically a frigate, yes. But modified a bit. That vessel's tops'l yards and royals were blocked for studding sails. That's done on occasion in the Mediterranean. Leeward shores, surface calms with winds aloft, that sort of thing. But it isn't a popular modification. It's unusual."

"On deck!"

"Aye, tops?"

"We have some visibility, sir. Clearing ahead a bit."

"Sightings, tops?"

"Nothing, sir, but I can see the sky."

As abruptly as they had entered the fogs, they left them. Now *Fury* sailed in clear airs, an eerie, contained clear with starry sky above and good visibility about — but for no more than a mile in any direction.

"Now we sail in a bottle," Dalton muttered, gazing around at the high cloudbanks that hid every horizon. "Weird waters, these. Very weird."

"Weird," Billy Caster agreed.

It *was* as though the snow sailed in a bottle, alone in a strange, starlit arena where the winds rose and fell in fitful gusts, a place where nothing existed except the ship, the dark sea and high, encircling walls of fog where lightnings flickered here and there. There was no sign of *Pride of Falworth* as far as they could see, nor of any other vessel or thing.

Abel Ball came aft, long-faced and pale in the lamplight of the deck. "Damage report, sir," he said.

"Report, Mister Ball."

"What broke yonder in the fore was our portside fish tackle," the sailor said. "The anchor is still there, a'dangle at the cat block, but the fish cable is broken at the channel. And we've . . . uh . . . we've lost a man, sir."

"What man?"

"Mister Finch, sir. Tommy Finch, one of the new lads. I guess he went overside when the line broke. It's where he likely would have been."

Dalton sighed, looking back the way they had come. A man lost. And no chance now of even finding him, much less rescuing him. If Tommy Finch had gone into that stormy sea, then Tommy Finch was dead.

"Spread and search, Mister Ball," he said. "We should —"

"Pardon, sir, but we've done that. His mates from old *Tyber* have gone stem to stern. He's gone, sir. Sorry."

"Aye. Well, then, there's nothing more to be done." Dalton turned to Ishmael Bean. "We'll want crew assembly in the morning, Mister Bean. Time of opportunity. All hands, for memorial."

"Aye, sir."

"On deck!"

"Aye, tops?"

"Eyes aft, sir! Weather coming!"

Behind *Fury*, the ring of cloud had bulged inward. Now it drove toward them, a wall of storm a'seethe, driven by sudden gale-force winds.

"Hands to sheets, Mister Ball," Dalton shouted. "Shrift sail and batten down. This bedammed weather hasn't finished with us yet."

To Billy Caster, it was obvious that his captain was worried. He wondered if it was the strange weather and "weird waters" that vexed him so, or the loss of a man overboard — or possibly the absence of any sign of Mister Duncan's prize bark.

In the darkness and the murk, Charley Duncan had no real notion of which way he was going, but he held *Pride* with the wind and hoped it had not changed.

Just once through the hours he left the quarterdeck, leaving Pliny Quarterstone in charge there while he felt his way forward to inspect the holds and the forecastle deck — glimpses by lamplight and lightning flash.

The transshipping of the cotton had relieved most of the hold space in the bark and — for the first time — all of the passengers and all of their livestock were below, secure from the drenching mist and the whipping rains that now came through it.

Making his way back, the length of the long deck, he went from rail to rail at each mast, identifying and encouraging the men stationed at pinrail and fife. "We'll be clear of this soon enough," he told them at each station. "We're on course and holding speed. It'll clear, and *Fury* will be close by to take up escort."

He saw no reason to mention that *Pride's* course had most likely changed. There was, after all, the off chance that what he said to them was true.

Part of it proved to be so. In the first gray light of dawn, *Pride of Falworth* broke free of the storms that had pummeled her through a long night. Fogs clung all about, drifting skirts of hazy mist taking on the first colors of morning, but there was a bit of visibility . . . a little piece of ocean where mists confused the eye, but better by far than the blindness that had engulfed them for so long.

All along the bark's dripping deck, sailors grinned at one another in sheer relief at being able once again to see.

"Far better," Charley Duncan breathed, looking around. "Very well, I think we should do a bit of inspection before those landspeople come up from below again. Mister Hoop, rouse two watches, please. We'll stand inspection on deck and rigging, and I'll want topmen aloft to have a look at clews and bindings."

146

"Aye, sir." The big man turned to go forward.

"And have a look at the fothering on our hull, if you please. If it's taken a bulge in the night, we'd best correct it."

"Aye, sir. I'll tend to that myself."

Pliny Quarterstone came from below, carrying a mug of tea. "By gor," he said. "We can see."

"That we can, Mister Quarterstone. And I've set a quick inspection stem to stern while we've a chance to move about without tripping over passengers and their livestock. Have you had your breakfast?"

"Aye, I just did."

"Then, maybe you'd take a watch while I go below and get a bit for myself?"

"Aye, I will."

Pride's deck and yards came alive as sailors scattered about the vessel, inspecting lines, ties, lashings and stowage. After a long, blind night of storm, they were a jolly, grinning lot on this misty morning.

The grins froze on stunned faces when a dark warship, as big as a frigate and heavily armed, nosed through the mists a half mile away, altered course and headed for *Pride* like dark destiny.

Sixteen

The instant *Valkyrie* cleared the cloudbank, her lookouts spotted the bark a half mile away. In the drifting tatters of fog and mist, painted brilliant by dawnlight, the merchantman might have been a phantom ship — elusive and indistinct, sailing on a cloud of surface mist among the gauzy hazes. It required only a moment's decision for Timothy Leech to give the orders to come to starboard and close with the vessel. "Target of opportunity," he told his helmsman. Then, "Misters Ames and Boyd! Crews to guns, please! Mister McNair . . . you, there! McNair! Look alive! Go below and tell the captain we've a merchantman at hand!"

The bark had seen *Valkyrie*. Across the distance, the ship now flew colors — what appeared to be the banner of one of the noncombatant trading companies — and was putting on sail. Leech grinned. "Look at him, Mister Trice. Claimin' disinvolvement while he makes to run." He squinted. "Is that a ship we've seen before? It seems familiar."

Dickie Trice studied the silhouette across the waters. "It's rigged much like old *Pride of Falworth*. If I didn't know she was at the bottom of the sea, I'd almost say it was her. But then, a bark's a bark. With better light an' a closer look . . ."

"Aye, I expect that's what struck me. It does look a bit like old *Pride*. No matter, though. Whatever ship it is, it's a poor, lost lamb for the takin' of the wolves, eh? And not an escort in sight."

"That little cruiser we passed in the rains — a brig or the like — maybe that was its escort, do you think?"

148

"Like enough." Leech nodded. "Separated in the storm. Well, our gain, then. Mister Strode! Increase sail for chase! The lost sheep is making to run for it."

Handling *Valkyrie's* big wheel, Trice peered ahead. "What do you make of that bit of color on the vessel's portside hull, Mister Leech. Could that be fothering? Is she patched?"

"If so, then all the better." Leech leaned big, contented hands on the bell rail and watched the distant bark putting on sail, trimming to the wind. "If he's wounded, he won't take so long to catch . . . aye! See there, Mister Trice! Whoever commands that deck has his wits about him, for all that. He hasn't come to starboard for distance. He knows where that bark's best wind is, and he's taking it — dead astern."

Jack Shelby came on deck then, and Leech pointed. "A prize of chance, Cap'n. We cleared th' murk and there she lay. What's your pleasure?"

Shelby studied the fleeing bark, and as the light of morning gained, his cold gray eyes grew puzzled. "I know that ship, Mister Leech."

"We had a chat about that, Cap'n. It does bear a likeness to old *Pride of Falworth*, for a fact. Course we know it isn't."

Shelby stood silent, staring after the bark now full-sailed and running, trailed by the billowing mists that lay upon the sea. The light continued to improve, though the tantalizing curtains of the fogs still hung all about. Shelby squinted, and the cold frown on his face deepened. Finally he stepped to the bell rail. "Mister Strode!"

The bosun hurried aft. "Aye, Cap'n?"

"Mister Strode, when we took *Valkyrie*, did you scuttle *Pride of Falworth?*

"We did, sir. Just as you said. A slow rip in her wales so she'd drift into deeps before she went under."

"Did you inspect the hulling yourself?"

"Aye, sir. Mister Trahan ordered the work, and I looked on as it was done."

"Where were the wales breached, then?"

"Portside bilges, sir. Just forward of the larders. Easy to get to, there. Beg pardon, but why do you ask?"

"Because that scuttled ship still floats, Mister Strode, and there are people aboard it who've fothered the hulling." He pointed, scowling. "That is *Pride of Falworth* yonder. I know the ship I sailed."

Timothy Leech frowned, but he kept his thoughts to himself. He remembered clearly how *Pride* had been dealt with. No one left aboard, and scuttled to sink, and no one about who might have made repairs. And he knew that if Misters Trahan and Strode said a ship was scuttled, it was scuttled. Jack Shelby was not a man to make mistakes, but Leech was sure he had made one now. That was a bark that resembled *Pride,* but it could not be *Pride*.

But then, it didn't really matter. Within an hour—two at the most—they would have the merchantman under their guns, whoever it was. And if Shelby wanted it sunk, they would sink it . . . after taking from it anything that it might carry, that they might want.

To have a close look at the hull's canvas patch, Mister Hoop—tagged after by his Frenchmen—had a small boat lowered alongside *Pride,* with a long tether from the fore portside channel of the bark. With this as a platform, and the Frenchmen and two others aboard to do his hauling, he could inspect the fothering closely, even though a heavy mist still clung to the sea, rising almost to *Pride's* gunwales. In the boat were all the tools he might need to inspect the ship's tied-on bandage and—if necessary—to make repairs.

They boarded the boat below *Pride's* channel hatch, with a man standing by to work the tether, but by the time Hoop had everyone in place, the boat was thirty feet astern of the still-moving bark, swinging on its line.

"Shoulders to the line, lads," Hoop instructed. "Heave away now, smartly."

With all of them playing in the tether, coiling it in the boat's bilges as they took slack, the boat caught up with *Pride* and came alongside her misted stern, heading forward. Then an odd sound caught Hoop's attention, and he held up a hand.

"Have we got something afoul there?" he pointed toward the bark's big sternpost with its iron-bound rudder.

They all listened, peering in the mist.

"Don't know as I can tell, Mister Hoop." Matthew Cobley admitted. "Can't see past arm's length down here in th' fogs."

"Might be seaweed," John Singleterry suggested. "Little enough harm in that, though. Just cut it away if it builds about the rudder."

"Well, let's see to the patch; then we can have another look," Hoop decided. "They went back to the tether, and the boat drew alongside *Pride,* riding the smooth waters of the ship's sidewake as it headed forward.

At the sailcloth patch, Hoop leaned outboard to peer at the repair, running a big hand along its surface. "We've took in some water," he decided. "The cloth is soft here, like a blister. One of you frogs hand me the pry bar there, will you?"

He held out his hand, waited a moment, then turned, scowling into puzzled faces. "Blast," he said.

"Blest," they agreed in unison.

"Pry bar!" He pointed.

"P'y ba'," the Frenchmen agreed.

"Well, hand it to me!"

"Ah!" Francois took his meaning. *"La torque! Oui. Tout de suite, m'sieur.* Rene, *la torque pour M'sieur 'Oop."*

"Oui." Rene picked up the pry bar and passed it across. *"Voila, m'sieur."*

"Thank you," Hoop breathed.

"De rien."

Using the pry bar against the thick wales of *Pride's* hull, Hoop forced a narrow breach in the cable cinching the sailcloth. Accumulated water flowed out, and gradually the stretched sail flattened itself against the hull, like a canvas skin.

"That should do it for now," Hoop decided. "Now, since we're here, let's swing back and have a look at that rudder." He raised his eyes and his voice. "Mister Reeves?"

Above, at *Pride's* gunwale, a tar-hatted head appeared. "Right here, Mister Hoop. Have you finished?"

"All done here, Mister Reeves. Now I wish you'd loose our tether there and walk it astern. I want to look at the rudder."

"Aye, I'll loose it, but don't go adrift now."

"We're not going adrift. Just give us a sternpost cleat, Mister Reeves."

Above, the rope was released, and the boat began to drift back along *Pride*'s towering hull.

Above and ahead, Reeves' voice said, "Hand here, Jaimie. Let's feed this line past the channels. There's a good . . . Jaimie! Blast it, don't . . . !"

Something splashed into the water ahead of the boat. Francois blinked, leaned forward and lifted the tether rope. It hung slack in his hand. *"Le corde,"* he said. *"C'est n'est pas attache!"*

"Mister Reeves!" Hoop shouted. "You've dropped the bleedin' tether!"

High above, a voice sang out, "On deck! Ship off the port quarter!"

Other voices followed, a chaos of them, and men appeared overhead, lining the rail, peering outward.

Pipes shrilled, and a voice said, "Hands to make sail! Stand by!"

Reeves' voice was nearly lost in the tumult. "Beg pardon, Mister Quarterstone, but Mister Hoop an' them are . . . Mister Quarterstone? Mister Quarterstone, sir, I . . ."

The boat neared *Pride*'s stern, and just overhead Charley Duncan's voice roared, "Up colors! Hands to sheets! Mister Quarterstone, let's have some order there! Helm, hold amidships! Ready all masts to make sail!"

"Mister Duncan!" Hoop called.

"Mister Reeves, did Mister Hoop complete his inspection of the patch?"

"Aye, sir, he did, but he's—"

"Never mind, Mister Reeves. Mister Nelson, quarter please! Misters Toddy and Sharp, see to the guns! Make sail, Mister Quarterstone! Trim full and by!"

Hoop stood upright in the rocking boat and cupped his hands. "Mister Duncan!" he roared.

"Moment, Mister Hoop. Let's get some way under us; then

we can talk. Mister Mudd! Mister Mudd, get tops aloft, please. Smartly now . . ."

"Mister Duncan!"

The bark's stern swept past, tall, dark and indifferent to the little boat bouncing now in its rolling wake.

"Mister Duncan! We're not aboard yet!"

"He's seen us, sir," a diminishing voice above the closing mist said. "He's making about to give chase."

"Sheet home! Sheet home there! Full and by the wind!"

"That's a warship, Mister Duncan! That's a blasted frigate! Where's his colors?"

"His colors may be entirely his own, Mister Nelson. I think that yonder is a pirate ship."

"Mister Quarterstone, I —"

"Not now, Mister Reeves! Get your back into that line!"

For a moment the voices hung in the air, receding with distance, overlying the thrum of the bark's big hull taking the sea in stride as it picked up speed, going away.

Then there was nothing. Only the lonely gurgle of water against the boat's planks.

Francois stared into the mist, then raised a forlorn hand in salute. *"Au revoir, vaesseau,"* he muttered sadly.

"C'est la vie." Rene shrugged.

"Rot!" Hoop rumbled.

Matthew Cobley and John Singleterry exchanged worried glances. The five of them were alone, fog-bound and adrift in a small boat without a mast, far at sea and hopelessly lost.

"I wish we at least had a bigger boat," Cobley said.

"Unship those oars, you," Hoop said. "There's no sense in just sitting here."

"Aye," Singleterry began unlashing the boat's two pairs of sweeps. "And where do you think we might make for, Mister Hoop? Back to that bedammed island, perchance?"

"Shut up and row."

With nothing else to do, they rowed, hoping that they were going in the general direction *Pride* had gone. Minutes passed, then tens of minutes; then Francois, in the bow, lifted his head and cupped a hand to his ear. *"Alons!"*

he said. *"Ecoutez avec moi! Autre vaesseau."*

Hoop glanced around. "What?"

"Ecoutez, s'il vous plait! Le bruit!"

"Brute?"

"Le bruit . . . le son! *Ecutez!"*

"I don't know what you're goin' on about—"

Rene put a finger to his lips and hissed, "Sh-h-h!"

"You hear something?" Hoop listened, too, then raised a big hand in command. "Belay that rowing, there. The frogs hear something."

They all heard it, then, somewhere aft and approaching—the unmistakable sounds of a ship under sail.

"Maybe they've come back for us," John Singleterry said. Shipping his oars, he cupped his hands to shout. Hoop's massive hands clamped his palms to his face.

"Quiet!" the big man hissed. "It isn't them. It's some other vessel. Now be still!" He stood, bracing himself on Singleterry's head, and stretched as tall as he could, trying to see above the mists. There was something there, vaguely. He stared, squinting, then dropped to a crouch. "Man those oars, you two. Pull with a will or we'll be run down. There's a warship bearing on us."

They pulled, while Hoop wrestled the tiller. The little boat swerved right, bobbed for a moment and scooted up the slope of a wave and down the other side. The growing sounds of the approaching ship had become a very thunder, seeming to be directly over them.

"Pull!" Hoop ordered.

Suddenly a tall, dark stem pierced the mists, thrusting like a thrown harpoon directly over them. The mists rang with the sounds of driving sails, straining lines and the thunder of waters keening past a rushing hull. The great, dark jib speared past above, and a wide prow with curling waters breaking from it bore down on them.

"Pull," Hoop rumbled.

They pulled.

For a moment it seemed the massive hull would grind them under. Then the little boat crested another wave and skittered aside like flotsam as the ship's bow wake slapped at it. A dark hull with ranked gunports streamed past, thundering through the waves, and the little boat spun full circle atop its wake. A moment, then it was past, a tall sternpost huge and shadowy spraying them with salt.

"Whoo," Hoop muttered. "Close, that."

The following wake of the big vessel spun the boat again, bouncing it like a cork a'bob on a rippled pond, and taut cables slapped it as another shadow bore down at it.

"Gor!" Matthew Cobley hissed. "Pull, mate!"

"Un autre bateau," Francois pointed out. *"Au compagnie le vaesseau travers le brouillard."*

"They got a launch in tow," Hoop told himself as a boat far larger than their own sliced past them. On purest impulse, he grabbed the coiled tether line and threw it. Its cleat hook bounced into the towed boat's bilges, caught on something there, and the line payed out as Hoop tried to bring the little boat's nose about. "Pull!" he bellowed.

The line came taut, sang with strain, and abruptly they were all clinging for dear life as their boat sliced through the waves, in the tow of the ship's tow.

"What the bejaysus did you do that for?" John Singleterry gasped, ducking the flailing shanks of his oars.

"I don't know," Hoop admitted. "I just did. Here, let's get those oars shipped before they brain us all . . . ah, that's better. Now, man that tether yonder and let's haul ourselves ahead."

Long minutes passed while they hove in tether, inching their way toward the stern of the towed launch. Then they were there, and Hoop tied off their line and clambered across into the larger boat. He looked around him in the flowing mist and grinned. "A sailing launch," he muttered. "A thirty-footer at the very least."

The others scrambled past him, crouching and crawling in the bounding launch. Amidships stood a sturdy mast with lateen rigging and a furled sail. Great sweeps four a'bank were lashed at the rails, and in the bow stood a swivel gun, ranked by stacked shot, a pair of powder kegs and all the loading and firing paraphernalia of a mounted cannon.

Francois and Rene hurried to the fore and hovered there, gaping at the great sterncastle barely visible above the mists ahead. After a moment, Rene burrowed into the sheltered supplies beneath the swivel gun and came out with a chest. Inside were strikers, fuse and the fittings of a linstock. *"E voila!"* he announced. *"Le feu!"*

"This here is no sniggin' punt gun," Cobley decided, admiring the mounted cannon. "This is a full four-pounder. An' it's charged."

"Keep your voice down," Hoop warned. "Whoever's ship that is, they're not friendly. This is why Mister Duncan made sail and got us lost, is because this ship was chasing him."

"Your frogs have become excited about something, Mister · Hoop." Singleterry pointed. In the bow, Rene and Francois were chattering about something while Rene squatted abaft the swivel gun, working at something under cover of the fore decking.

Francois gestured at Hoop and pointed upward, through the mists. *"C'est la* Valkyrie," he said emphatically. *Le criminel . . . les . . . les* pirates!"

"Pirates?" Hoop gawked at the escutcheon dimly visible on the tall stern ahead. "What pirates?"

"Oui, m'sieur. Malsaiteures. Brigands. Pirates. *N'importe lequel* pirates . . . *ceux la!* Pirates!"

"Keep your voice down, then," Hoop tried to hush him. "Best we not . . ."

Just behind him, Rene came up with a glowing fuse on a linstock, smoke trailing from fresh-sparked punk in the firebox, and said, determinedly, *"Pour mons potes . . . Le feu!"* Before Hoop or anyone else could react, the Frenchman cranked around the swivel-mounted four-pounder, raised its notches toward the stern ahead of them, and set off its vent.

Smoke blossomed in the mist ahead, obscuring all sight of the ship at the other end of the towing cable, and the four-pounder's roar was echoed by a crash just ahead.

". . . let them know we're here," Hoop finished lamely, his eyes growing wide, then "Jesus have mercy!"

156

"My God in Heaven," Cobley muttered as shrilling voices clamored in the mist just ahead. "That's capped it off nicely." He almost collided with Singleterry as the two of them raced for the mast with its furled sail. "For mercy's sake, Mister Hoop, cut us loose!"

While Hoop wrestled with the towing line, Rene and Francois were reloading. The stench of smoke in the flowing mist receded, and just ahead and above they heard shouted commands, and the unmistakable sound of big deck guns being run out.

As the launch swung free, grasping at the wind with its squat sail, Francois LeBlanc squinted at the stern rails of the tall ship just ahead. Suddenly his eyes went wide. *"C'est* m'sieur Leech,*"* he pointed.

"M'sieur Leech?" Rene glanced up and saw the familiar face at the rail. *Ah . . . mais oui! C'est le malsaiteur! Le brigand . . . le ma'chant . . . le . . ."*

"Fils de pute?" Francois suggested.

"Oui! Le fils de pute!" He aligned the swivel gun again and brought the smoking fuse down. *"C'est pour vous,* m'sieur Leech! *Le feu!"* Again the four-pounder roared, and again there was a crash echoing back through the blinding smoke.

"Touche, M'sieur Leech," Rene muttered.

The launch swerved on tossing wakes as far greater thunders crashed and bellowed in the mist ahead, and tall spumes of water erupted on either side to rain down on them. Hoop half-ran, half-stumbled the length of the launch to throw himself onto the bucking tiller. "Get that sail up all the way!" he roared. "We are in serious trouble here!"

Seventeen

On an eerie sea where morning light slanted through trailing skirts of fog, swept aloft from the blanket mists by topsail winds, *Pride of Falworth* fled northward while eyes aboard looked back — back at the tall, stacked sails of the dark ship in pursuit, back across an emptiness that gave no sign of *Fury* . . . back at the drifting fogs where five crewmen had been left behind, adrift in a little boat.

Her hatches were battened, her decks alive with sailors who knew that the bark was no match for the stalking frigate slowly closing on their wake, and in the holds below frightened passengers huddled. Of the passengers only three — Squire Aaron Fairfield, Caleb Smith and a burly young farmer named Darling — had gone a'deck before the battening, and those remained there.

"What kind of seaman loses his escort?" Fairfield had demanded at first sight of the warship bearing down upon them. Then, "And what kind of escort loses his charge?"

"Mind your tongue or go below," Charley Duncan had snapped in response. "I've no time for chatting."

Now the landsmen huddled beside hammock nettings at the foot of the quarterdeck ladder and watched in horror as the dark ship grew astern. Dimly across the waters had come the sounds of cannon fire, just moments before. Several distinct thumps they had heard, though the range was yet far too great for shooting.

And looking up at Duncan on the quarterdeck, they knew that he was as puzzled as anyone as to why guns had

158

been fired. There was no doubt, though, that they would hear the sounds again once the pursuing ship was in range. For the dark ship had shown colors as the chase began — arrogant colors intended to create panic aboard the bark. A black flag.

At *Pride's* stern rail and along her beams, hands were at work quoining up the merchantman's inadequate cannons. Commander Duncan, it seemed, was not a man to meekly strike colors in the face of overwhelming force. If all else failed, he intended to fight and had made that clear to one and all.

But first, he would run, and with the wind at his back and sails stacked high on the bark's four masts, he would make it as difficult as possible for the sleeker frigate to overtake them.

"I wonder what Patrick Dalton would do now," he muttered as he watched the errant winds aloft. "I know he would find some way to amuse those people back there . . . but how?"

"Sir?"

Duncan turned and shrugged. "Nothing, Mister Nelson. I was talking to myself."

"Aye, sir."

"How do we read, Mister Nelson?"

"Twelve knots steady by log and line, sir. We are full and by the wind."

"Twelve knots." He frowned, glanced aloft at the gauges at their spars, then looked astern, scowling at the big cruiser back there. It was closer than it had been, and coming into line with their course. He watched its great sails align and trim, and frowned again. There was something about it . . . he shook his head, puzzled. "Twelve knots on a wind that's making eighteen to twenty. He'll do better than that, Mister Nelson. A ship-rigged vessel of that size, he'll make fifteen easily, when he's trimmed . . ."

Again he squinted, studying the ship a half mile away. By his own estimates, it would be within range of big guns

159

within the hour. And it carried big guns. He had no question on that score. Though not quite a proper frigate by Royal Navy standards, the pursuer was the size of a frigate and designed for the same thing—to seek and destroy. And it had the legs and the teeth for its purpose.

He stood silent for long minutes, watching the ship astern, then pointed. "Mister Nelson, what would you say he is doing now?"

"He's chasing us, Commander."

"I mean his maneuver. What is he doing, exactly?"

Nelson hesitated, gazing aft, then shrugged. "He angled to dead astern of us, and now he's coming over a bit—a point I'd say—to follow up our wake until his bow chasers can reach us. And that won't be long, either . . . sir."

"Shouldn't a frigate make about more smartly than that, Mister Nelson? Should it balk at the turn, as he seems to?"

"I don't know, Commander. I sailed under the Union Jack for a time, but I was posted to a brig. I never sailed on a frigate." He squinted, trying to see what Duncan was getting at. "Maybe it's because of his rigging. He has run-outs on his tops. Could it be that gives him a balky rudder? I don't know."

"Possibly." Duncan nodded.

"Mister Quarterstone, he sailed aboard a frigate, he said, his last tour before going aboard old *Tyber*."

"That's right, I heard him say that." Duncan turned and strode to the bell rail. "Mister Porter!"

"Aye, sir?"

"Please find Mister Quarterstone and ask him to come aft if he will."

"Aye, sir."

Quarterstone arrived within moments, and Duncan met him at the ladder. "Come astern, please, Mister Quarterstone. I'd like your opinion of how that vessel back there handles its course corrections."

"Aye, sir."

Side by side they headed for the stern rail. In the net-

160

tings, Aaron Fairfield growled, "Blast all sailors! Here we are, running for our very lives, likely to be blown out of the water at any moment, and they discuss the sailing habits of the enemy."

"Maybe Mister Duncan is making a plan," Keith Darling suggested. He was silenced by the scowls of the two older men.

Astern, Pliny Quarterstone planted himself at the rail and squinted aft. Even in morning light, the sea had an eerie, otherworldly appearance with its low cover of heavy mist from which curtains seemed to rise and swirl as the topsail winds drew skirts of fog upward. The phenomenon played puzzles with the eyes. But the dark prowler was clearly visible, even so. Less than half a mile astern, it had come onto *Pride*'s track and was pursuing under full sail — even the odd-looking studding sails at its tops were full of wind.

"Not just exactly a frigate," Quarterstone judged, "but close kin for certain. What did you want me to look at, Mister Duncan?"

"How he makes his turns," Duncan said, realizing as he said it that the pursuer was no longer turning. It had come to course. "Stand and watch for a bit." He turned to the helmsman. "Bring us a point to starboard, please, Mister Mudd."

"Aye, sir." The helm spun, and the bark shivered as its rudder fought the trim of its sails, then took control.

Duncan went to the bell rail and called, "Hands to trim, please, Mister Porter. We are exercising the ship."

"Aye, sir. Hands a'sheet! Trim to course!"

"Now the fool is conducting sailing practice," Aaron Fairfield muttered darkly in the nettings.

Pride lost a bit of way, trimming to a new course, but she took the wind again and made it back. Astern, the dark ship had gained a bit, but now was off course, and still beyond good range of even heavy guns. As they watched, it altered to match course, and Pliny Quarterstone frowned and shook his head. "Sloppy, that," he muttered.

Duncan was beside him. "What do you see?"

"Poor helmsmanship. I'd expect better."

"Be more specific, can't you?" Duncan demanded. "What are they doing wrong?"

"I'd call it a lazy rudder, myself." Quarterstone shrugged. "He is slewing on his helm. Very sloppy."

"What could cause that, do you think?"

"Some bumbling landsman at the helm would." Quarterstone glanced pointedly around at the three passengers in the nettings.

Duncan ignored the jibe. "Not too bloody likely, that," he said. "What else?"

"Any number of things, I suppose. Do you think we might have another look at it?"

"Mister Mudd, bring us a point to port, please." Duncan again went to the bell rail. "Mister Porter, we are turning again. Hands to—"

"I know very well what we're doing!" Porter sounded a bit testy. "Run your quarterdeck, Commander. My lads know what to do with the sheets."

"Sorry." Duncan scowled. "Just get on with it, then."

"Aye, sir. Hands a'sheet! Retrim!"

At the stern rail, Quarterstone watched carefully as the pursuer again corrected, coming onto their course again.

Duncan said, "Well?"

"That's a right trim warship yonder," Quarterstone opined. "Beats me why he'd sail it with such a handicap."

"What handicap, Mister Quarterstone," Duncan asked through clenched teeth.

"Why, with the couplings askew on the rudder, of course. That's his problem. His rudder's fouled, in its bandings. Hard as the devil to sail a ship that way. Any captain worth his salt, with a problem like that, why he'd lay over and fix it, he would."

"Will it keep him from catching us?"

"If he lays over to fix it, it probably will."

162

"And if not?"

"Oh, if he keeps coming, he'll catch us, right enough. In an hour or so, is my guess. But he's having a devil of a time with course changes. He really should repair that rudder."

"Thank you, Mister Quarterstone." Duncan looked aloft at the gauges, judging the wind. "Two points to starboard, helm," he ordered. He started toward the bell rail, then changed his mind. Mister Porter was surly about being told to trim, so he wouldn't bother him with such things. But trim they would, and trim again. "If that villain yonder is suffering his turns," he told Finian Nelson, "then let's give him as much suffering as we can."

"Sir?"

"We zig," Duncan said. "And when he zigs to follow we zag. Then when he corrects we zig again."

Sweating at the helm, Raymond Mudd muttered, "I never thought I'd miss Mister Hoop, but I do now."

"If it's muscle you want, just show me what to do."

They all turned at the unfamiliar voice. It was the burly young passenger, Keith Darling. He had come to the helm box and stood there, glaring at Pliny Quarterstone. "Landsman at the helm, eh? I be no sailor, swabby, but I can turn a bloody wheel as well as any man."

"You don't belong—" Duncan started.

"Take these spokes here," Mudd cut in. "Just hold them firm . . . like this, you see. Nothing much to steering. Just turn the wheel when I turn, and stop when I stop."

Leaning and shivering, hands at eight pinrails racing to trim and retrim sails, *Pride of Falworth* began a random zig-zag course northward, pursued by a dark and bitter frigate with a sore tail.

Though Charley Duncan had no way to know that two four-pound iron balls, fired point-blank from a launch in tow, had fouled *Valkyrie's* rudder, he did know that the pursuer was lamed in some manner. He knew also that—even lame—the stud-sail frigate coursing behind him still had the power to run down and kill his ship.

Hands clasped behind his back in the way he had seen ship's masters do, Duncan paced *Pride's* quarterdeck deep in worried thought. *What would you do now, if you were me, Patrick Dalton,* he wondered. *And for that matter, where the devil are you? We sorely need you now.*

"Frenchmen!" Timothy Leech hissed, peering into the baffling mists that ebbed in to hide *Valkyrie's* wake. "I swear they were Frenchmen, Captain, though how they managed to get aboard our whaleboat is beyond me."

"Beyond you, Mister Leech?" Jack Shelby turned cold eyes on his big second. "Then, you should ponder upon it. They obviously came from that merchantman there ahead, to attempt sabotage upon us. Purest luck that they were able to do so, but that is what they did."

"Then, you think that's who has *Pride* now—if that *is Pride?* Frenchmen?"

"That would be the obvious deduction, Mister Leech." Shelby turned toward his helm, where four men were struggling with the double wheel. "Confound it, helm! Must we slew about that way? I don't care to devote the entire day to the taking of that bedammed bark!"

"Sorry, Cap'n," a crewman puffed. "We're doin' the best we can."

"Like I told you, Cap'n," Leech put in, "they've maimed our latches. The rudder binds at every turn."

"And that captain is taking every advantage of it," Shelby spat. "He alters course every time we correct. He knows what he's done, right enough. Likely it was what his boat party was set to do."

"I don't see what Frenchmen would be doing in these waters."

"Harassing the British, obviously. It's well known that they've taken an interest in the Colonial cause. As to how they came into possession of *Pride of Falworth,* we'll know more about that when we have them under our guns—or

164

sunk. I shall need a few prisoners to chat with, Mister Leech . . . though I shan't need many. Keep that in mind when we catch them."

"Aye, Cap'n." Leech turned away, shaking his head. There was much about the loss of the towed launch that just didn't make sense in any way that he could see. Still, there was no question what had happened. Someone had boarded their whaleboat and fired its swivel gun — twice — into *Valkyrie*'s stern. And the shouts he himself had heard were in the French tongue.

With a good sail set on a stubby mast, the big launch coursed to its best pace — a broad tack that held such wind as could be had three points abaft the port beam. The little work boat followed on a tether.

"I'd say we're makin' two-three knots at best, Mister Hoop," John Singleterry announced bitterly. "What is it about these waters, that the winds can sing aloft so and yet not come down to where our sail is?"

"Weird waters." Hoop shook his head. "Myself, I like the trade lanes better. A man generally knows what God has on his mind there."

"How far do you suppose it is to America, then?"

"I haven't got the slightest idea. But I think we're going the right direction."

"How come your Frenchies opened fire like that on that ship that had us in tow?" Matthew Cobley wondered.

"They're not *my* Frenchies." Hoop glared at him. "Anyway, how does a body know why Frenchies do anything they do? Some way or another, they decided that was a pirate ship, so they just naturally opened fire, that's all."

"Seems to me the prudent thing might have been just to quietly cut loose and go away."

"That was what I was about to suggest when the shooting started. Have you finished looking at the stores aboard?"

"Not much to look at." Cobley shrugged. "Two casks of

165

water, a bit of biscuit and a stack of netting that's all fouled with bits of wood and twigs. I'd say this launch had spent some time bein' hid someplace, by the looks of it."

"I'd feel better if you'd get those two away from that cannon," Singleterry suggested. "The way they act, they might take a notion to turn it around and open fire on us."

Hoop frowned, turned to glance at the smug-seeming Frenchmen in the bow, then turned back. "Why would they do a thing like that? We're all in the same boat."

"They *are* French," Singleterry pointed out.

Hoop thought it over and turned toward the Frenchmen again. "You frogs! You keep that gun stowed unless I say otherwise!"

Francois and Rene looked at each other, puzzled, then shrugged in unison. *"Oui, M'sieur 'Oop,"* Francois agreed. Stepping carefully aft, squeezing under the sail's lower edge, he made his way astern and began hauling in the little boat's tether. When it was snugged against the launch he lashed the line, leapt across into the boat, then returned to the launch. *"Voila!"* he said, handing Hoop the pry bar. *"Le torque."*

"We'll stand shifts of two," Hoop said tiredly. "Tiller and watch. That way we can take turns getting some sleep."

North of Bahamas Passage, under cloudy skies, the packet *Cricket* was making its own way northward by a bit west, bound from Cape Jane to Wilmington with news of ship losses . . . and with a passenger.

Lewis Farrington, once commander of His Majesty's Sloop *Wolf,* more lately in command of escort for a pair of lost merchantmen on the Indies run, leaned forlornly on *Cricket's* gunwale. "Its name was *Valkyrie,* all right," he repeated. "I saw it clearly, just as my ship was destroyed."

Beside him, Captain Nat Simms frowned. "But *Valkyrie* was Thibaud's ship. The pirate. And he's gone. I heard fishermen found his corpse washed up on one of the cays . . .

him and several others. Not a lot left of any of them, but it was Thibaud, fair enough. They knew him by his beard and by the locket he always wore. Everybody figures the *Valkyrie* for sunk."

"Thibaud or not," Farrington said, "that pirate was *Valkyrie,* and the man commanding her was as black a villain as I've heard of. No signal, no call nor quarter . . . he just opened fire on us and kept shooting until there was nothing left."

"Lor'." Simms shivered. "I hate to hear about a thing like that. And I'd hate to be the one to tell Squire of it. What do you plan to do then?"

"Plan?" Farrington blinked, glancing around. "I don't know," he said vaguely. "Except I need a ship."

"You'd go out again . . . after that?"

"I *have* to go out. If I don't get back under sail now, I'll never sail again. I need a ship," he said it slowly. "A fighting ship, if there's one to be found."

"On deck! Sail ho!"

Simms straightened, peering aloft at *Cricket's* single masthead. "Whereaway, Toby?"

"Off the starboard beam, Cap'n. Hard down."

"Can you read it?"

"No, sir, but I'll keep an eye on it."

It was later in the day when Toby advised that the sail abeam looked like a boat. "Maybe a whaleboat or sailing launch, sir!" he called.

Simms shook his head. What was a boat doing way out here? He thought it over, then called aft, "Bring us hard to starboard, helm. Whoever that is yonder may need some help."

Eighteen

With fair light, *Fury* had eyes aloft in both tops, searching for sign of *Pride of Falworth,* but nowhere on the obscured horizons was there any sail at all. Patrick Dalton read a memoriam for young Tommy Finch, able seaman once of His Majesty's Royal Navy, now lost to the sea; then splicers and pulley teams went to work to repair the snow's broken port fish tackle while Dalton looked at his charts and read the morning's fairing.

"We haven't overrun them in the darkness," he decided. "Mister Duncan would keep his sail aloft in those winds. Nor have we altered course by more than a mile or two. Therefore, he has changed course for some reason."

"But where?" Billy Caster traced the markings on the makeshift chart. "And in which direction?"

Dalton was thoughtful for a time, his eyes scanning down the list of watch reports and conditions. "North, I believe," he said, finally.

"That warship that passed us . . . it was going north, wasn't it?"

"Yes, it was. Mister Wise, how are the repairs forward?"

"We haven't fished the anchor yet, sir," Cadman Wise said, "but the tackle is in place. All the work's a'deck now."

"Very well, Mister Wise. Have hands to station please, to trim to course. We are going to look for Mister Duncan."

"Aye, sir."

"Mister Locke, two points to starboard if you please. Bring us a point east of north. Mister Mallory, I shall want all possible sail very shortly. At my call, please."

168

"Aye, sir."

With topsails and topgallants spread to take the wind, *Fury* shook off the slumbers of the night and leaned into a new course, lifting a jaunty jib above the mists of morning as the rising keen of her sleek hull echoed in the spray at her bow.

"How do you fare the morning, Mister Caster?" Dalton asked offhandedly as topmen swarmed aloft to stand by the studding wings and others made ready the run-out gaff and boom of the snow's great ringtail astern.

"Odd weather, sir," the boy said. "The gauges aloft read a wind of twenty knots or more and rising, though here on deck it's hardly ten."

"Weird waters," Dalton muttered. "What else?"

"The mist seems to be shredding, sir. The winds are drawing it aloft. It's . . . it's pretty, sir. Like ladies' skirts sweeping across a ballroom."

Dalton glanced at his clerk. The boy did have a way with words sometimes. "I have eyes, Mister Caster. I can see all that. What will it do?"

Billy hesitated, looking again at the blowing gauges in the tops, the swirling, dancing motions of curtains of mist rising from the fog-covered sea, then spread his hands. "If it keeps doing what it's doing now, sir, I'd warrant the winds will rise to thirty knots or near it, and once the mists have cleared we'll have low overcast and a good general wind that's as fresh down here as it is up there."

"Interesting," Dalton said. "How do you come to that prediction?"

"I don't know, sir. It just seems as if that's what it's trying to do. Am I correct?"

"I don't know, Mister Caster. Your guess this time is as good as mine. But I find no fault with it."

He stepped to the quarterrail. "Double your hands at the sheets, please, Mister Wise. We are putting on more sail."

"Aye, sir. How much?"

"All of it, Mister Wise. Studding sails top and topgallant

yards, royals aloft, top main staysail and the ringtail. By the numbers, Mister Wise."

"Aye, sir."

"You lads is in for a show now," Purdy Fisk announced to some of the new hands at the main fife rails. "What would you wager this vessel's hull speed to be?"

"Fourteen, maybe fifteen," Virgil Hemingway judged. "A king's brig of this size might do that or near."

Fisk grinned. "Aye, that would be proper—if *Fury* was a brig. But a snow is somethin' else again. I'll wager a week's pay that Captain Dalton gets eighteen knots out of her . . . no, by heaven, I'll wager he gets twenty."

"Why would you wager such a thing?" Noel Ransom frowned at Fisk. "That isn't even . . ."

Ishmael Bean, hurrying past, paused. "Don't jeopardize your wages on that, lads. Remember, some of us have sailed with Dalton longer than any of you." He cocked a brow at Fisk. "And there's some who don't hesitate to take advantage of others' ignorance."

High aloft, the tall royals billowed on *Fury's* fore and main skymasts, then snapped taut as brawny men at the pinrails below trimmed them to the wind. *Fury* seemed to shudder, like a racehorse quickening its gate, then leapt forward as rollers of bright water cut through the mists riding along her hull. She surged again when the upper staysail unfurled from its gaff above the spencer, and as the big ringtail ran out astern, increasing the size of her driving spanker by a third. She twitched her behind like a stalking cat and pranced upon the waters. Above her jutting prow great bat-wings of jibsail and fore topmast staysail arched aloft, taking the wind's angle a'fore just as the spanker took it astern.

Twelve great sails she spread now, only her main course furled up to give the spencer advantage of the tacking wind.

Like a dancer at center stage she took spray in her teeth and rose on a throbbing keel to race across blanketed waters.

Then at Dalton's command, the studding sails ran out, at

port and starboard, six on the foreyards and four on the mains — big, bright extensions of the tops and topgallants, great wings spread from the forecourse. Here aside and aloft was the best wind, and the ship's rigging sang like harp strings as the structure of masts, shrouds, yardarms and stays adjusted to take the massive press of sail. Aloft, topmen clung to pitching, surging footropes, while all along the deck men grabbed supports to keep from falling.

"Sweet Jesus," Noel Ransom gasped, then turned to stare at the beaming face of Purdy Fisk.

"Told you." Fisk grinned. *"Fury* isn't a brig."

Just forward of them, Ishmael Bean had taken his first cast with log and line, and turned to relay his report. "Seventeen knots by log, Mister Wise! Seventeen and climbing!"

The whine of singing waters along the hull rose in pitch, and rose yet more as surging gusts settled from aloft to thrum and snap in the ringtail and spanker. The curling spray off both bows had become tall, bright cockscombs of clear water, rising as high as the deadeyes where the shrouds were cleated before curling out and down to fall back into the misted sea.

From the quarterrail, Dalton gazed at the quivering, driving spanker with its ringtail extension aft, and nodded. "You've faired it well, Mister Caster," he said. "The lofty winds are lowering to give us their advantage."

"By log eighteen and climbing!" Ishmael Bean called from ahead.

Bell by bell, the weather changed. Sea mist was swept aloft and settled there to canopy a gray sky. The high winds came down to replace the mists, and increased to a steady twenty-eight knots on *Fury*'s port quarter, and the visible world became steadily wider as the air was swept clean between sea and sullen sky.

Fury thrummed northward, booming deep in her hull as she overran and clove the rolling waves, her wake a long sheen of foam where she had been. A gust sent the gauges flying to thirty-plus knots, and the snow growled like thunder deep in her knees as rigging aloft shrilled at the press of sail on the delicate counterbalances of mast, yard and stay. On the working decks men glanced around, wide-eyed at each new sound and rumble.

"By the log . . . and a half, twenty!" Ishmael Bean called from the fore.

"The captain's a madman," new hands muttered. "He'll destroy us all if he keeps this up."

"I'm for taking in a bit of sail," one suggested. "No ship can—"

"I'd mind my tongue if I were you, swabby," Cadman Wise growled. "Captain Dalton says what sail we press, not the likes of you."

"But he'll kill us!" another said. "Listen to the footings, man. He'll break us apart pressing the ship so."

"I think I agree," another said.

Wise turned, surprised. "You, Mister Tucker? You, a first-rate seaman with line duty behind you?"

"I've sailed a fine ship or two." Euclid Tucker nodded. Heavy muscles corded and rippled in his bare shoulders. "And with fine commands. But no man can press a ship so and not come to ill. Are they right, Mister Wise? Is Captain Dalton mad?"

"Not mad." Wise shook his head. "Sanest man I've met, for an officer."

"Then, what drives him so?"

Wise shrugged. "Maybe it comes of bein' black Irish. They sometimes aren't like other folk, you know. Moody, that's the way of 'em. And it's my notion that the captain's in a black mood right now. But if Captain Dalton says this vessel shall take wing and fly, then I for one intend to find myself a good spot at the midships rail."

Credence Tapp squinted at him. "A spot at the rail? Why?"

Wise grinned. "Because I've never seen what the earth looks like from above the clouds."

"Somebody needs to talk to him," Tucker persisted. "If

172

you won't do it, Mister Wise, then I will."

"Suit yourself." Wise shrugged. "Though I'd advise against it."

"Who's with me?" Tucker raised his voice. "Who'll demand caution with me?"

Several raised their hands, and Wise shrugged again, glancing at the knowing faces of Claude Mallory and Purdy Fisk. "And if Captain doesn't agree?"

"Then, by the Lord we'll press our point."

Dalton was, as Wise had guessed, "in a mood." Long weeks on lonely seas, the frustration of the fugitive — the grounded fox waiting for the hounds to abate their chase — the uncertainty of what to do next, to keep both the ship and the honor that he had fought to win, and now the anxiety of the lost *Pride,* somewhere on an unfriendly sea where predators lurked, all weighed heavily upon him as he pushed *Fury* to new limits and scanned the seas ahead.

Cloud cover still limited the view. Low and jumbled the clouds lay, narrowing the span between sea and sky. Murky distances playing tricks with the eyes. Bell succeeded bell, and no sighting came from the mastheads, nor even from the agile topmen who braved the topgallant shrouds for a bit now and again, clinging more than a hundred feet above the deck on a racing snow that skimmed and pitched as she ran.

Far below, on the quarterdeck, Patrick Dalton worried and paced. "I've an ill feeling about that frigate, Mister Locke," he said, not so much to his helmsman as to himself. "Neither trader nor escort that, nor yet a proper instrument of belligerents." He glanced around. "Is the helm behaving as it should? At this press of sail, it could become skittish."

"Docile as a lamb, sir." Locke nodded, then braced himself as a surge of wind belled in the taut ringtail and the ship tried to turn of its own accord. "Best I should say a weaned colt, I expect, sir. She does have a friskiness to her at this speed."

"Manageable?"

173

"Oh, yes, sir. Manageable, aye."

"Keep a good grip, then, Mister Locke. If we've no sign of *Pride* in the next hour, I shall add more sail."

Behind him a querulous voice gasped, "More sail?"

Dalton turned. Several sailors were massed at the quarterdeck ladder, some on the steps and one or two already on the command deck.

"You men!" Abel Ball snapped, from the bell rail. "Avast there. You've no business on the quarterdeck!"

"Business with the captain." The lead among them frowned, then straightened and faced Dalton. "Sir!"

"Well?"

"Sir, we've come to petition you to ease sail a bit. It seems to us that we are likely to break up at this press."

Dalton gazed at them, one by one. "We?" he asked. "You six?"

"Aye," the leader hesitated; then his face grew pugnacious. "Aye, we bring a fo'c'sle mandate, Captain. Slow down this ship, or we will."

"You will," Dalton breathed. Near at hand, Billy Caster was edging toward a rack of belaying pins. Dalton halted him with a raised hand. "You men, do you recall the articles you agreed to when I gave you berths on *Fury*?"

"Aye, sir," the leader said. "And we mean no breach of articles, sir, but by God we aim to save our skins if you won't."

"By mutiny?"

"No, sir. By persuasion, sir."

"And who here would like to do the persuading, then?"

"I might attend to that, sir, by your leave. Euclid Tucker, sir. Able seaman, at your service."

"I know you, Mister Tucker." Dalton sighed, then removed his sword and buckler and handed them to Billy. "Very well, Mister Tucker. You have leave. Feel free to persuade me."

Tucker blinked in surprise, then shrugged and grinned. "No hard feelin's, Captain?"

"Not in the slightest. Begin."

174

Like a pouncing cat, Tucker launched himself at Dalton, knotted arms swinging, hard fists clenched. The sailor was shorter by inches than Dalton, but widely built and equipped with broad, powerful shoulders and burly arms as hard as shroud cable. And he was quick . . . though not quick enough. His first rush carried him directly through where the Irishman had been an instant before, and he sprawled on the deck, tripped by a booted foot.

Dalton called over his shoulder, "Mister Caster, pass the word. I am not yet persuaded. Ask Mister Mallory to break out the flying jib, please. That should give this bumbling tub a bit more speed."

"Aye, sir."

Tucker scrambled to his feet, wild-eyed. "You are a madman!" he shouted, then lowered his voice. "Beg pardon, sir, but the calling of names is part of leave, isn't it?"

"Right you are." Dalton nodded. "Call away."

"Madman!" Tucker repeated, then came in low, rushing the captain with arms spread wide to grapple. He didn't see the hard fist that took him at the cheekbone and looped him around, but he felt the booted foot that connected with his posterior and sent him sprawling exactly where he had been before.

Dalton straightened. "Mister Caster, ask Mister Mallory to break out that spritsail we carry, and sling it below the spreaders."

"Aye, sir." Even as he responded, *Fury* seemed to leap into a new stride, answering to the pull of the high-flying jibsail at her nose. "Mister Mallory, Captain would like the spritsail, if you please."

Tucker got to his feet more slowly this time, dizzy and shaking his head. "You're still adding more sail?" he coughed.

"I have not been persuaded otherwise, Mister Tucker."

Like a bull fighting flies, Tucker shook his head from side to side, muttering, and braced himself to charge again. The charge never began. Dalton stepped in front of him, ducked

175

a roundhouse swing and bent the man double with a fist to his midriff, then straightened him up again with a blow to the chin. Tucker wobbled, almost fell, then crouched, hands on knees, trying to catch his breath.

"Mister Mallory," Dalton called. "Sheet and trim the main course, please."

"The main . . . ah, aye, sir."

Like fiddles in torment, *Fury's* singing shrouds howled as the big sail dropped home and took the wind. Deep within her hull the snow crackled and boomed, mast footings straining and grating against their keelson stays. Timbers rumbled and chattered as her knees took the strain. She leapt forward as though she would take flight, and the thunders of her torment were deafening for a moment, then eased.

From forward, the amazed voice of Ishmael Bean shouted, "By log, twenty-two . . . no, twenty-three! Ye Gods, twenty-three?"

Dalton listened to the sounds of his ship, his dark eyes alight with interest, a brow cocked in judgment.

"Marvelous," he breathed. He looked at the groaning Tucker. "You still have leave to continue, Mister Tucker, though I've run out of sails, I'm afraid. We've pressed on every stitch of canvas that we've anything to hang it from, unless we invent something new. What is your pleasure?"

Tucker looked up, dizzy and battered. "Twenty-three?" he croaked. "Twenty-three knots?"

"It seems so," Dalton said happily. "To be honest, I wouldn't have thought it could be done. I owe you a debt of thanks, Mister Tucker. Without your . . . ah . . . persuasion, I might never have had the nerve to really try all sail in such a wind. Good to know what we can do if we set our minds to it, though, isn't it?"

"Twenty . . . three?"

"On deck!" The hail from aloft was distant, but clear.

"Aye, tops?"

"Sail, sir! Ahead and a point aport, a mile at most! Two

ships, sir, and cannon fire! One is *Pride of Falworth!* The other wears a black flag!"

"Ah," Dalton said. "It's time we earn our keep, then." He straightened himself, retrieved his sword and slapped Euclid Tucker on the back, urging him forward. The man's companions backed away before him. Dalton waved them forward. "To stations, lads. We've work to do. And by the way, Mister Tucker, well done! I was in something of a mood, but I feel much better now."

Nineteen

Despite the best of Charley Duncan's evasions, as the hours passed the dark warship bore down relentlessly — closing, ever closing on the fleeing bark. Though awkward in its corrections because of its binding rudder, still the frigate was fast and lean. Its three masts carried as much sail — and in greater variety — as *Pride*'s four, and its timbered hull was sleek and trim.

Though strongly manned now, despite the loss of Hoop and his companions aboard the little boat, *Pride* with all the weight of sail that could be pressed onto her stacked spars was yet only a bark — a merchant sailing vessel designed and rigged for the transport of cargoes — and no match in speed or agility for the ship-rigged cruiser on her tail. Nor were her guns — a mere handful of antiquated cannons, the largest of which were the brace of old nines at her stern — any match for the banked guns of the frigate, as Charley Duncan saw clearly when the first smoke-roses bloomed at the pirate's nose.

"Ranging guns," he muttered as a pair of balls whined overhead, tearing gaping holes in the courses there. "Long twelves. He'll tear us to pieces with those if we don't heave to."

"Aye," Pliny Quarterstone said darkly. "Then bring his broadsides to bear and blast us out of the water when we do. That ship is not inviting surrender, Mister Duncan, nor offering quarter. I believe he intends to kill us, no matter what we do."

178

Duncan squinted through a glass, then lowered it with a sigh and handed it to Quarterstone. "You likely are right," he said. "Read her name."

Quarterstone glassed the pursuer. "*Valkyrie*," he read. "Isn't that the ship that . . . ?"

"Aye. The one the Frenchmen told us about. The same people who had *Pride* once, then tried to scuttle her."

Again the frigate's bow chasers blazed. A ball skipped across the waters thirty feet off *Pride*'s portside beam, to sink in a geyser of spray ahead. A second whined across stern timbers astarboard, gouging out a half-moon of bright wood.

"He's aiming to hull us at waterline!" Finian Nelson shouted.

Duncan counted the seconds, clicking his tongue in slow rhythm to keep the count. Then he turned. "Point aport, helm. Bosun, trim to—"

"I know, I know!" Porter's growl carried astern.

Pride came over into a graceful turn as the smoke-roses blossomed again behind them. This time both shots were wide to starboard, but Duncan shook his head. "That likely won't work but once," he admitted. "Mister Reeves? Where's Mister Reeves?"

Reeves came racing aft, skidding to a halt at the netting ladder. "Sir?"

"Mister Reeves, when Mister Hoop inspected the fothering, what did he find?"

"A blister, sir. The patch cloth had taken in water. He let it out."

"Then, likely it has taken more, and it's dragging on us. Was there water below decks from the patch?"

"I don't know, sir, I . . ."

"It's dry below," Keith Darling said. "Nothing's leaking that we could see down there."

Duncan made a decision. "Mister Reeves, break out axes and cut away that fothering."

"Aye, sir. Shall we hoist it . . ."

179

"Cut it away and let it go," Duncan said. "Now!" He turned to the helm. "Point to starboard, helm . . . no, belay that! Just a bit more to port, then lay over two to starboard."

"Aye, sir." Again *Pride* veered to the left, and this time the fire from the pursuer's bow chasers was farther off to the right.

Duncan let out a deep breath, then sighed and shook his head. "That's another move that won't work again," he muttered. "Stern guns, do you have his range yet?"

"Not bloody likely," a hand at the nearest of the ancient nines growled. "Not with these popguns."

"Well, damn it, shoot anyway!"

"Aye, sir."

As the nines bellowed in ragged volley of two, *Pride* answered to her helm and swung gracefully to the right. Smoke rode across her tail, but its shredding mist could not obscure the twin clouds that grew at the nose of *Valkyrie*. Too late to reverse, Duncan knew that this time the pursuer had outguessed him. He braced himself for the impact of iron ball, then staggered as *Pride* seemed to shoot forward, gaining speed as though kicked from astern. Aport, a sprawl of sailcloth drifted past her beam.

Twin iron balls threw spray from her wake, missing by scant yards.

"That fotherin' was full of water!" someone called forward. "Like we was draggin' a lake around."

"Trim to course!" Duncan shouted.

"We're trimmin', blast it!" James Porter snapped. "Stop tellin' us our bedammed job!"

In the nettings, Squire Aaron Fairfield's caustic voice was raised, "What sort of officer takes that kind of backtalk from his crew?"

Duncan looked around, fuming, then stalked to the quarterrail hatch. "I am not a damned officer!" he roared at the startled passengers just below. "And if you call me that again, I'll have you thrown overboard. Now will you be silent?"

Fairfield blinked at him. "I was only just . . ."

"Will you be silent?"

"Well . . . yes."

"What?"

"Yes, I said!"

"Yes . . . what?"

"Yes, *sir.*"

"That's better." Duncan nodded, turning away. "Laxity aboard ship is not to be tolerated," he muttered.

Between *Pride's* sudden release from the bondage of her hull patch, and the pirate's binding rudder, the bark had gained a bit of space. But *Valkyrie* had compensated now and was coming on, hard in pursuit.

"Well, Mister Duncan, do you have any more tricks?" Pliny Quarterstone asked bleakly.

"On deck!"

Duncan peered aloft, then turned to look astern. The grim set of his freckled face softened, then became a vicious grin. "Aye," he said. "One more. Mister Porter!"

"I know!" the grumpy voice bellowed. "Trim to —!"

"Mister Porter, shut your bleedin' mouth and listen! I want you to stand by to come about."

"Come about?"

"Come about?" Quarterstone echoed.

"Into the wind?" Nelson gaped.

"You're daft!" Aaron Fairfield yelped, then clapped a hand over his mouth.

Duncan ignored them all, gazing out at the killer in his wake, his grin feral. "At my call, helm," he said evenly.

At the helm, two pairs of wide eyes stared at him, but without argument.

"Squire Fairfield," Duncan said, "you can make yourself useful now. Go below and get all of your people into the after holds. No person is to be forward of the foremain footings."

"Now see here . . ." Fairfield blustered.

"Do it now!"

Fairfield and his shadow scurried away, muttering.

"Mister Nelson, hands to all guns, please. I want every gun we have hauled to the bow, three each side of the sprit. Secured, loaded, primed and aimed straight ahead level."

"Are you sure you know what you're doing, Mister Duncan?" Pliny Quarterstone scowled at him. "Sure, an' we come about for a fast bow volley, we'll do a bit of damage . . . but then that blaggard will blast us out of the water."

"I know what I'm doing," Duncan gritted.

"Well, what *are* you doing?"

"I am amusing the enemy. Keeping him entertained, just as Captain Dalton might do. I hope . . . ," he added under his breath. Then, "Lend a hand with those guns there."

"Aye . . . sir."

Valkyrie was closing again, and again her long twelves thundered. A ball smashed into the bark's sterncastle, taking out bulkheads below deck, and emerged howling through the steerageway to demolish a yard of starboard rail. Its companion gouged splinters from the mizzen mast.

"Whatever you're about to do, you'd best do it now!" someone shouted.

"Aye," Duncan breathed, still grinning. "Hands to all guns in the fore! Fire as your target bears! Ready? Now, strike our colors!"

The trade pennant crawled down its lanyard. Duncan watched it until it was taken in. Behind, very close now, he could see the faces of men at *Valkyrie*'s rails, the smoke of burning fuse at linstocks poised above cannon vents. "Do I have your full attention now, ye bleedin' cutthroats?" he muttered. "Well, watch closely, for there's more yet to see." He turned. "Helm hard astarboard! Come full about, smartly!"

Pride reeled like a drunken thing as her rudder bit the current and her tail sidled out of line. Her sails fluttered uselessly, and for a moment it seemed she would come dead in the water. But her momentum carried her into the scudding turn, and abruptly she came about, her nose swinging into and through the wind.

Only a few hundred yards away, now suddenly dead ahead on a collision course, *Valkyrie* fought her stubborn rudder, edging to port. Two more shots blossomed at her nose, but both went wide. Then *Pride's* bow guns began to speak, a ragged rhythm of thunders that washed great clouds of acrid smoke back along her decks. Six roars sounded, and ahead there was the sound of balls striking. Six shots, then silence except for the shouts of men and the growing thunder of the big warship closing on its treacherous prey.

Quarterstone was at Duncan's side. "Well, that was a bit of sport, right enough, though I can't see that it has done us much good."

"Can't you?" Duncan pointed. "Look yonder, then, beyond him. See what has closed in while we kept the blighter amused."

Quarterstone raised his eyes, and they went wide. Beyond the pirate ship were other sails—massive, stacked sails above a lethal hull that seemed to fly across the waters. Like an angel of mercy, or an angel of death, *Fury* bore down on the frigate at near twenty knots—a sharp-toothed, dashing fox on the wolf's blind side, roaring in to bite and rend, to tear and maim. At twenty knots, she closed on a collision course.

Aboard *Valkyrie* they saw the bark veer and hesitate, then saw the trade flag descend its lanyard.

"He's done, Cap'n Shelby." Timothy Leech grinned. "He strikes his colors. What signal shall we make?"

The man who had been John Shelby Butler scratched idly at his whiskered chin, cold eyes gazing out at the four-master under his guns. Then he clasped his hands behind him. "No signal, Mister Leech," he said. "We shall speak with our

183

guns. When we've closed to three cables, have the bow guns take down his mizzen mast, then recharge and break down his stern post. Starboard batteries stand by to hull him at the water when he's crippled."

"That'll sink him, right enough." Leech nodded. "But don't you want to see who's aboard?"

"We'll pluck a few survivors from the sea to question," Shelby said. "That will be enough. I want that bark sent to the bottom, so get on with it."

"Aye, Cap'n." Leech wondered at the man's determination to destroy what yet might be a prize, but he didn't press it. He had learned long since that John Shelby Butler—now Jack Shelby—made his own plans for his own reasons, and that those reasons were valid, whether expressed or not.

At his relayed command, the gun crews in the bow bent to their long twelves, waiting for the order to fire. The bark was dead ahead now, the range nearly point-blank for the ranging guns. At three cable lengths the slaughter would begin, and they would not miss.

The bark had not veered again, but now—abruptly—it did. It responded to hard rudder, shook itself like a tormented bear, and came hard over to the right.

"Bear on him, helm!" Leech roared. *Valkyrie* slid into the turn, trying to keep her nose in line with the vessel ahead, then suddenly was charging down upon it. The bark had continued its turn, had come right about into the wind, and now sat motionless, head-on to its charging pursuer.

"Rudder aport!" Leech shouted. "Veer off! Veer off!"

"He's insane," Shelby muttered. "He wants us to collide with him."

Valkyrie had barely begun to answer her helm when smokes erupted at the nose of the bark, now less than two cables away. Ragged thunders rolled across the water, and iron balls screamed into the nose of the frigate, ripping and tearing.

In an instant there was chaos in the bow as *Valkyrie* struggled to bear aside, to avoid collision. The binding rudder balked and struggled stubbornly. In the fore, stunned gunners got their feet under them and fired the twin ranging guns, realizing as they did that they were no longer on point. The shots went wide, uselessly, thrown off their mark by their own ship's turn.

In the same instant, a panicked cry rang down from aloft, "On deck! Attacker on our port quarter, bearing in . . . lor', but he's dead on us!"

The echoes of the shout were massed thunders riding on the wind. Those on the quarterdeck turned as screaming shot ripped into their structures and whined across their decks. The ship there was under full sail—twice the sail that it seemed so small a vessel could press—and it bore down on the larger frigate at an impossible speed. Again guns volleyed, their smokes riding ahead of them to mist the specter of imminent, grinding collision.

"Port batteries!" Shelby shouted. "Align and fire. Stern guns hard over! Fire!"

Somewhere within *Valkyrie* big guns thundered, rocking the ship, but they were not those aport. The starboard batteries, ready to fire, *had* fired—wildly—not at the attacker but in the direction of the wind-locked, motionless bark just now sliding past to starboard.

Timothy Leech gripped the rail and stared at the ship thundering down on *Valkyrie*. A brig, his mind registered, then corrected itself in an instant. No brig could put on such sail. No brig could move so fast—and the speed was headlong, directly toward the larger ship. "He's making to ram," he muttered, gaping. Nearer and nearer, faster than seemed possible, the attacker swept in, a deadly, blasting phantom shrouded in the smokes of its cannons—smoke that rolled with the thunders of its guns, that billowed and spread, that rode on the wind and seemed a part of the ship.

In *Fury's* bow and abaft both her catheads, Ethan Crosby and Floyd Pugh worked furiously, directing four gun

185

crews—quoining, aiming and firing as fast as searing-hot guns could be run in, charged and run out. Steam from scorched swabs rose in clouds as dense as the acrid smoke of the volleys.

Amidships, Cadman Wise danced from rail to rail, setting his sail-handlers to their tasks, his eyes turning at each breath toward the quarterdeck where Patrick Dalton directed the attack. Through the smoke, the figures there—Dalton and others—looked vague and far away, but Wise knew that when Dalton called or raised his arm to signal, he must respond instantly . . . as must the entire working deck. "Maybe now you swabbies will learn why the captain ran you through all those drills," he barked, for any who might hear. "Now is when it counts!"

Aft, Dalton ceased his pacing and stood, squinting, peering ahead through the smokes. *Fury* was closing rapidly on the larger ship now, her speed unabated, all of her sails set aloft and all of them full of wind. Dead ahead, the pirate seemed to falter uncertainly. And beyond was the bark, wind-locked and helpless now but in the position it had taken to decoy the attacker. *Well done, Mister Duncan,* Dalton thought. *A nice ploy, indeed.*

He had heard the muted roar of a broadside fired by the frigate, but not at himself, and his eyes went flat and cold. If not at *Fury,* then it was at the helpless, wind-locked bark standing "in irons" just beyond the pirate. Round after round flew from *Fury's* guns, and he could only guess at their effect. The smoke rode on the wind, shrouding everything.

He knew almost to the second the point at which the pirate had spotted *Fury,* and he estimated the reaction time aboard. Counting seconds by counting the beats of his heart, he squinted, judging distance, then turned to the helm. "Hard astarboard now, if you please, Mister Locke. Smartly!" In the same instant he raised his arm and brought it slicing downward, trusting to Cadman Wise to see his signal.

Fury shook like a warhorse, crested a wave and bit water with a wide rudder. For a moment she seemed to hang suspended; then she leaned hard over and skidded into a tight turn, sheeting bright spray from her portside hull. Rumbling growls of torment erupted below as timbers and bracing took a sudden new strain, then eased as the yards above swung into new positions, hauled about by those on the sail deck.

"Gunners aport!" Dalton shouted, signalling with his arm. "Fire as she bears!"

Shrouds screaming, sails drumming and timbers grinding, men clinging to whatever was at hand to avoid being thrown over, *Fury* braced her keel against deep waters and turned, skidding and sheeting spray. Through the smokes an abrupt darkness grew off her port bow, then amidships — the great, dark silhouette of the frigate, so close it seemed they might reach out and touch it. Faces along the rails came clear, faces gaping, faces shouting, faces cursing . . . and disappeared in smoke, fire and thunder as beam guns on both vessels roared. Crashing, rending sounds echoed and re-echoed through the turmoil.

Aloft, above the smokes, big yardarms crashed against shrouds as the high structures collided, spar against cable, spar against spar, a confusion of timbers and stays in swift opposition. Somewhere a man . . . or more than one, Dalton could not tell . . . screamed, plummeting from high above.

The chaos dinned, peaked and suddenly stopped. Dalton's breath hissed through clenched teeth. "Rudder amidships, Mister Locke! Gunners aft, to the stern chasers!"

"We've been hit, sir." Billy Caster's adolescent voice broke in pitch as he turned from the rail, his face pale against a curtain of smoke that almost hid the frigate, now off their port quarter and receding. "I heard a hit . . . or maybe two or three."

In the waist, sailors hauled at sheet lines, trying to correct the battered set of spars aloft. Crosby and Pugh raced past, others following, to train and fire the twin stern chasers while yet they had a target. The guns thundered, and a ball came in response, singing overhead. Guns quoined high for the decks of a tall bark were too lofted for the much smaller snow.

"Run in studding sails!" Dalton called. "Run in the ringtail! Loose courses fore and main!" He turned. "Point to port, please, Mister Locke. Hands a'deck, ease topgallants and royals! Down the flying jib!"

As abruptly as the engagement had begun, it was over. Smoke drifted down the wind, and revealed a sea where ships stood at odds—the bark still nose to the wind, in irons, the snow just coming about off its flank, and the frigate still moving, under sail, retreating northward with a quartering wind.

"Do we go after him, sir?" Victory Locke strained at the helm, his eyes glittering with excitement.

Dalton shook his head. "Not this time, I'm afraid, Mister Locke. We've reclaimed our prize, and drawn first blood, but our duty is to *Pride*. I'm afraid *Valkyrie* shall have to wait for another time, to join us in a sport."

Billy Caster gazed out at the retreating frigate. It was still going, making no effort to turn. "Mightn't he come back, sir? He outguns us. He might . . ."

"I think not," Dalton said. "We've damaged him, and we have the weather gauge. He knows that I won't give him the upwind position. Bring us over, helm. Let's have a look at Mister Duncan and his command."

Twenty

Aboard a ragged and crippled *Valkyrie,* Jack Shelby paced his deck, staring darkly back at the pair of vessels diminishing behind. The armed snow had made no attempt to pursue. Having completed its surprise attack, it stood now, alee of the far larger bark, letting the merchantman drift down to it.

He was not surprised that the snow did not continue the engagement. Its attack had been sudden and ferocious, conducted with either extraordinary skill or extraordinary luck, but it was still only a small cruiser. Hardly a match for a frigate-class vessel in head-to-head combat. And the captain had his escort to worry about. He would hardly jeopardize the merchantman by heading off into a lopsided engagement.

Neither could he, himself, go back now. *Valkyrie* had extensive damage. Nothing that couldn't be repaired, but enough to cripple her for now. Almost overhead, on the mizzen, a broken spar dangled from its tackle, swaying afoul of the stays. Torn sailcloth whipped and fluttered in the wind. Belowdecks, the entire sterncastle was a chaos of debris thrown by iron balls smashing through the frigate's timbers. He had lost six men—four dead and two so wounded as to be of no use to him. The ship's galley was out of service, the after pumps heavily damaged and the cable tiers awash in the muck of shattered kegs from ship's stores.

All of that, and the crippled rudder.

189

Valkyrie would lay by for repairs. And his chance of destroying *Pride of Falworth,* that floating evidence of his treachery, was gone.

Sooner or later, now, Ian McCall would have an answer to the riddle of what became of his merchantman.

But would McCall deduce that it was his own trusted captain who now sailed *Valkyrie?*

Shelby pondered on that. No, he thought, that might remain a mystery, even now. For who alive could tell the squire that Jack Shelby was John Shelby Butler?

And as long as that was secret, Jack Shelby's career could continue. As long as no one knew who he was, he would know what cargoes were shipped and where they might be intercepted.

Timothy Leech appeared beside him, big and dour. "Beg pardon, Cap'n," he said. "We've listed th' damages. Mister Strode expects we'll need a week to get her shipshape again."

"A week," Shelby muttered.

"Aye, and we'll need to make land first, to do it right. That blighter has bled us. Luck was on his side this day."

"Luck?" Shelby spoke the word as though holding it suspended, studying it. "How much luck can one renegade Irishman have?"

Leech turned to gaze at him, puzzled. "You know who that is?"

"I know the vessel," Shelby said. *"Fury.* A snow that Ian McCall commissioned as a privateer, then lost. And I've heard of the man they say has it now. I expect you've heard the name as well. Patrick Dalton."

"Dalton?" Leech's eyes widened. "The Britisher that brought so much grief to the king's ships back . . . ?"

"That one." Shelby nodded.

"But he's dead, isn't he? Seems like I heard that."

"Not dead. Escaped and missing, along with that snow. Bring us over to westerly, Mister Leech. We'll make for the cays, and Mister Strode can have his week while you and I go to visit the Spaniard. There are messages to be sent and things to be done."

190

"Aye, Cap'n. What of the dead and wounded? What do you want done?"

"Drop them overboard," Shelby grunted impatiently.

"Wounded too, sir? Some of the others might . . ."

"Every man aboard this ship knows our articles, Mister Leech. And every man has agreed to them. We carry no dead weight aboard *Valkyrie*. Drop them overboard."

Pride's prow was a shambles, as were her forward holds. Though most of the pirate's broadside, fired wildly and without aim, had gone astray, the bark had taken several solid hits. Six crewmen were gone, including the prize ship's only veteran bosun. A ball had smashed into one of *Pride's* nine-pounders, throwing the old gun entirely off its carriage. It flipped and fell, and when it hit the deck, James Porter was under it. George Reeves was dead, as were William Anglen, Clifton Foote, Terry Harp and a joking, laughing young topman named Romeo Martell.

In the forward hold there were dead animals. At least a third of the island refugees' livestock had fallen to cannon fire coming through the ship's nose. Blood was everywhere.

Surprisingly, there was only one casualty among the passengers. A farmer named Whitworth was dead. A panicked milk cow had broken through a plank bulkhead and gored him.

As *Pride* drifted down on the wind toward the waiting *Fury*, Charley Duncan turned the deck over to Finian Nelson and sent Pliny Quarterstone forward to begin a damage assessment. He directed hands to assemble the remains of the dead and cover them with sailcloth, and to carry the injured, of whom there were several, below to the galley for treatment. These things done, he went amidships and let himself down the midden ladder to inspect the passengers.

In the murky belly of the bark, nightmarish chaos ensued. Forward, still mostly contained by the plank "fences" the landsmen had hammered together, animals of all sorts stood among the bloody remains of their fallen mates.

191

The stench of blood and manure was eased by the fact that *Pride,* drifting without set sails except her fore-and-afts, had turned her tail to the stiff wind. Open hatches became breezeways, carrying the stink away.

One of the low plankings had been broken, and men were working to repair it while others labored in a sweating line. Some were tearing up decking in the after holds, some carrying the planks forward and others beginning the erection of chutes for hauling the dead beasts up to the foredeck where grapples could reach them. Duncan gazed around, shaking his head in disbelief. It was hard to tell who had done the most damage here — the pirates or the passengers.

Farther back, in the rearmost spaces just short of the stores and galley, were huddles of women and children. Aaron Fairfield was flitting here and there, trying to direct all the activities, and generally was being ignored.

As Duncan approached, a small figure broke loose from one of the huddles and hurried toward him, skirting perilously close to one of the gaping holes where decking had been lifted away.

"Here! Be careful!" Duncan barked, and rushed to catch the child before it could trip or fall. He grabbed the boy up, and shuddered as he looked beyond, down into the deep bilges of the bark — a maze of timbers, treenailed structures and dark holes filled with the great heaps of metallic rubble that were *Pride's* ballast.

"You should stay with your mother," he told the boy. "It isn't safe to run about like that."

"I was looking for you, sir," Henry Cabot said as Duncan set him on his feet. The boy's eyes were bright with excitement. "I heard all the cannons shooting. There was a lot of noise."

"Yes, there was," Duncan agreed. "Where's the lady your mother, lad?"

"She's back there, in the shed."

"Shed?"

The boy pointed.

Duncan shook his head. "Ships don't have sheds, lad.

192

Yonder is the capstan track. On a cargo vessel like this it's housed so men can work there without fear of shifting loads. Come along, then." He took the boy's hand.

"But I have something to show you," Henry balked. "Something I found."

From the "shed" came the sound of a woman's voice, raised above the clamor. "Henry? Henry, where are you?"

"Women!" the boy muttered, then tugged at Duncan's sleeve. "What I found is —"

"Later, lad," Duncan said. "Come along. Your mother is worried about you."

"But there's a whole lot of —"

"Whatever it is will keep. Come on now. Let's return you to Mistress Cabot."

With the youth firmly in tow, Duncan approached the capstan housing, peered inside, then removed his hat. Somehow the passengers had converted the little space into a sleeping accommodation for women and children. Hammocks lined the entire enclosure, and the stubby capstan in the center had become a hold-high pillar, extended by stub-nailing braces of hardwood that could only have been ladder rails. All around it were slung small hammocks and trundles for children.

"Bleedin' hell," Duncan swore, then blushed as several women turned to gape at him. "Pardon, ladies," he said. "I just never realized how much damage a bunch of refugees could do to a perfectly good sailin' vessel." He gazed around at other modifications the people belowdecks had made to accommodate themselves. "Worse'n bore-worms," he breathed.

Priscilla Cabot pushed through the crowd, a vision of large, frightened eyes in a pale face. She glanced at Duncan, then turned her attention to the boy. "Henry? What have you done now?"

Duncan released the boy and gazed at the woman. "He did nothing, Mistress Cabot. I only came below to inspect the damages, and Henry came to bid me hello."

"No, I wanted to show you the —" the boy started.

Priscilla's color returned somewhat. "Thank you, Captain. Is the . . . the cannon-firing over for now?"

"It's over, mistress. The bedam — the foul pirate has been chased away by our escort. Are you . . . ah . . . is everyone here well?"

"Very well, thank you . . . thanks to Squire Fairfield, who had the foresight to move everyone to the back of the ship . . ."

"Stern," Duncan corrected.

"Yes, he can be that at times, though he's mostly bluster. But he said for everyone to stay in the cellar and . . ."

"Below deck," Duncan put in.

"Pardon?"

"It's *below deck*. Ships don't have cellars."

"Oh. Well, downstairs anyway. Oh, it was awful, though. So much noise, and those poor beasts . . . and then I couldn't find Henry. Would you care for tea, sir?"

"I think not, right now," he said, backing away. He noticed again how large her eyes seemed. Abruptly he felt confused and disoriented. "I have inspections to make . . . and repairs. Ah . . . good day to you, mistress." He backed away, put his hat on his head and turned, nearly bumping into Aaron Fairfield.

"We could use some help building the chutes," the squire said, "since you seem to have impounded our only carpenter to help you turn your wheel."

"Helm." Duncan glared at him.

"Call it what you like." Fairfield shrugged. "And we could use some more lumber, as well."

"You people are doing more damage here than that pirate did," Duncan hissed. "Look at that. And that! I warn you, sir, the first man to take a pry to my hull timbers will be stretched over the bore of a cannon." He spun away. Nearby, men were wrapping a body in quilts. It was Whitworth, the man gored by the cow. Duncan turned back. "My sympathies for your loss. Have the man brought on deck and we'll bury him with honor, along with the others."

A small hand tugged at his sleeve. "Here, sir," Henry Cabot chirped. "This is what I wanted to show you."

Duncan glanced down. The boy held a canvas sack, which he lifted with difficulty. Absently, Duncan took it and glanced inside, then stared. "Where did you get this, boy?"

"I found it in the basement when they took up the floor, sir."

"Bilges," Duncan said.

"Oh, no, sir, I really did. And there are a lot more of them, too. I . . ."

Shoving the sack into his coat, Duncan shouted, "Squire Fairfield!"

Nearby, the squire turned, frowning.

"You said your party has money," Duncan said. "Is it secure?"

"It is." Fairfield nodded. "I checked it myself."

"None of it is missing?"

"Not a penny." Fairfield scowled at him suspiciously. "Why?"

"Never mind, Squire. Go about your business." Taking Henry Cabot by the hand, Duncan strode forward to the midden ladder, raised his head and shouted, "On deck!"

A sailor appeared at the hatch. "Sir?"

"Find Mister Quarterstone, please. And Misters McGinnis and Mudd. Tell them report to me immediately, below deck at the shed."

The man looked blank. "At the what, sir?"

"The sh—I mean, the aft capstan housing. Look alive!"

"Aye, sir."

"Now, boy"—Duncan looked down at Henry Cabot—"show me where you found this."

Though the wind had shifted through the day, coming now from east-southeast, its force held steady at close to thirty knots—a stiff wind that fought the surface currents and put rolling waves upon the ocean's face.

On such a sea, there would be no snugging together of the two vessels, though Dalton could see clearly as the bark drifted down toward him that a lay-by for repairs would be needed. *Pride's* prow had taken some shot, including one that had cut the spreader stays on the starboard side. With her jib weakened, she would not be able to mount staysails in the fore, and without the staysails the big vessel would be impossible to control on a long run.

Fury also had damage, though of lesser consequence. Two twelve-pound balls had punched through the snow's portside hull just below the after channel. One of the wounds was a gaping hole between the channel and the chain plate that would have to be reinforced or jeopardize the mainmast shrouds.

As *Pride* neared, Dalton maneuvered *Fury* around the larger ship on jib and jigger, assessing need, planning approach. Finally he edged the snow as close as he dared, staying to windward of the bark, and had Billy Caster bring up a speaking horn. With this at his mouth he hailed the bark. On *Pride's* high quarterdeck a man stepped to the rail and responded.

"Who are you?" Dalton called.

"Nelson, sir," the other answered. "Finian Nelson. Commander Duncan's second. He's below with Mister Quarterstone."

"Report your condition, Mister Nelson."

"Damage in the fore, Captain. Above waterline. A bit astern, too, though that's minor. Six men dead, sir. Seven, counting a passenger. Five missing. Mister Hoop had the dinghy out, with Misters Singleterry and Cobley and those two frogs. They're gone. Several injuries, being tended in the galley. Bleedin' merchantman's got no orlop deck . . . but I guess you know that, sir."

"What is the activity in your fore, Mister Nelson?" Dalton responded. "Have you begun repairs?"

Nelson turned to gaze forward, then called, "That's the passengers, sir. They're building ramps or something, to fetch up dead livestock. The animals took the brunt of the pirate's volley."

In the strong wind, the two ships had begun to drift

apart, *Pride* on the downwind side taking more wind on her high stern than the smaller snow. Dalton studied the westward sky, the lowering sun, the angle of drift, and called, "I'll want tethers fore and aft, Mister Nelson, with fenders. A pair of yardarms should do nicely. Splice them into the hawser and drift them out when they are secured. We will fish them out at this end and lash the ships together for assessment and repair."

"Aye, sir."

Dalton turned away, looking for Billy Caster, and found the young clerk at his elbow. "Mister Caster, I'll need the rosters of recruits, both vessels."

"Aye, sir. I have them right here. Seven of the men from the island have done at least a bit of carpentry, and of course all of us who were originally aboard have done a bit, but I can't find any real carpenters. We'll have to—"

"Ahoy *Fury!*"

Dalton turned. The voice that hailed them was a different voice than before. The man who stood at *Pride's* rail was a large, broad-shouldered young man holding Finian Nelson's speaking horn. Vaguely, Dalton recalled seeing him among the Mayaguana refugees. "I hear you!" he responded. "Who are you?"

"Keith Darling," the man shouted. "You'll be needing a carpenter here, sir. That's what I am. A carpenter."

The sun was afloat on the west horizon when they got the two ships tethered in the only manner that the wind and running sea would allow—snugged by hawsers at bow and stern, with yardarm timbers between them to keep them apart.

When it was done, *Fury's* launch was brought around and lashed between the vessels, below the fending yards. The boat made an adequate bridge between the two ships.

As Dalton turned his deck over to Purdy Fisk and started across, he saw others coming from the other deck, and stepped back to await them. The one in the lead was Char-

197

ley Duncan. He and the three following him were bent under heavy, wrapped parcels resting across their shoulders. Long moments passed, and Duncan hailed *Fury's* deck from below. Hands went to lift aboard the thing he carried . . . a canvas sack that seemed far too small for the heavy thump it made when it was deposited on the deck.

Duncan scrambled aboard, saluted Dalton bleakly, then turned to help lift aboard the burdens carried by the other three men. When their loads were aboard *Fury*, he sent them back to *Pride*.

That done, he turned to Dalton, gesturing at the canvas-wrapped packs at his feet. "Thought this would be safer here than yonder, sir," he said. "A boy found all this hid in the aftermain well."

"What is it?" Dalton prodded a sack with the toe of his boot.

Duncan glanced around and lowered his voice. "What it is, sir, is a bloody fortune. A treasure. Jewels and goblets, crucifixes, everything under the sun. And coin, sir. Silver and gold. More flamin' money than I ever even imagined there was."

Twenty-one

For days, the turning winds of spring had held traffic on the Delaware to a minimum. Square-rigged vessels tended to avoid the precarious closeness of river channels in seasons of chancy wind, and those fore-and-afts in merchant service in the middle colonies—states, they called themselves now—plied mostly out of Chesapeake because that was where the big carriers were.

As for warships, few were to be seen now. General Washington had come forth from Valley Forge, and the king's ground forces were aligning in the north. Where armies campaigned, there were the navies to support them, and His Majesty's White Fleet was deployed off New York to give aid and transit to Clinton's forces . . . and off the New England shores to guard against French troops being imported by adventurers such as the marquis de Lafayette.

Along the Delaware it was a time of quiet . . . almost a time of tranquility. And the seasonal winds that often swung about to blow strong and steady upstream, adding their force to the incoming tides, made it a good season in which to launch ships.

Despite business losses which seemed insurmountable and unexplainable reverses—ships and cargoes that sailed away and never returned—which had him to the point of distraction, Ian McCall had come across from Chesapeake at John Singleton Ramsey's grudging invitation, to witness the christening of the schooner *Faith II*.

Accompanied by his most trusted commercial factor and a

pair of clerks, McCall went first to Eagle's Head, where Ramsey waited. Colly met them at the great door, showed McCall and his associate into Ramsey's study, then led the clerks away to show them where they would sleep the night.

As the two men waited in the plush study, McCall paced the floor moodily, still thinking of the latest reports his factor had brought him. "Two more," he muttered. "Just disappeared somewhere. No word, no sign, no report even on their escort?"

"Nothing, sir." The man shrugged. "I am sorry."

"First *Pride of Falworth,* then the *Kerry,* and now three more — both *Christopher* and the *Lady Chance* . . . and even the brig, *Pliny!* Disappeared without a trace. I am being bankrupted, Evan. And we don't know what is happening!"

"No, sir," the man said quietly. "I have inquiries out in every quarter I can reach, sir . . . especially regarding the first one, of course, but for all. But there is nothing. Just . . . nothing."

He sounded so distraught that McCall turned to him. "Of course you do, Evan. I have no doubt you're doing your very best. My God, I realize it's your own brother you're searching for, as well. But . . . just nothing? No word at all?"

"Nothing, sir."

"Pirates," McCall muttered. "It must be pirates, but blast it all, what kind of pirate can operate without anybody knowing about him? I've never encountered the like."

"Nor have I, sir."

McCall paced a bit more, then shook his head. "Well, to the matter at hand. You have secured the . . . ah . . . special cargo we discussed?"

"Of course, sir. It is under guard on Chesapeake. Your own guards, as you instructed. Do you know what ship is to carry it, sir?"

"I know," McCall said. "Though I doubt you'll believe it when you see it, Evan. It's the schooner we came to see launched. The *Faith.*"

"Ramsey's daughter's own schooner? He'd chance that ship with such cargo?"

"So he says." McCall shrugged.

Evan tugged at his lip. "I'd have taken Squire Ramsey for a

more . . . ah . . . conservative gentleman than to risk such . . ."

"I expect he had little enough to do with the decision. You haven't met Constance Ramsey, have you, Evan?"

"I've not had the privilege."

"You probably shall, shortly. And I caution you, good Evan, should you ever find yourself in disagreement with that young lady, it's best to simply concede defeat and retreat as gracefully as circumstances allow. It's my studied opinion that there's only one man alive who's a match for Constance Ramsey."

"And who is that, then?"

McCall's brow lowered. "Patrick Dalton," he snapped. "Ramsey's damned Irishman."

A door had opened across the study, and a voice heavy with protest said, "How many times must I tell you, Ian? Dalton isn't *my* Irishman!"

McCall turned, still scowling. "If he isn't yours, John, then why didn't the scoundrel make off with one of your ships, instead of one of mine?"

"Oh," Evan muttered. *"That* Dalton."

"He *did* make off with one of mine," John Singleton Ramsey huffed, glaring at his friend and guest. "In case you have forgotten, it was him that wound up with the first *Faith* . . . through no doing of mine."

"As I recall," McCall gritted, "you had already lost *Faith* to that black-hearted devil's spawn Jonathan Hart, and it was *that* gentleman from whom Dalton took it."

"And you lost *Fury* to a bitch-whelped Spanish pirate, not to Dalton. He simply took it from *that* gentleman."

Behind Ramsey, a lovely young woman appeared at the door, and Evan straightened his shoulders admiringly.

"Don't you two *ever* get tired of this argument?" the girl snapped. "Mercy!" Then her frown became a dazzling soft smile, and she curtsied. "Good day to you, Squire McCall. So nice of you to come for *Faith's* christening."

"I wouldn't have missed it." McCall bowed. Then he turned. "Mistress Ramsey, I don't believe you have met my personal factor. Evan, may I present Constance Ramsey.

201

Constance, this is Evan Butler. He accompanied me from Fairleah because of press of business."

Evan bowed smartly. "Mistress Ramsey. A right honor."

Constance curtsied again. "Mister Butler." Then, "Please, gentlemen, do be comfortable. I've asked Colly to fetch tea."

"And grog?" Ramsey glanced around. "You did order a tot of grog, didn't you?"

"And grog." She nodded. "Though if either of the gentlemen would prefer brandy . . ."

"In my house we'll drink grog," Ramsey stated. He indicated chairs, and they sat, the three men in a semicircle facing the hearth, Constance demurely to one side. "Well, then, Ian," Ramsey opened. "I take it you have a cargo for me?"

"I do." McCall frowned. "Evan has secured it at my docks on Chesapeake . . ."

"The Wilderness Dock," Evan added. "Below Selden Road. It can be shipped aboard your vessel there, sir. Might I ask where it is bound?"

"For Savannah," Ramsey said after a pause. "You'll understand, I'm sure, that all of this requires the utmost secrecy."

"Certainly." Evan nodded.

"You may rely on Evan's discretion, John," McCall assured. "I trust him completely."

"Of course." Ramsey waved it off. "I simply —"

"You simply can't abide the idea of anyone realizing how active a patriot you are," McCall said. "You've postured as a damned — pardon, Constance — fence-straddler for so long that it galls you to have it known that you've taken sides. You're an American Patriot, John. Admit it."

"I'll admit no such thing!" Ramsey growled. "This is strictly business, and I am simply a businessman. I disdain politics."

"Of course you do," McCall drawled, winking. "A shipload of the best Austrian small arms for the colonials in Georgia certainly has nothing to do with politics . . . even if they *are* delivered on credit."

"Who said they are consigned on credit?" Ramsey demanded.

"Don't beat about the bush with me, old friend. I've done a bit of business with Andrews and his lot myself. On credit."

"Hmph!" Ramsey snorted.

The servants' door opened, and Colly entered, bearing a silver tray with a jug of rum, a pitcher of water and three pewter mugs. Behind him was a maid with a tea service. Constance took charge and busied herself serving the three men. As she poured tea for Evan she said, "I'm so glad you came, sir. I hope you can come to South Point tomorrow for the launching of *Faith.*"

"Faith the Second," her father corrected.

"Of course. Whatever. You will come, won't you, sir?"

"We shall both be there," McCall said. "I've already mentioned to—"

"I'm sorry," Evan said. "I must make my apologies, but I shall have to start for Chesapeake at first light. There are things I must attend to."

McCall turned sharply to stare at him. "Return? But I thought . . ."

"I'm sorry, sir. I've just this moment recalled some things that must be attended to, immediately. Somehow I had forgotten them. Forgive me."

McCall shrugged. "Very well, then. If you must, you must." As Constance chatted with Evan, McCall turned to Ramsey, speaking in a muted whisper. "An excellent employee," he said. "But he hasn't been quite himself of late. Not since his brother failed to return from a voyage to the Bahamas."

"His brother?"

"Aye. One of my best merchant captains. John Shelby Butler. Evan is his younger brother."

Dinner that evening was to have been a sumptuous affair, replete with roast partridge, greens from Ramsey's kitchen garden where the great man enjoyed experimenting with such notions as stepped irrigation, crop variety rotation and dustings of wheat flour to confuse the insects—all to the exasperation of his servants—and a cobbler made from fresh-gathered dewberries. Dinner was to have been all of that. It was, in fact, a disaster.

Midway through the roast partridge, Dora appeared at Constance Ramsey's side, bending to whisper in the young lady's ear. Constance listened for a moment, then scowled and

said, "Bedamme!" As the gentlemen looked up in astonish-
ment, she gathered her skirts about her, rose to her feet and
turned to Ramsey. "I'm sorry, Father, but you'll have to excuse
me. I must return to South Point immediately. Dora has my
coach waiting."

"Return? Now?"

"Now. My apologies, gentlemen."

"But what is it? Has something happened?"

"Has something . . . oh, no. Nothing much. It's just that
one of your yardmen got a hauling winch afoul of *Faith's* way-
blocks and decided to break it loose by main force. Now *Faith*
is atilt on half a running rail, and my men are standing off
your drydock crewmen at gunpoint to keep them from doing
any more blasted damage! Dearest father of mine, I've asked
you ever so nicely to keep your dolts away from my ship. Now
I must go and see if it is necessary for me to shoot the bleedin'
arses off a brace or two of them." Amidst stunned silence she
straightened her sleeves, brushed her auburn hair into her
bonnet and put on a pretty smile. "Gentlemen, do have a nice
evening."

She was gone then, Dora trailing after her, and the three
men looked at one another.

"You see now what I meant about her," McCall whispered
to Evan.

"Afoul of the way-blocks?" Ramsey muttered to himself.
"How on earth would anyone get a hauling winch afoul of
way-blocks, unless . . . unless he was using draft animals and
they strayed . . ."

"Remarkable," Evan breathed.

Colly had just served the cobbler when there was a caller at
the door. Colly disappeared into the front hall and returned a
moment later. "Gent'man to see Mist' Evan Butler," he announced. "Urgent, he say."

Butler frowned, surprised, then wiped his lips and stood.
"By your leave, gentlemen. I was not expecting anyone, but
whatever it is, it shouldn't take a moment."

He hurried out as Colly leaned over John Singleton Ramsey's shoulder to serve his cobbler. "Gent'man outside's got a
horse that's rid near to death," the servant whispered.

Ian McCall squinted at the lamp-lustered oak of the door that had closed behind his employee. "Must be important," he said. "I wonder if it's news of his brother . . . and of my ship." In silence the two businessmen tasted their cobbler, both of them noticing how abruptly the dining hall had become spacious.

Evan Butler was back within minutes, his expression oddly reserved, as though he were holding a fear hidden behind his hooded eyes. "Squire, I must apologize," he said, bowing slightly toward McCall. "Something unforseen has come up. I must return to Chesapeake immediately."

"Is it about your brother?"

"Ah, no, sir, though I wish it were. It's just a . . . ah, there's been a minor disturbance at the Wilderness Docks. It's something I must attend to, so that we may be sure that nothing goes amiss with your . . . ah . . . the special cargo consigned to Squire Ramsey's new schooner. Don't trouble yourself about it, sir. It really is only a minor thing."

"Then, you'll certainly miss the christening!" Ramsey put in, then reconsidered. "If there is a christening." He shook his head. "How could a hauling winch become afoul of wayblocks? I've never heard of such a thing."

Another odd thing occurred to him as Evan Butler put on his greatcoat, retrieved his tricorn hat and headed out to begin his trip overland to Chesapeake. Why would a man ride a horse almost to death, all the way from below Fairleah to Eagle's Head—from the Chesapeake to the Delaware—just to report a disturbance so minor that one man could attend to it? And why had Evan Butler seemed frightened?

Ramsey glanced at his remaining guest, wondering just how well McCall *did* know his trusted employee.

By evening sunlight filtering through the upright poles that were the wall of a sturdy cargo shed, Mister Hoop paced among bales and kegs, his face a study in huge worry. Since the packet *Cricket* had stood off the east bank of Chesapeake to disgorge its passengers into the towed launch with its towed dinghy, since they had bid their benefactors goodbye—or, in two cases, *adieu* — and pointed the launch's bow toward Squire Ian McCall's lower docks, much had happened, but nothing that made sense.

The packet's passengers were six — three ex-British tars and a pair of Frenchmen picked up at sea, and a young ex-British officer named Farrington who, the others gathered, had been in command of a civilian trading convoy but had lost his command to pirates.

He was on his way to report to his employer, Squire McCall. Having nothing better to do, the others — Misters Hoop, Singleterry and Cobley and the two Frenchmen — tagged along behind him.

With the launch and the dinghy secured at a rough pier, they went ashore. The Wilderness Docks were at the rear of a small, dredged harbor, a busy and businesslike place recently reopened after removal of activities from the Delaware. Dairy roads and barns, sheds and low warehouses clustered above empty docks now. The only sailing ship in sight was a corvette at anchor just off the upper quay. Its escutcheons proclaimed it the *Resolute*.

"All this is Squire McCall's," Lewis Farrington told the others. "His main operations are up the bay at Fairleah, but a lot of cargo is assembled down here at the wilderness docks."

"Some bein' done now." Hoop pointed. In the distance, men worked at a group of barns or sheds, preparing stacks of tarp-covered goods for skidding down to the docks to be shipped aboard a vessel, though there were no ships there.

Farrington led the way up the slope toward the buildings, and was confronted by armed men patrolling the area. "Lewis Farrington," he told them. "I've come to report to Squire McCall."

A beady-eyed man with a full beard pushed through the guards. "Squire ain't here," he said. "What is it you want to report?"

"It's for McCall's ears," Farrington said. "Or for his personal factor. Where is he?"

"Not here either," the man said. "So you can just tell me about it. I'm Budge. Mister Evan left me in charge here."

"I'll wait for the Squire," Farrington decided.

"Suit yourself." Budge frowned. "But stay away from the sheds." He glanced at the others behind Farrington, his eyes lingering on the giant form of Mister Hoop. "Who be these? Yours?"

"Not mine." Farrington shrugged. "We found them at sea. They're off a ship that was taken by pirates, then reclaimed as salvage."

Budge's eyes narrowed. "Reclaimed, ye say." He looked at the others, one by one. "An' what ship might that be, now, mates?"

Hoop decided he didn't like the man, but he held his temper. *"Pride of Falworth,"* he rumbled. "That's her name, if it's any of your business, *mate."*

For an instant, Budge looked as though he had been swatted across the face. *"Pride of . . .?"*

"Falworth."

What happened then was abrupt and startling. Budge made a signal with his hand, and suddenly the newcomers were surrounded by levelled muskets.

"Take them to the stowage barn," Budge growled. "All of 'em. Lock them in and guard 'em. Somebody bring me a horse. Evan needs to know of this."

Now they were locked in the barn, all six of them, trying to make sense of it all.

It was Farrington who expressed a course of action. "If we could get out of here," he suggested, "I'd go and find Squire McCall. He can sort out whatever misunderstanding there is here."

"Do you know where to find him, then?" Hoop stopped his pacing and turned.

"No, I don't. Not that it matters. We're barred in here until somebody decides to —"

"Oh, that's nothin'." Hoop shrugged it off. "But if you don't know where he is . . ."

"I really don't."

Hoop ran big fingers through his untidy hair. "It's a notion, though," he said. "We don't know where that squire is, but I know where there's another squire. Squire Ramsey. Cap'n Dalton thinks fair of him, so maybe he'd help us."

"But we're locked in!"

Hoop shrugged. "Misters Singleterry and Cobley, do you have a calculation on the guards out there?"

"Aye," Singleterry said. "There's two of them, one on each side of that barred double door."

"Do they have muskets?"

"Aye, they both do."

"Good. We might want some muskets with us, for we've a night's hard travel ahead."

"Where we goin', then?" Cobley blinked.

"I just told you. Across to the Delaware to see Squire Ramsey. Stand clear now." As the others scurried aside, Hoop looked around at the stacks and provisions in the stowage barn. In one corner an anvil stood, stud-mounted on the sawn top of an oak log two feet across and four tall. "This should do nicely," he said, inspecting it.

"You intend to do a bit of smithin', Mister Hoop?" Singleterry drawled.

"Thinkin' of a ram," Hoop said, squatting beside the anvil and butt.

"That?" Cobley frowned. "Lord's mercy, man, that thing must weigh three-four hundred pounds."

"Likely," Hoop agreed. Sucking in a great breath, the big man wrapped his arms around the log and stood, balancing on spread legs as he shifted it, holding it horizontally under one arm, bracing with the other. Veins stood out on his bull neck. He steadied the massive thing, anvil to the fore, then turned, sighted on the crack where the two doors met, and charged.

Hoop and his ram hit the door dead center, and beyond it a drawbar shrilled and cracked. The twin doors flew open, smashing back against the outer wall on each side of the portal. Hoop set down his ram and stepped through, catching the echoing doors as they rebounded. Sodden thuds sounded beyond them, where battered men fell to the ground, unconscious.

"My Lord in Heaven!" Lewis Farrington breathed.

"Bring along the muskets," Hoop said. "Lively now, lads. We've some ground to cover."

"C'est magnifique!" a wide-eyed Frenchman chirped as they all followed Hoop out of the barn and toward the nearby forest, making northeastward.

Twenty-two

Askew on her way-blocks, her nimble stern standing dry above the dredged cut on the Delaware's right bank, *Faith II* stood aslant in the midday sun, her tall masts casting shadows below, where nearly a hundred men labored to right her for launching.

Virtually every man in South Point was involved in the enterprise. Most of them were in the employ of John Singleton Ramsey and had found their services abruptly requisitioned by the great man's daughter. Others working shoulder to shoulder among them were innocents who had happened to be in or about South Point's three inns and five taverns when a squad of Colonial sailors led by the Virginian, Michael Romart, made a sweep of the village for "volunteers." They worked now with a will, intensely aware of the armed sailors standing watch at the schooner's rails overhead.

At first they had tried to careen the vessel to port, to lift its hull away from the damaged slideway under its starboard timbers so that the slideway could be repaired. But the schooner had only settled more securely into its gap, and the plans were revised.

Great hawsers now led from the tops of both mainmast and foremast, firmly cleated there, out to a row of buried "dead man" stanchions fifty yards away, and with the schooner held in check against further shifting, work was progressing on the lowering of the portside way so that it would match the fallen one at starboard. Meanwhile, beneath the jutting stern, almost at the heel of the great rudder, men with teams of mules were dredging a deep trench for the hull to settle into when it was released.

Beyond the works there were spectators — there had been spectators since the initial crash when the dry-docked new ship had lurched off its starboard way — and among them were grizzled veterans of the yards who, in many years at South Point, had seen almost everything. These scratched their heads now and stared in awe at the work in progress. They had seen nothing quite like this before.

Yet the man in charge, a ship's carpenter named Joseph Tower, went stolidly about his business with the assurance of a man who knew exactly what he was doing. "It will work," he assured Constance Ramsey as she prowled the yards, fretting. "It may be a unique launching, but launch her we will."

"In a ditch?" the girl asked, frowning. "Wouldn't it be as easy just to set winches and drag her to the water's edge?"

"We'd likely mar the coppering if we did that." He shrugged. "Then she'd have to be careened for repairs. Seems to me it bodes bad luck to have to repair a vessel from its own christening."

"There is that," she admitted. "But Mister Tower, how did you decide on such a . . . well, unusual procedure as this?"

"Oh, that was nothing. I just asked myself, 'What might Captain Dalton do in such a situation?' And the answer came to me, just like that."

"On deck!"

They looked upward, squinting against the sun. High aloft, clinging to the slant of *Faith's* foremast fighting top, Phillip Ives cupped his hands and repeated the call, "On deck!"

On the schooner's foredeck, Michael Romart responded, "Aye, Mister Ives?"

"People coming, Mister Romart. Crossing the cartage road. One of them seems to be Mister Hoop."

"It can't be Mister Hoop," Romart said. He turned, shaded his eyes and peered westward. "Mister Hoop is with Captain Dalton and *Fury.*" Then he grunted and his eyes widened. "By all that's proper, I believe that *is* Mister Hoop! On de — I mean, on the ground!" He looked down, waved at Constance and Tower and pointed. "There's Mister Hoop yonder, com-

211

ing this way with some other men! What do you suppose he's doing here?"

"Mister Hoop?" Constance looked around.

"One of Dalton's Britishers, miss," Tower said. "You might recall him from when we all had supper that time, over on Chesapeake. When we had th' orchestra. Hoop was the big one. Twice the size of any other man I ever saw."

"The man with the flat nose," she recalled.

"That's the one. I've always wondered who managed that."

The party coming down from the road was in sight for them now, Mister Hoop hulking huge, followed by five other men. Beyond them, up on the road, Squire Ramsey's carriage had just come into sight, heading an entourage coming down from Eagle's Head.

When the walkers approached, Michael Romart called from the rail, "Ahoy, Mister Hoop! Is that you?"

"As ever was," the bull voice bellowed back. "Who's that, then? Mister Romart?"

"Aye! Where did you come from, Mister Hoop? Has *Fury* landed?"

"I don't know! We haven't seen *Fury* since just after the storm!"

"What storm?"

"That weird one, off—oh, you weren't there, were you. Anyway, we got set off in the bark's dinghy and—!"

"What bark?"

"One we found. But Mister Duncan had to run from pirates, so when we got on their launch and the frogs opened fire, we . . . !" They pushed through a scattering of spectators, and Hoop spotted Constance. In sudden confusion he stopped in his tracks, oblivious to those who bumped into him from behind. "Miss Ramsey? Ah . . . Miss Constance, is that you?"

"How do you do, Mister Hoop." Constance curtsied.

"Where is Patrick?"

"Who, miss?" Hoop shouted, then realized that he was still bellowing. His face went scarlet, and he lowered his voice. "Who, miss?"

"Patrick. Captain Dalton. Weren't you with him?"

"No, miss. Not just lately. Commander Duncan took us as prize crew on *Pride.* An' now we don't rightly know where anybody is because we got lost." He glanced at the carpenter. "How do, Mister Tower."

"Mister Hoop. Who are these with you?"

"These? Oh." He pointed. "That's Mister Singleterry there, and that's Mister Cobley. They're first-rates. An' those two yonder, grinnin' at the lady, they're frogs, the both of 'em."

Realizing that introductions were being made, the Frenchmen executed elegant bows toward Constance. *"Bon soir, mademoiselle,"* Francois said.

"Mon dieux," Rene muttered. *"C'est magnifique, la jeune fille."*

Hoop rounded on him with a roar. "You mind your mouth! There's a lady present!"

"It's quite all right, Mister Hoop," Constance said. Then she curtsied again. *"Bon soir, m'sieurs. Comment allez-vous?"*

Francois beamed. *"Ah! Tres bien, merci, mademoiselle. Enchante. Je m'appell Francois LeBlanc. Presente mon ami, Rene Escobier, vient de Marseilles."*

"Enchante," she said. "Mister Hoop, I don't recall Patrick having any French people in his crew. Where did these gentlemen come from?"

"France, I expect, miss," Hoop managed, confused by the sudden torrent of foreign language. "But where I got them was out of the chain locker of the bark. They was drunk as lords, they was."

Above them, Michael Romart repeated his earlier question, "What bark, Mister Hoop?"

"Pride of Falworth's its name. We found it an'—"

"Pride of Falworth?" Constance cut in. "But I think that was the name of Ian McCall's ship that . . ." She looked around, suddenly aware of the sixth newcomer, a tall, ruddy young man with deep blue eyes. "Oh, I'm sorry. You, sir? I didn't get your name. I'm Constance Ramsey"

He bowed slightly, smiling. "Lewis Farrington, miss. At your service."

"He ain't exactly with us," Hoop explained. "It was just that, well, we went with him to see Squire McCall; then when they locked us in the barn, he come with us to find Squire Ramsey."

"Locked you in the barn?" Tower frowned. "Why?"

"We don't any of us exactly know. That's why we come to find Squire . . ." he broke off, just noticing the odd angle of the schooner looming over them. "Do you realize this ship is tilted? What be ye doing with it?"

"We're trying to launch it. I don't understand . . ."

"I can see that. Generally, ships are launched straight up."

"Upright," Singleterry corrected. "Not straight up."

"Haven't we met before?" Constance asked Farrington. "You look familiar to me."

"And you to me, miss. And this odd schooner even more so. When I commanded His Majesty's sloop *Wolf,* there was a schooner with fighting tops . . ."

"Ah! Was that you who ran aground there in that bay?"

"And you were aboard the schooner! Yes, I saw you there, later, firing a cannon. Quite remarkable."

"It was an ordinary enough cannon," she said.

"What about the bark?" Michael Romart stormed above them. "And where the blazes is Patrick Dalton? And Charley Duncan?"

"M' sieur le commandante Duncan," Rene brightened. *"C'est bon!"*

Hoop's face registered immense confusion. "Miss, can you tell what these two is chatterin' about? None of us has been able to make head nor tail of it."

"I believe we must all compare notes," Constance decided. "Mister Romart, send down a scaffold, please. We can talk better aboard." She turned and waved at the men stepping down from the carriage which had just arrived. "Father! Bring Ian with you and come aboard *Faith!* We have mysteries to unravel."

Farrington turned and spotted Ian McCall. He raised his hand and called, "Ah, there you are, Squire! I tried to report to you at the Wilderness Dock but . . ."

McCall's eyes widened. "Farrington? What are you doing here? Why aren't you on . . . ?"

"We can talk aboard," Constance said. "Come along, everyone." To the Frenchmen she said, *"Par ici, s'il vous plaît."*

"C'est un plaisir, mademoiselle." Rene grinned.

"Mercy," Tower muttered, shaking his head in confusion.

"*De rien, m'sieur,*" Francois assured him.

It was a somber and uncomfortable conference that was held that day on the bright-planked afterdeck of *Faith II.* Some of the discomfort came from the acute cant of the schooner's deck. Chairs, benches and stools were hoisted aboard for the visitors, but the furniture tended to slide to starboard at every opportunity, and the discussion kept winding up athwart the after rail or in the racks. Mostly, though, it was the story that began to piece itself together as Constance questioned the Frenchmen, and Hoop and his mates added their information to the weave.

Ian McCall sat stunned, shaking his head in disbelief as the betrayal aboard *Pride of Falworth* unfolded.

"I can't believe it," he muttered, again and again. "I simply cannot. Not of John Shelby Butler."

"There is a lesson in this," Ramsey noted. "Revolution or not, this piracy situation has gotten completely out of hand. We fight the British and the British fight us, and the field is so open to freebootery that even the most trusted of men can be seduced. I believe it is time to press our case with the Continental Congress, Ian. We need a coastal patrol, whether or not there is a war."

"The Continental Congress turns a deaf ear to such pleas." McCall frowned. "They see coastal patrol as a provincial matter, to be dealt with by the individual colonies."

"Then, let's call on Governor Henry, by God!"

Through it, Lewis Farrington sat pale and silent. He had reported, briefly, on the loss of his brig and his charges, then sat in dismal resignation, wondering what would come next.

Now, though, Constance was talking to the Frenchmen again, and suddenly Farrington's head came up. "*Valkyrie?* Did they say the name *Valkyrie?*"

"That was the name of the pirate ship that was lured and taken," she said.

"The same ship!" Color flushed his cheeks and his eyes went steely. "It was *Valkyrie* that sank me, and took my escort. Squire, I swear that devil knew exactly where I would be and

215

when. Do I understand now that it was one of your own captains who did that?"

"So it would seem," McCall rasped. "It seems I've had a very conspiracy amidst my most trusted people. I think there can be little doubt that Butler did know precisely where and when to find you."

Ramsey turned to him. "His brother?"

"Evan." McCall nodded, looking bleak and gray. "My own true Evan."

There were sudden crashing sounds, and *Faith* lurched violently, then resumed her sedate slant. In the fore, a voice shouted, "Let's be a bit easier with those hawsers, you men! There's gentlefolk aboard, here!"

John Singleton Ramsey picked his dignity up off the deck and retrieved his chair. "I don't suppose we could hold off on the construction long enough to lay our plans?" he suggested. But the only answer he received was the ring of hammers and the creak of winches as those around *Faith* resumed their activities with renewed enthusiasm.

As the meeting came to order again, the Frenchmen were a few steps aside, chattering and gesturing. Constance listened for a moment, then said something in French.

"What are they arguing about?" McCall wanted to know.

"Something about a treasure," she said. "They are trying to decide whether to tell us about it."

"Treasure?" Ramsey's brows went up. "By all means, tell them to tell us about it."

She spoke with them for a moment, then said, "They are worried. It seems Mister Duncan signed them aboard as crew when they were found, and read them their articles, but they don't know what restrictions those include, because they were in English."

"Confound it!" McCall stamped a buckle-shoed foot. *"Pride of Falworth* is my ship and I'll say what articles—"

"Not if Patrick has claimed it as salvage," she pointed out. "In that case, I imagine it's his ship."

"Not bloody likely! That confounded Irishman has already done me out of one ship, and he'll not do it again. Tell them they answer to me!"

Constance's chin went up in determination. "If Patrick claimed a ship you had already lost, Squire McCall, then he has 'done you out' of nothing."

"Don't look at me, Ian." Ramsey shrugged. "I can't argue that."

Again *Faith* lurched and thrummed, and they clung to stays to keep their balance. In the distance Mister Tower's voice called, "That's getting it, mates. Now let's pull back those dredges and . . ."

"Hell's humping haggards," McCall swore. Then, "Pardon, Miss Constance."

Francois was beside Constance, trying to get her attention. *"M'selle . . . l'argent?"*

"What about it?" she snapped, then said, "Oh, I believe they have decided to tell us about the treasure. *N'est-ce pas. m'sieur?"*

"Oui. L'argent." He nodded vigorously, took a breath, and said, *"Quand ils monterent abord du bateau, deux d'entre eux trouverent de l'argent. Certaines pieces etaient en or. Ils le ranamerent dans dis petite sacs —"*

"What the blazes is he saying?" McCall glared.

"Hush!" Constance raised a small, imperious hand. *"Oui,* Francois?"

"Les sacs," he continued. *"Petites sacs. Encachette du Capitaine."*

"The captain? Captain Butler?"

"Oui. Bood'lair."

"Boodelair!" Hoop said. "That's the Frenchy pirate they was goin' on about when we found 'em."

Constance ignored him. *"Por qua encachette de* Butler?" she asked.

"Ils voualient le garder pour euxmemes." Francois shrugged.

She waved him to a stop and turned to the squires. "He says that when they went aboard the other ship, they —"

"Other ship? The *Valkyrie?"* McCall prodded.

"Q'uell bateau. Francois? Valkyrie?"

"Oui. Valkyrie."

"Yes. When they went aboard, some of them found money. A lot of money and other things, including gold. They brought it back . . . back to *Pride of Falworth,* apparently, in

217

little sacks, so that the captain wouldn't see it. They hid it."

"From their captain?" McCall sounded outraged.

"Easy, Ian," Ramsey said. "It's pirates we're talking about here."

"Oh. Right. Go on, Constance. What about the treasure?"

"If you'll let me, I'll find out. Francois?"

"Oui, m'selle. Ji les ai vous avec l'argent avant quils le cachent, mais j'ni sais pas du ils l'ont mis. Mais abord du l'Pri'e o' Falwort'." He turned to Rene. *"N'est-ce pas,* Rene?"

"Oui."

"He saw them . . . the other men . . . with the treasure before they hid it, but they don't know where they put it."

"What about the men who hid it?"

Constance translated the question. Francois sighed. *"Ils sont morts maintenant. Ils faisarent partie de ceux qui le capitaine avait mis a'mort."*

"They are dead," she translated. "They were among those the captain had put to death."

"Incredible," Ramsey muttered.

"Oui," Rene agreed. *"C'est incredable."*

"I don't wonder these two was hidin' in th' chain locker," Mister Hoop allowed. "Bloody business, that."

"Shocking." McCall shook his head. "John, there's no question about it. That villain must be run down and punished. And others like him, as well. I am ready to petition Patrick Henry for a coast patrol and hang the cost."

Faith shuddered, then shuddered again, and a clamor of voices erupted below, on the surrounding ground. Rising above them was Joseph Tower's strident shout, "She's righting herself! You there! Cut away those hobbles!"

The schooner seemed to convulse itself, its deck wobbling as ominous rumblings erupted below. Then, suddenly, its slated masts rose tall overhead, and the entire ship seemed to fall, as though into a hole. The crash was horrendous, and muddy water shot upward in great sheets along both rails. On deck, people rolled and flipped in all directions. In the pitching foretop, Phillip Ives clung to shrouds, swinging like a monkey in a tree.

Constance rolled over, untangling herself from a pair of

Frenchmen. Even sprawled on the deck, she noticed, they seemed determined to give her far more of a hand — or of their hands — than she required. She got to her feet and planted her little fists on her hips. "Mister Romart! What was that?"

In the fore, Michael Romart was unwrapping himself from the stem rail. He peered over, then turned. "Looks to me like *Faith* has just launched herself, miss. We're afloat . . . and so is most of the yard crew."

Lewis Farrington had gotten his feet under him. Now he ran from rail to rail, looking over, then shouted, "Hands aloft! Make sail! Make sail! Forecourse, jib and jigger! Let's get this vessel out of this ditch before we ground ourselves!"

An instant's surprised silence answered him, then a chorus of "Aye, sir!" and the crew aboard swarmed into action. Farrington planted himself at the tiller and shouted, "Two men aft to raise the gaff! Lively now! You . . . whoever you are, loose those sheets and trim to the wind. Ready? Haul away! Ah, that's it. She's coming free. Hands aloft, trim until we're clear of the bank, then let them luff. I'll bring her around on her spanker."

"Aye, sir."

Amidships someone asked, "Who the blazes is that givin' the orders?"

"I don't know," someone else said, "but he's doin' it right, so don't argue."

Constance gazed at Farrington with calculating eyes. She *did* still require a captain for *Faith* if she was going to use the schooner as she planned.

Jaunty as ever a proud topsail schooner could be, *Faith II* eased out of her ditch and into the swelling lap of the Delaware. With Lewis Farrington at her tiller, she slid about in a graceful arc, dropped sail and nudged gently against the pier.

"She's a sweet lady," Farrington said, his eyes alight with the love of a seaman for a fine ship. "I'd warrant she has fine legs, and I can see she has teeth."

For an instant, Constance Ramsey felt disoriented. The young man was certainly not Patrick Dalton, but just in that moment he had sounded like him.

Twenty-three

The White Fleet's blockade of the central shores was stretched thin now as more and more of the Admiralty's hardware cruised northward to support General Clinton's sortie against the winter-hardened forces of General Washington. Thus, though the blockade continued, those ships that might have sighted the battered bark nearing Colonial waters were small cruisers widely spread, and none inclined to test the temper of the fierce-looking little snow that rode herd upon it. By its maneuvers and its general aspect, the snow conveyed clearly that it would like nothing so much as a reason to blow somebody out of the water.

Therefore the cruise from asea to sight of land was uneventful for *Fury* and *Pride*. When their tops raised the light at Cape Henry, they adjusted course and steered for Chesapeake, *Fury* in the lead.

The bark still limped from its wounds, and Charley Duncan held a sedate seven knots on a quartering southerly wind while the agile snow seemed to surge and fret at its bonds at such a pace; but Patrick Dalton was content. The luck of the Irish had shone upon him once more. He had now what he had lacked before—a fully crewed ship, the wherewithal to dictate his own destinies for a time, and tasks to complete. The refugees from the islands could be put ashore at Ian McCall's wilderness yards, and would be safe enough from there. The bark in his custody was a questionable salvage claim at best, but it would serve as a trading point with McCall. And there was the treasure, now safe aboard *Fury*.

Every man involved in the adventure would receive a share, of course. He wondered whether any of them realized that they stood to be wealthy men very soon. But even after the sharing, there would be a staggering fortune left over. And Dalton had some ideas about that.

"It would be folly for me to ever return to England," he had told Billy Caster. "There are no charges against me now; but there is nothing there for me, and I have come to terms with that knowledge. So, I will stake my destiny in this land. It has much to offer, it seems to me."

Including Constance Ramsey, the clerk thought. But what he said was, "There is still a war, sir."

"Aye, there is a war." Dalton's moody eyes roved the morning sea and the approaching land. "And that's a problem."

Billy said nothing. He knew exactly what his captain's quandary was. Despite having resigned with honor from His Majesty's service, Dalton still felt an allegiance—or at least a respect—for the Union Jack and the nation it represented.

Not once in all the time since his escape from false charges at Long Island had Patrick Dalton dishonored that respect. Oh, they had fought against vessels that flew the Empire's colors. When they had to. But never once had a ship under Dalton's command, whether the captured schooner *Faith*, the poor, slogging ketch *Mystery* or the little warship that now was his by right of recovery, the *Fury*, ever initiated such an encounter. And not once had he ever fired the first shot.

"There's honest work for a fighting ship," Dalton said finally. "There's work that has nothing to do with politics or war."

If he had a plan in mind, Billy had not yet heard it. But the boy had come to know that when Patrick Dalton mapped a course, however devious it might seem, there would be a proper destination at the end of it.

Past Cape Henry they sighted only one vessel—an armed corvette coming downbay toward them. The ship had sails laid on and was tacking for best advantage of the wind, but still was moving slowly, fighting the spring tides. As they closed to scanning range, Dalton glassed it. It was a ship he had seen before. Taken as a prize by a Royal Navy frigate two or three years ago, it had stood for a time at anchor in New York Harbor, waiting to go on the auction block.

He read the escutcheons at a half mile. The corvette *Resolute*. The same vessel. He recalled seeing it again, since, either on the Delaware or off one of the Chesapeake ports. Probably some Colonial merchant had bought it for escort service. Well-armed on its single deck, the corvette could be formidable in an encounter, though the axe-blade shape of its hull would allow barely room for stores and none for cargo.

"Show him our colors," Dalton said.

"The East India flag, sir?"

"No. Our true colors. We're past the cordons. We have as much right as any to be in these waters."

It took a few minutes for Billy Caster and Purdy Fisk to find and bring up the tattered flag. It was a long time since *Fury* had worn the blue and white of what some called the "freeman's flag," the pennant of the private armed vessel on private business, aloof from any conflicts around it.

By the time *Fury*'s colors were aloft, Charley Duncan had already run up colors on *Pride*'s lanyard—the prize flag of a claimed vessel under armed escort.

They had introduced themselves. Now they waited for the corvette to respond to the civility. But no colors showed on the stranger.

Ill-mannered, then? Or hostile? Dalton's eyes went dark. "Stand to guns afore and aport," he said.

"Aye, sir." The snow's deck came alive as men scurried to battle stations.

"If he doesn't respond to colors, we'll try a salute presently," Dalton said. "Steady on, Mister Locke."

"Aye, sir."

The corvette came on, still showing no colors, then broke off just beyond gun range. Hauling about its yards, the stranger hesitated, angled to the left and took a new wind, skimming ahead on a starboard reach to cross the incoming ships' path and make for the east shore. Within minutes it was again a half mile away and gaining distance. At a mile or more—almost within the shallows of Cape Charles – it corrected again. Beating southward now, it headed for the open sea.

"Standoffish sort of person, that," Billy Caster suggested. "He didn't care to show us any colors at all."

Dalton gazed astern at the fleeing corvette. "Odd," he muttered. Then he shrugged and faced forward. "Bring us a point to starboard, please, Mister Locke. If the fairway is clear at Squire McCall's harbor, we'll have Mister Duncan anchor there and see about debarking his passengers."

Fury answered her rudder with an easy grace, coming a point to the right. A few cable lengths back, *Pride of Falworth* adjusted to follow. Dalton looked back once more, past the bark with its crowded decks – at this distance he could even see a few of the ubiquitous chickens that seemed to roam everywhere – and frowned as his eyes caught the distant sail that was the corvette. The slender vessel now was making for the point of Cape Henry, beating its course with a press of sail aloft. Someone there was in a great hurry, to push the vessel so. No one was pursuing it, no one threatening it, yet the corvette called *Resolute* had bent on enough canvas to swamp her should she catch fair gusts past the point.

"On deck!"

Dalton peered upward. "Aye, Mister Livingston?"

"Smoke ashore, sir! Dead ahead!"

With his glass, Dalton found it. Tendrils of smoke drifting above the treetops beyond the screened mouth of an inlet. He turned, glanced at the chart that Billy Caster had unfolded, and frowned. The inlet was Ian McCall's lower yards, what the trader called his Wilderness Dock.

"Buntings, please, Mister Leaf. To *Pride*. Say to stand off and wait. We shall have a closer look."

"Aye, sir."

"Give us topsails and gallants, Mister Ball. Trim to course. Mister Locke, bring us off that inlet yonder and stand by to come about smartly."

"Aye, sir."

"Man guns afore and both bows. Mister Fisk, take a squad into the tops with rifles, please."

223

At the bell, *Fury* stood off the inlet, and Dalton glassed the clearings beyond. The smoke arose from what might once have been a barn or shed, but was now just a shattered hulk of a structure, still burning.

"Powder magazine?" Billy Caster supposed.

"Or stores." Dalton nodded. There were men in the compound, some of them waving at sight of the snow. The only vessels in sight were a launch and a dinghy, lying at the stub dock. He raised his eyes. "Tops?"

"Something exploded yonder, sir. I see men, but they mostly aren't armed. Some of them are waving at us. And I see a few on the ground, sir. Dead or injured."

Dalton put away his glass. "Take us in, please, Mister Locke. We'll see what has happened there."

As *Fury* came to a standstill in the little bay, her guns covering the whole area, men put out from shore in the launch and came alongside. Dalton recognized several of them — workers employed by Ian McCall.

The story they had to tell was simple. Squire McCall was away, but his personal factor, Evan Butler, had come galloping into the yards on a spent horse, ordered everyone off work, and — backed by the compound's guards and foragers — begun looting the stores. Some of the yard crews had objected, and several had been shot before they organized themselves and found muskets with which to fight back.

Faced with opposition, the Butler band had blown the powder magazine for diversion, then boarded the corvette *Resolute* and made their escape.

Which explained the odd actions of the corvette that had passed *Fury* in the outer channels.

With *Fury* riding at anchor, her guns at the ready, Dalton signalled Charley Duncan to bring *Pride of Falworth* in. The mystery of the Wilderness Docks would wait. First, there were things to do.

As the hours passed into evening, *Pride of Falworth* disgorged passengers, livestock and gear, oddments of cargo and stores, until the yards above Wilderness Docks had the look of a bustling town. The four-master was no proper fighter; but her decks and holds were capacious, and when they were empty, Ian McCall's clearing was full. People were everywhere, it seemed — penning cattle, chasing down errant sheep, devising shelters, building cookfires, chattering, exploring and, in the case of Aaron Fairfield, Esq., complaining bitterly.

"This is no destination!" the good man shouted at Charley Duncan for the seventh or eighth time. "This is a wilderness! If we had to come to the Virginias, you might at least put us off at Baltimore or Williamsburg, or Philadelphia . . ."

Duncan had developed the knack of simply not hearing Fairfield's voice, consigning its mouthings to the category of meaningless sound much as the keening of wind in shrouds or the lowing of cattle on the foredeck. He saw no reason to change this happy decision now that he was rid of the man and his motley followers. Brushing past the man, Duncan gave his arm to Priscilla Cabot to walk the lady down the gangway to the dock.

"You'll be in good hands here, mistress," he assured her. "All of this belongs to Squire McCall, and as Captain Dalton says, the squire is a fair man. You'll not have to worry about that island governor following you here . . . or any other for that matter."

"I'm sure of it, Commander." She smiled up at him. "You've really been most kind through all of this. I can't understand why Mister Fairfield considers you uncivil."

"Why he what?"

"Oh, it's just something he says. I'd pay it no mind if I were you. For myself, I find you quite civil." She reached into the bag she was carrying, brought out a length of stiff rope and showed it to him. "And instructive, as well. Ah, if you'd care to join us, I expect I can find something to cook this evening."

"I should like that, mistress, I . . ."

A man hurried past them, carrying an armload of folded canvas, and Duncan stared after him, then looked beyond, where the clearing rose away from the docks. There seemed to be tents springing up everywhere. Tents, hammocks, trestle tables, livestock pens. . . .

"I . . . ," Duncan started to continue, then frowned. "Excuse me, mistress." He turned and headed back up the gangway.

Keith Darling was coming down, carrying a large trunk on his shoulder. As Duncan approached, the big landsman said, "I think that's all of us, Commander. If you'll find Mister McPherson, he can settle accounts with—"

"That's between him and Captain Dalton." Duncan brushed past him, cleared *Pride*'s rail and headed for the hold coamings. "Mister Quarterstone, bring a lantern! We're going below."

Three of them descended into the holds—Quarterstone with a lantern, Charley Duncan and little Henry Cabot, trailing after Duncan as though he were his shadow. By the lantern's light, Duncan stared around in amazement. The entire enclosure forward of the aft capstan had been gutted—planking pulled up for the building of pens and trestles, every scrap of loose cable, every keg and barrel, everything that wasn't nailed down and much that should have been, had been pressed into service by the busy refugees. And what they had used—as though theirs by right of service—had gone ashore with them. In the bowels of *Pride of Falworth* there was nothing except a cat stalking a pair of stray chickens.

"May God have mercy," Quarterstone muttered.

"Sweet Jesus." Duncan shook his head.

"Watch where you step," Henry Cabot warned. "Most of the floors and walls got used for pens."

"Deck and bulkhead," Duncan breathed.

"What?"

"It's deck and bulkhead. Ships don't have floors and—what are you doing down here?"

"Nothing," the boy assured him.

Quarterstone handed the lantern over, moved away, then returned. "They emptied the sail locker," he said. "And cleaned out the larder and stores."

"Worse than bore-worms," Duncan muttered, shaking his head in disbelief.

Distantly, from *Pride*'s tops, came the call, "On deck!" Finian Nelson's response followed, then a pause, and Nelson appeared at the hatch. "Mister Duncan, you'd best come on deck. The snow has signalled that there's sail off the quay."

Still stunned by the stripping of the bark's interior, Duncan hurried to the main deck, strode astern and peered toward the open bay beyond the inlet, where *Fury* stood at guard. A ship was just coming into sight beyond. Past the forest screen a jaunty jib slid into view, batwing sails billowing above a sleek bowsprit . . . then a graceful bow, a jutted foremast with spencer sail on its gaff and topsail above, partly obscuring a sturdy fighting top.

Charley Duncan's mouth hung open, and he stared, a man seeing a ghost. Two years ago — more than two years — he had seen the shattered carcass of a lovely schooner hauled to final rest on the banks of the Delaware. A proud, fighting schooner that had done heads-on combat with a frigate, then had limped home to die.

He had sailed on that schooner. He had seen its destruction. Yet now, just standing in the mouth of the inlet, was — so far as he could tell — that same schooner, as fresh and bright as new.

"It's *Faith*," he said, to no one but himself. "Sweet Mary, holy mother, that's *Faith*."

As empty as Ian McCall's "Wilderness Docks" had been just a day before, now they were as full. The compounds and clearings were full of people, and the inlet was full of ships.

The big four-master, tied off, dwarfed the stub dock while the snow and the schooner stood at anchor in the moonlight beyond, and although the hour was late, fires still burned brightly here and there, lamplight was everywhere and boats of all descriptions plied back and forth. There was so much to report, so much to sort out, so many questions to be answered, so many decisions to be talked through, that it would be morning or beyond before most of them took time to rest.

The story of the brothers Butler had been related, Dalton

227

and Duncan adding their accounts of their encounter with *Valkyrie* at sea, and of the escape of Evan Butler and his men aboard the corvette *Resolute*.

The finding of *Pride of Falworth* adrift in the Indies Lanes had been hashed and rehashed, though each time the mention of treasure came up, Dalton and Duncan either changed the subject or went silent. Ian McCall was almost beside himself, about almost everything, until John Singleton Ramsey breached a keg of rum and began the quelling of his friend with repeated tots of grog.

Mister Hoop had become caught up in the general reunion of ex-British fugitives who had arrived aboard *Fury* and ex-Colonial fugitives who were part of the crew of *Faith,* and had wound up being carried to a hammock by two Frenchmen and six Americans as a result of too much rum.

Charley Duncan and Michael Romart had exchanged grins, back-slaps and mutual insults, and Patrick Dalton and Lewis Farrington had exchanged remembrances of a time that now seemed long ago when their two vessels had stood each other off in a foggy little bay on upper Long Island. Another thing the two young captains exchanged was veiled, cautious glances each time one or the other set eyes on Constance Ramsey — which was at every opportunity.

By the time the encampment had quieted itself some-what — well past midnight — the courteous demeanor that had been between the two of them had become something else. Something that bordered upon hostility.

And it came to a head when — a dozen of them sitting around a blazing fire in the wilderness — Constance Ramsey mentioned her own plans.

"I have decided to go ahead with my shipment," she told Ian McCall. "I understand your special cargo is intact in the barns there, so you can have your men begin the loading of *Faith* at first light."

"Right you are," McCall slurred, staring at the fire.

"I can fill out a complete crew from among the extra sailors Patrick found," she said.

"Right you are," McCall mumbled, as one mesmerized.

"Of course, we shall replan the route to Savannah," she said. "And I'm sure you won't mind that I have offered the command to one of your captains, will you, Ian?"

"Right you are," he said.

John Singleton Ramsey leaned over and waved a hand in front of his friend's eyes. McCall didn't even blink. "Ah, the efficacy of two-water grog," Ramsey beamed. "You'll have to tell him all of that tomorrow, Constance. I doubt he's heard a word that's been said the past hour."

Across the fire, though, Patrick Dalton had looked up from his own contemplations of grog and philosophy. "You are making a shipment, Constance? Aboard the new *Faith?*"

"I am." She nodded. "Ian has gathered a load of Austrian musketry, which will find a market in Savannah. Father is sponsoring it, and *Faith* can serve a noble purpose on her maiden voyage."

"I see." Dalton nodded gravely, glancing beyond at the moonlit waters where the ships stood. "It tugs at my heart to see the new schooner, Constance. She looks so very like . . . like *Faith*. You, ah . . . mentioned a captain for her?"

"Why, yes. I have asked Captain Farrington to undertake the voyage. He has experience of fore-and-afts."

"Oh."

His voice sounded so distant that she looked up, startled by a sudden intuition. "Well, I couldn't very well ask you, Patrick. I mean, you have *Fury* now, your own ship . . ."

"Ill-gotten gains," the glaze-eyed McCall muttered.

"Of course," Dalton said. "I understand."

"I was sure you would," she said. "Of course, once we return and I square accounts with my father, then perhaps you and I might —"

"We?"

"What?"

"You said, 'when *we* return.' We, who?"

"Well, of course I am going along on my *Faith*'s maiden voyage. I mean, after all . . ."

The bench on which Dalton had been sitting crashed over backward, his booted feet hitting the ground with a thud as he came upright. "The devil you are!"

She blinked. "What?"

"I forbid it! I absolutely forbid you to go sailing off on some wild adventure with . . . well, with anybody!"

John Singleton Ramsey also came to his feet, somewhat unsteadily. "Patrick, I advise you, this is not the way to — "

"You . . . *forbid* me?" Constance's eyes narrowed.

"I most certainly do. I won't have it!"

Now she was on her feet, too, small and resolute, her eyes blazing, hands on her hips in battle stance. "You . . ."

"You've made a serious tactical error, Patrick," Ramsey pointed out. "I can tell you from long experience that . . ."

Lewis Farrington appeared at Constance's side, quick eyes assessing the situation, glaring across the fire at Dalton. "See here, Dalton, if you have offended this lady . . ."

"Stay out of it," Dalton growled, a hand on his sword.

"Stay out, yourself," Farrington snapped, his own sword at the ready.

"Oh, shut up, the both of you!" Constance commanded. "Captain Farrington, I'll want *Faith* loaded and ready for sail at the earliest opportunity tomorrow. You shall be in command, and I intend to go along."

"See here, miss," Farrington hesitated. "Yourself? I don't know if that is such a good — "

"Do you want the command, or not?"

"Yes, miss, I believe I do."

"Then, don't argue!"

"No, miss."

"God's name, Patrick," Ramsey said sadly. "I thought you were wiser than to set her off. I've told Ian the same, a hundred times, haven't I, Ian? I've said . . . Ian? Where . . .? Oh."

Ian McCall had fallen off his perch and now lay curled in sleep on the grassy ground.

With nothing else to do, Patrick Dalton glared for a moment longer at Constance Ramsey, then turned and strode away, tall and stiff-backed. Charley Duncan, Billy Caster and a few others followed, silently.

At water's edge, Dalton stopped and looked out at the moonlit schooner riding a cable's length from his own proud snow. "Jaunty," he murmured. "Proud and steady and ready for the winds and what they'll bring."

"Aye, sir," Charley Duncan said, for lack of anything else to say.

As though he had not heard him, Dalton sighed. "As beautiful as ever I'd remembered," he muttered. "Aye, even more so. Graceful and proud. Spirited. Give her a course and she'll leap to it. Aye, with a vengeance she will. But it'll take more than a strong hand on her tiller to hold her to tack. A wise hand is what's needed. Wise, indeed."

Duncan and Billy Caster glanced at each other, confused, each suddenly uncertain whether their captain was commenting about the schooner at all, or whether he had some other subject in mind.

Dalton turned, noticed them standing there, and sighed again. "Mister Duncan, round up our crew, please. There'll be tide at first light. *Fury* sails on it."

"Aye, sir. Ah, where are we going, Captain?"

"We are going to find ourselves a fight, Mister Duncan. You've no objection to that, I trust?"

The glint of Charley Duncan's grin in the moonlight matched the feral gleam of his eyes. "Not in the slightest, sir. Not in the least."

Twenty-four

There had been traitors in Ian McCall's company — traitors in positions of trust who knew the sailing schedules, cargoes, itineraries and course charts of merchant vessels, traitors who somehow passed that intelligence to a bloody pirate lurking in the Indies Lanes. The pirate had waylaid McCall's ships — and maybe others sailing from his ports — and taken what he wanted from them. Cargoes, valuables, even the ships themselves, sailed by prize crews to some freebooter haven where they could be sold.

A bloody pirate. A deadly pirate with a deadly, killing ship.

The traitors were Evan Butler and his men. The pirate was John Shelby Butler, who now — from what the Frenchmen had overheard — called himself Jack Shelby. The killing ship was *Valkyrie*, and Patrick Dalton had seen that ship and would not forget: a dark, heavily armed vessel of frigate class, with the distinctive silhouette of yards blocked for studding sails. A ship designed for battle and modified for piracy by men whose business was piracy — commanded now by a ruthless master seaman.

A murderous vessel, sailed by murderous men.

The errant weather of coastal spring was changing again now and *Fury* sailed under low, sullen skies as she crooned down lower Chesapeake toward Cape Henry and the sea. The shifting of weather in the night had given her a solid wind on her starboard beam, and runnels of spray curled from her bows as she knifed along on a beam reach, great

232

sails thrumming aloft.

The foreboding clouds seemed a reflection of the moody set of Patrick Dalton's face, a gloom that seemed to deepen as the snow came to course east of the cape light, trimming sails to a tighter tack in the steady offshore winds.

He would not have been surprised to see the wreckage of the corvette that had come this way. Those aboard had been pressing the sleek vessel hard for speed, hard enough for the narrow hull with its press of sail to be in jeopardy of capsizing when it reached the open sea. But the corvette apparently had made it to sea, and he knew it had turned south.

"How do you fare the day, Mister Caster?" Dalton asked, not looking around.

Billy Caster hesitated, studying the sky and the run of the waves, then said, "Wind westerly, sir, at about twenty and a bit, heavy sky and a running chop. The tide is with the wind."

"And what will it do?"

"It will hold steady through the morning, sir, and there'll be squalls now and then. Limited visibility, generally a few miles at best."

"Very good, Mister Caster. You saw the corvette that gave us wide berth yesterday. Where would you think it is now?"

"I . . . ah . . . that would depend upon where it was going, sir."

At the bell rail, Charley Duncan glanced around. "I'd wager I know where it was going, sir. From what we heard, it's heading right down to the islands to make rendezvous with that pirate ship. They're in league."

"A fair assumption, Mister Duncan. But suppose you were Evan Butler, and your brother were the pirate, and you had to make regular contact to report on ship movements without any one suspecting you. How would you do it?"

"I don't rightly know," Duncan said. "It's a long way from Chesapeake to the Indies Lanes for the like of a trader's coastal packets."

"Precisely." Dalton nodded. "So maybe Evan Butler's little packets don't go all that far. I've a hunch there is a contact base much closer . . . somewhere nearby, where messages can be relayed to swift sails, for relay to *Valkyrie*. To operate from Chesapeake, there would have to be a base closer than the lanes."

"Closer? But where? This is all Colonial coastline, most of it either patrolled or blockaded . . . ah! Wait a bit! There's the Carolina barrens, and the Hatteras shores. Where we played tag with that Spaniard, when we had the ketch."

"Right," Dalton said. "Albemarle Sound, Pamlico, the Currituck and the Croatan . . . desolate waters, those, and all fronted by Hatteras. The only shores north of Florida where the Spaniard still plies his trade. I've a hunch that corvette hasn't gone very far. I've a hunch we'll see him soon enough."

"Him . . . and maybe his relays as well," Duncan pointed out.

"They said Butler knew of the plan to ship small arms aboard the schooner," Billy Caster said, troubled eyes watching the distant shore. "Is that what you're thinking, sir? That the pirate might lay in wait somewhere . . . that *Faith* and . . . and Miss Constance might . . ."

Dalton's eyes were as dark as the clouds overhead. "A proud and jaunty lady," he murmured. "A proud and headstrong woman. She's made it clear that she does not appreciate interference with what she sets out to do."

Duncan looked at him, quizzically. "Then, you don't mean to attend to the safety of Miss Constance, sir?"

"Miss Constance? Of course not," Dalton growled. "I would not presume to take such liberties. Not unless she asked me to, which she has not done." A shadow of humor lurked behind his eyes. "Not that she and the schooner will require assistance in these waters, any time soon."

"Well, beggin' your pardon, sir, in that case just what *are* we doing here?"

"I propose to exercise my ship," Dalton said. "Sail handling and gunnery drill. We've been too long in escort duty, gentlemen. Escort duty can lead to laxity, and I'll have no laxity aboard my ship."

"Oh." Billy Caster looked confused for a moment, then grinned. "Aye, sir. Sail handling and gunnery."

Duncan also had begun to grin, the fierce, hard-eyed grin of the natural fighter. "Might be we should give *Fury* a real shaking down, sir. I mean, cutting capers on an empty sea is no proper test for a warship, is it? A cotillion is far better if there's someone to dance with."

"And gunnery," Billy Caster added. "Cannons do sing better when they have a target. And a pirate's corvette might render a pleasant tune."

"My thoughts exactly," Dalton agreed. "So, let us keep a sharp eye out and see if we can find someone willing to play."

Through the last hours of day while the found bark had been unloaded, the provisioning of *Fury* had been under way. What Dalton needed he took, from Ian McCall's barns, while Billy Caster had kept meticulous accounting. There had been much to resolve—the claim against the bark, its cotton sold at sea to the Portuguese trader, the fate of the island refugees from Mayaguana, the recovered shipwrecked mariners, damages to the bark in transit, sums owed for ships' stores and provisions, wages and shares to those who had become crew . . . and the strongbox in Dalton's quarters aboard *Fury*. Counting claims, contracts and fees, there was a wonderful lot of sums owed by various people to various people, all of which accounts must be settled.

Dalton had shrugged it off earlier. "I have made certain arrangements, Mister Caster. Just keep the tallies and accounts, please."

For the moment, then, it was Billy's job simply to keep records of everything so that all the accounts could be made good when the time came.

235

Dalton's abrupt decision to put to sea had added to the recordkeeping. *Fury's* crew now was a select forty-seven, most of whom had arrived on the snow, but some of whom had been with Mister Duncan aboard *Pride.*

Billy Caster had added one requisition lot to Dalton's bill. The rosters, musters, tallies and logs the clerk was keeping had become sizeable. He drew fresh supplies of foolscap, ink and nibs from the squire's stores.

Now as *Fury* cruised southward on a somber wind, Billy completed his muster and day notes and took them below to put away . . . and made a discovery. Pale and frightened, he hurried a'deck and tugged at Dalton's sleeve. "Sir," he whispered, "did you move the strongbox? It isn't there."

Dalton glanced around, seeming distracted. "I had Mister Hoop carry it ashore last night," he said. "Don't fret yourself, lad. It is in good hands. I told you I had made certain arrangements. Have you completed the crew muster?"

"Aye, sir." Billy breathed a sigh of relief, though he remained puzzled. Of all those who had remained at the Wilderness Docks, who might Captain Dalton have so trusted as to leave with him a recovered pirate treasure that amounted to a fortune?

Fury now was manned as a warship should be. At stanchions, rails and tops, at sheets, trims and helm, at gunnery and greves, from stem to stern, from captain to clerk to the one-armed cook Nathan Claremore, every man was an experienced first-rate. Fourteen of them had sailed with Dalton since the day he acquired the snow, and of those, seven were from the fugitive crew of the original *Faith.*

All the rest were hand-picked from the sailors brought from the shipwreck island, and most of those had Royal Navy experience gained aboard HMS *Tyber.*

The men Dalton had wanted for *Fury*, he got, and to a man they came willingly. Only nine might he have wanted who were not aboard. Michael Romart and the other eight Colonials who had once sailed aboard *Fury* now were com-

236

mitted to berths aboard *Faith II*. Dalton and Duncan did not even approach them. They had sworn their service to the lady.

Off the Back Bay cut where the shoreline became that string of bays and estuaries that opened toward Albemarle Sound, Dalton had the snow trimmed to a new course, closer in, and put fresh eyes in the tops. "Ready all guns, Mister Ball," he said. It was a task of only a moment. *Fury's* guns were trimmed and ready, with each its complement of tub and pail, ram and swab, ball and deck loads, quoins, grapples and linstock. All that lacked was ready fuse and fire, and these now joined the stations that were *Fury's* fighting teeth.

The snow strode southward, leaning to a beam wind from the misted shore astarboard, Victory Locke at the helm holding her in check against the pressure of her sails. The land they scanned was barrier island, with bays and inlets beyond where incipient squalls rolled and tumbled. Tricky waters, inshore and at sea. Behind the fronting island were shallows, with only here and there a channel deep enough for the draft of a sailing vessel, and much that was there was hidden by thickets and forests of seashore pine. And offshore were shoals and sandbars where the unwary could run aground.

A proper hidey-hole for pirates, Dalton thought. A lair where one who knew the channels could go to ground, and from which a killer could sail forth to strike his prey.

Instinct told him the corvette had not gone far. Hunch told him the larger pirate ship was nearby, waiting for word of prey. And his seaman's senses told him that neither, in these circumstances, would be easy to flush out.

As though reading his mind, Charley Duncan said, "If the scoundrels are in there, sir, they'll have the advantage of us. If we go in after them, they have a hole to defend, and if they come out in this wind, they'll have the weather gauge."

"We shall see." Dalton nodded. "Mister Caster, do we still have the charts from *Mystery?*"

237

"Right here, sir. I thought you might have use for them."

"Thank you, Mister Caster. I recall that there is a cut just ahead that showed on no charts."

"It does now, sir. On these. I drew it in."

"I remember that cut, sir," Duncan said. "But it was barely deep enough to allow a ketch draft, an' that with good tide. *Fury* would ground there."

"The launch wouldn't," Dalton pointed out. "I'm thinking of a scouting party if we —"

"On deck!"

"Aye, tops?"

"Sail, sir. Dead ahead and hard down."

"Can you read it, tops?"

"Not rightly, sir, though it is something less than a frigate."

"The corvette, do you think?" Duncan squinted, trying to see what the tops saw.

"That would prove my hunch, wouldn't it?"

Ian McCall, still red-eyed and shaky from the night's bout with John Singleton Ramsey's rum concoction, watched in irritated disapproval as the loading of cargo aboard the bright new schooner continued. Bale after bale of canvas-wrapped merchandise was hoisted on the schooner's spencer gaff, swung inboard and lowered to stowage in the holds.

"Contraband," McCall said for the dozenth time as he held back velvet curtains to peer from the loft window of his main warehouse. "Contraband aboard a ship owned by a fool and ordered by the daughter of a fool." He turned, scowling at the servants and clerks busy around him, and caught the eye of one of them. "Claremore," he beckoned.

The clerk blinked at him. "Me, sir?"

"Of course you," the merchant snorted. "Would I have called out your name if I wanted someone else?"

"No, sir. But you said, 'Claremore,' sir. My name is

Clarendon, just like it's always been."

"Clarendon." McCall rubbed his aching temple and closed his eyes tightly, then sighed. "Right you are, Clarendon. What is keeping Squire Ramsey, do you know?"

"Not exactly, sir. He said he had matters to attend this morning, but he's somewhere about. Do you want me to go and find him, sir?"

"Never mind, Clarem . . . Clarendon. I shall go myself. The fresh air might do me good."

"Yes, sir."

McCall went downstairs and out the main door, pausing again to stare at the schooner being loaded at the stub dock. Down there, in the midst of the feverish activity, was Constance Ramsey, stalking about, issuing orders as though she owned the place. On the schooner's deck, he could see the men who would sail her. Lewis Farrington was there, directing the preparations aboard.

A hundred yards away, tied and silent, stood the four-master *Pride of Falworth,* and McCall gritted his teeth. Once again he had lost a ship only to have it turn up in the hands of that wild Irishman Dalton, claimed as prize or derelict. He had meant to have it out with Dalton today, to stand toe to toe with the rascal if necessary and explain to him the civilized way of doing things. But Dalton was gone. He had boarded *Fury* in the predawn hours and sailed away somewhere, and none seemed to know where he had gone.

With a growl that echoed in his aching head, McCall turned away, then growled again at sight of the sprawling tent city that occupied most of his clearing. Refugees, they had said. People fled from some island, and dumped on his doorstep like so many waifs in the wilderness . . . by Patrick Dalton.

"Ye gods," he hissed, shaking his head.

Near the north tower he found John Singleton Ramsey, in cheerful conversation with several men McCall did not know.

As he approached, Ramsey raised a hand in greeting.

239

"Ah, Ian! Up and about, I see. Top of the day to you, sir. While you rested, I have been taking care of some of your business for you."

"What business? Who are these people?"

"Ah. You haven't met your guests? Let me present Aaron Fairfield, Esq., recently of the island of Mayaguana, and some of his associates, Claude Dunstan, Prosper McPherson, Caleb Smith and Manning Renfrow . . . and the sturdy young man just over there is Keith Darling, an excellent carpenter. Gentlemen, I present your host, Ian McCall, Esq., the owner of these properties."

The men bowed curtly, and McCall returned the gesture, then squared about at Ramsey. "I don't know what I am expected to do with all these people . . ."

"Why, lease them space, of course, and give them employment. Didn't Patrick tell you?"

"I haven't had the opportunity for private conversation with your damned Irish fox," McCall growled. "Though I certainly intend to. What kind of idiotic claim is that that he has against my bark? 'Salvage of flotsam'? What idiocy . . ."

Ramsey raised a hand. "Calm down, Ian. Patrick asked me to attend to some things for him, and I am doing so. One of them is to help you get these people settled. In return, he has warranted their full passage fee — which they will pay in good coin — to you."

McCall squinted. "Why would he do that?"

"The only provision of the agreement," Ramsey continued, "is that you employ such of the men as want to work, long enough for them to build cabins and plant crops. You will, of course, receive rents when the crops are in."

McCall started to sputter, then hesitated. It was, in fact, a godsend to him — an opportunity to turn the Wilderness Docks into a year-round, profit-making investment. A settlement.

"Then there's the bark, *Pride of* — "

"Which is, by God, mine and not Patrick Dalton's! I shall

240

fight that claim, John, I swear I will . . ."

"No need for that, Ian. Patrick has empowered me to issue a quit-claim to you. You can have the bark back."

McCall raised a suspicious eyebrow. "In return for what?"

"In return for your quit-claim against the snow, *Fury*. In Patrick's own words, Ian, 'Let's put an end to this rubbish about what ship is whose.' *Fury* is his, fair and square, and he wants to hear no more about it. And the bark is yours if you accept it . . ."

"Done," McCall said.

". . . as is."

"What?"

"Nothing. You said, 'done.' The deal stands."

Walking back toward the warehouses, McCall felt confused and a bit light-headed. Still, he scowled as he pointed toward *Faith*. "I may be a fool, John, but you're a bigger one. Don't you realize your daughter will be in critical danger, sailing southward with a cargo of muskets?"

"She isn't sailing southward," Ramsey said happily. "She thinks she is, but she isn't."

"Then, where in blazes is she going?"

"To Philadelphia. The British have pulled out of there, you know. They're off chasing General Washington. So the muskets are going to Philadelphia as legitimate cargo."

"How did you arrange that?"

"Oh, I'm only following instructions from the owner of the vessel . . . and of its cargo. When *Faith II* sails, its ladings and orders will read, Philadelphia."

"The owner . . . but *you* are the owner."

"Not anymore." Ramsey grinned. "Patrick Dalton bought the ship from me, cargo and all. It's his now, and must go where he says. I must say, I got a good price, as well. It seems the lad has come into a good bit of money in his travels. In his absence, he has entrusted me to handle his affairs."

"Oh, Lord." McCall let the enormity of it sink in. "Your daughter is going to . . ."

241

"Yes, I know." Ramsey's grin widened. "She is going to pitch a royal fit. And, when it's done, if she still wants to take passage aboard 'her' schooner—and if Captain Farrington still wants to command the vessel—then we shall have a pleasant journey up the Delaware. To Philadelphia. You're invited to come along, if you care to."

Twenty-five

A white squall swept down from the North Carolina coast, and for a time there was nothing to be seen to the south, even for those in *Fury's* tops. The gusting storm was no more than two miles wide as it tracked out to sea, but it spread wings of chilly rain as it passed, and the sea and sky were joined by a curtain of weather.

One tantalizing glimpse of distant sail, and then nothing. Dalton held his course on shrift sail and waited, grim and impatient. Hunch as strong as the Celtic blood in his veins said the vessel ahead — eight to ten miles, he guessed — was the corvette *Resolute.* But the weather — his clerk had fared the day properly — had betrayed him. The weather, and his position. This close to a bay coastline, offshore winds became squalls abruptly, offering no chance to plan around them. As *Fury* had sighted the corvette, it was likely that the corvette's spotters also had sighted *Fury.* Eyes worked both ways at sea. And if the corvette knew of its pursuer, the squall creeping along between them would give it plenty of time to design an escape.

"If he's seen us, he'll put the wind on his starboard quarter and run for sea," Charley Duncan allowed, thinking the same thoughts. "That knife-keeled weasel can be hard to catch if it has a start."

"Aye . . . he can run to sea, or he might make for the bays. He could hide from us there, at least for a time."

"Maybe he didn't see us," Billy Caster suggested. "It was

only a moment, and not everyone has the eyes of Mister Mallory."

"It could be, lad." Dalton shrugged. "We'll know soon enough."

Driving rain swept in sheets across the snow's deck as *Fury* nosed into the trailing edge of the squall, blind at eight knots, not even the barrier islands of upper Hatteras visible now. In the rains were gusting winds which pushed and tugged at the half-press of sail aloft, making the decks roll. From the partially open companionway forward of the bell rail came a clattering of pans and kettles, and a string of sulphurous curses. Nathan Claremore was below, in the galley, trying to prepare a meal from newly stowed stores.

Dalton wagged a thumb at Billy Caster. "Please tell cook to batten down, Mister Caster. We shall be through this weather presently, but then we may have a corvette to fight."

"Or chase," Charley Duncan added. "Or find."

Billy went below. In the gloom of the tight little galley, lit by swinging lanterns, the one-armed veteran was cursing through clenched teeth, kicking fallen copperware about as he tried to wield a mop with his only hand. Billy took the mop from him and began collecting pots. "Captain says to please batten down, Mister Claremore," he said. "We've come into a squall, and beyond it is a ship that will run, fight or hide if it can."

Claremore subsided, accepting a handful of pot-bales from the clerk. "Ah? The pirate's in sight?"

"We had a sighting. Captain believes it is the corvette that fled Chesapeake. I don't know whether those people are pirates, but they're in league with pirates."

"Pirates be pirates." Claremore nodded. "Them as does an' them as gives comfort to 'em, they be all alike, an' all deservin' of the same."

"The same?" Billy looked up from his mopping.

"Aye. Hang them from a leeward yard or send them to the bottom with grapeshot and hot ball."

The grizzled man sounded so fierce that Billy paused.

"That is much like Captain Dalton's opinion of pirates," he observed.

"Aye, I thought so. The captain wasted neither time nor concern on that black-flag cutter yonder in the islands. Man after me own heart, he is."

"You've dealt with pirates, then, Mister Claremore?"

"You might say that, lad. It's how I lost my arm. I made a miscalculation. We had a pirate in custody, an' I was with the prize crew. I took the word of a cutthroat that he'd mind his manners. I took it for an honest vow, and turned my back on the blaggard. It cost me an arm, and cost two of my mates their lives."

Billy shivered, his eyes on the stump of the cook's lost arm. "I'm sorry, Mister Claremore," he said.

Claremore shook his head. "No need of it, lad. Twas a long time ago. But mark my word well, never put your trust in pirates, not even for the blink of an eye. There's no honor in men who'd sail under the black flag, lad. Not even among themselves."

"Captain Dalton says much the same. He says pirates are to be despised."

"Aye, an' right he is, too." Claremore chuckled, righting a stack of parcels on the galley table. He used his good arm and his stump as one who had long since learned such arts. "I believe it's a thing even enemies can agree on. I've seen the time a pair of warships locked in fray raised flags of truce long enough to sail together after a pirate. They were enemies, ye see, but civilized men all the same, an' no civilized man tolerates pirates."

Distantly, beyond the companionway, they heard the hail from the tops. "On deck!"

"I'll be needed on deck," Billy said. He set the mop aside and headed for the ladder, then paused to glance back. "Thank you, Mister Claremore."

"Aye, lad." The cook was stowing bundles in his pantry.

On the snow's little quarterdeck, Patrick Dalton had his glass to his eye, looking ahead. "It is the corvette, Mister

_..erself

_.. the sedate pace of shrift canvas,
..eeth. Almost as though she were a thing
..eemed to drum a war chant as she crested
..._ siuing waves and raised her proud nose to taste the
wind.

Billy Caster squinted, peering ahead. The corvette was
fully visible now, hull up and adding sail, but not to run or
hide. Its narrow hull slender under stacked sail, it leaned
from the wind, gained way and headed toward them.

"He's coming to meet us," Charley Duncan said, confused.

"Aye, an' raising his colors," Victory Locke noted. "The
audacious blaggard intends to fight!"

Dalton rubbed his chin thoughtfully. The corvette had
guns, right enough. It was well-armed and well-manned, a
vessel capable of putting up a fight and inflicting damage.
Yet, in final analysis, a corvette was hardly a match for a
snow. Odd, that it should challenge so readily. "Stand by
chasers," he said. "Stand by starboard batteries. Mister
Locke, when we close I'll give him the courtesy of a demand
and a warning. If he does not strike colors, we shall engage.
Bow chasers and starboard broadside, then stand ready to
come through the wind, full about. Bow guns, quoin to
rake his deck. Starboard and port batteries, level for waterline at four cables."

"Aye, sir."

Charley Duncan stood, grasping the bell rail in hard

hands, a grin of sheer anticipation on his freckled face. A born combatant, Dalton thought, just spoiling for a fight. Keeping his voice level, Dalton said, "Mister Duncan, you did well, bringing that bark in."

"Aye, sir." Duncan didn't look around. "Thank you, sir."

"Burden of command is not easy for any officer, Mister Duncan."

Duncan's grin slipped as he looked around. "Aye, sir, but . . . please the captain, I never felt right. I mean, tryin' to be an officer an' all. It doesn't come natural."

"I see. Mister Duncan, would it amuse you to command the batteries when we engage the corvette?"

The grin returned, bigger than ever. "Aye, sir. It would."

"Then, by all means, go forward and command the guns."

"Aye, sir!"

At half a mile, closing on opposite beam reaches, Dalton glassed the corvette again. Like a knife through water it came, its slim hull bladelike below massed wings of slanting sail. He could see the guns at its bows, the figures of men a'deck making ready for battle. *"Resolute,"* he read its escutcheons. "Resolute indeed, but overmatched. Odd that they didn't run." He lowered the glass. "Signals, please. Tell him to strike his colors and stand to."

The signals ran high on their lanyard. There was no response from the corvette.

"Fore battery, lay a shot ahead of his bow, please."

"Aye, sir." Echoing the words, one of *Fury's* bow chasers thundered. Moments passed, then a plume of spray rose just ahead of the approaching vessel. In answer, twin clouds of smoke billowed at the corvette's nose, and a ball cut water alongside *Fury's* driving hull while a second one skipped across the waves farther out.

"We have his answer." Dalton nodded. "Helm dead on, Mister Locke. Forward guns, fire at will."

The ships closed to five hundred yards, then four hundred, and the corvette's bow guns blossomed again. A ball sang through *Fury's* rigging, punching holes in two sails.

Duncan had held off, judging range, but now he let fly. Both bow chasers roared, dense smoke drifting seaward on the wind. The corvette's starboard bow seemed to explode, a shower of shards and bright splintered wood erupting there.

"Point aport, helm," Dalton ordered.

Victory Locke spun the big wheel. Responsive as a coursing hound, *Fury* edged to the left, swinging her thrusting jib off line with the corvette. At a distance of four cables the ships passed, beam to beam, and thunders rolled and roared. Dalton heard several hits on *Fury,* and the sounds of chaos astarboard where drifting smoke hid the corvette.

"Bring us about, helm," Dalton ordered. "Hard astarboard, through the wind. Hands a'deck, to sheets for a full about!" Answering her rudder, the snow shouldered starboard seas and began a graceful turn toward the wind. Sails aloft went luff, yards making about to resheet for a port reach, as momentum carried her into her turn. In the near distance, the corvette also was turning, but not through the wind. Instead, the lean vessel had turned downwind, seaward, and the wind in its sails pushed it into a long arc away from shore.

"He has made an error, there," Dalton said judiciously. "Tell me, Mister Caster, what is his mistake?"

Billy glanced around. He was at the stern rail, where he had been trying to count the adversary's wounds. There were several. "He turned the wrong way, sir," he said.

"How so?"

"Well, by coming through the wind, sir, we have held our ground. When we complete, we will be where we were, only faced about. But he is turning with the wind. By the time he is about, he will be seaward of us . . . and downwind. He has given us the weather gauge, sir."

"And can you think why he has done that?"

"No, sir. Poor seamanship, I suppose."

"One might assume that." Dalton nodded, frowning as he considered it. Poor seamanship? Possibly. Certainly in making such a come-about the corvette had lost any chance it might have had for an equal battle. It had given *Fury* a huge advantage. But then, *Fury* had held the advantage from the outset. The corvette was not the warship that a snow was. Even if the master of *Resolute* were not familiar with snows — even if he thought *Fury* to be a brig — still he would have been better advised to run than to fight.

Fury completed her turn, and a bit more. With her stem aligned on the corvette — now a quarter-mile away and taking the wind on its starboard beam — the snow's wind was aft, on the port quarter. No better wind could an attacker ask.

"Sheet home," Dalton ordered. "Hold on him, helm, and a bit ahead. Fore and portside batteries, at the ready."

Big sails booming, *Fury* raised her prow above twin sheets of spray and picked up speed, seeming almost gleeful as she raced toward the corvette.

In the forecastle, Charley Duncan was directing gun crews. The long bow chasers would have first fire, quoined to deck level and aimed at the corvette's masts. Then the port beam guns would broadside as they closed, aiming at waterline to hole the hull and break down the timbers within.

The corvette's guns thundered at them as they closed, but the shots were wild, the rhythm ragged as though no one were directing their fire. At nearly eighteen knots, *Fury* closed, content to wait for shots that would not miss.

"On deck! On deck!"

The shouts aloft were almost a scream. Dalton glanced up, then turned. Behind *Fury* another vessel had shouldered through the rolling mists — a big, dark ship with stacked sails full of wind and curling combs of spray angling back from its driving hull. He knew the ship the instant he saw it. *Valkyrie!*

"It's a trap!" Victory Locke rasped. "The corvette was only bait."

"A trap, aye, and we've fallen into it." Dalton's eyes were

as cold as winter storm. Impelled by great weight of sail, the frigate was already within range of ranging guns, and now it began to speak. Smokes billowed at its nose, obscuring everything below its courses, and a ball screamed through *Fury*'s rigging. Lines aloft sang and snapped. Something crashed astern, and the snow lurched crazily, fighting its rudder. "Steady on, helm!" Dalton shouted. "Steady ahead. Mister Duncan, finish the corvette!"

Fury's forward guns thundered and roared.

"Point to starboard now, helm!"

Fury eased to the right, and great balls from astern threw spray where her tail had been. Dalton did not look back. "Broadside now, Mister Duncan," he muttered.

As though he had heard the command, Charley Duncan barked at his beam crews, and guns all along the snow's port side crashed, the ship rolling from their recoil. Just off the port beam, the corvette seemed to come apart. Ball after ball tore through its hull, some of them going entirely through to open gaping wounds on the far side.

People ran through the smoke, coming aft, and Billy Caster dodged aside as a lurching figure nearly bowled him over. Abruptly, *Fury*'s twin stern chasers were manned, stooped figures at the starboard gun working to align it while two men at the port gun seemed to be wrestling with it. Billy gaped, his eyes stinging from the smoke. No quoining or aligning there. Only two men, but now he saw them. One was a huge bull of a man, great arms wrapped around the cannon's midsection. The second man held a smoking fuse aloft with the only arm he had.

"A bit more, Mister Hoop," Nathan Claremore shouted. "Up a tad . . . just . . . there!" The linstock came down upon the vent and the gun roared. Just aft, invisible in the rolling smoke, wood and metal disintegrated. A second later the second stern chaser thundered, and again there was chaos astern . . . chaos and the clear roar of a single large gun. Something exploded directly in front of Billy. In a roaring, stinking darkness full of shouting voices and crashing things, he felt himself lifted and thrown. For an instant that went on and on, he hung suspended it seemed, floating like a gull on wind currents . . . or like a proud and beautiful sailing ship cresting a wave that had no end.

Then there was nothing.

Twenty-six

Where there had sailed three ships, dancing to the deadly song of great guns a'thunder, now there was only one. Bloodied and torn, it limped and faltered as it took the seaward wind on its beam, and the sound of it whining across shattered railings was a low chorus of regret.

As men labored a'deck to mend what could be mended and clear away what could not, they looked often astern, their eyes bleak with the mourning of lost mates . . . and with an outrage that all of them shared. Far astern now was the drifting wreckage of what had been a handsome corvette. *Resolute* had been bait for a trap. As bait, she had been expendable. She had gone down by the bow within minutes of *Fury's* final sweep.

But beyond the grave of *Resolute,* somewhere in the murking distance, was the target of their outrage.

The pirate frigate, *Valkyrie,* had made one run at *Fury.* Like a hunting cat the big ship had hidden in the mist while the corvette played out its role — luring *Fury* into position to be killed. *Valkyrie* had made her move then. In a single pass she had raked and hammered at the snow. But then, taking two fair hits in the bow, the pirate had changed his mind. Faced with a ship that yet had teeth to bite him, he had simply turned away. Turned, and gone south without so much as a salute for those sacrificed to his purposes.

Expendable. The corvette . . . and his own brother aboard the corvette. Expendable.

Valkyrie had attacked, then simply sailed away, and *Fury* stood alone on the sea. Battered and crippled, her decks red with the blood of good men, she stood, then turned away in disgust.

Silent and somber, the snow turned northward. Repairs would be needed, the mending of what could be mended.

They had tried to carry Charley Duncan below; but he fought them off, and finally they had brought splints and wraps and set his broken leg there on the midships deck where he fell. Through it he clenched his teeth and went pale, but not once did he utter a sound. When it was done, he lay against the bell rail and stared back the way they had come.

Patrick Dalton was everywhere for a time, seeing to the tending of his injured and the wrapping of his dead, the clearing of his decks and the splicing of his rigging. Only when there was nothing more to be done did he return to the quarterdeck. Purdy Fisk came from below then, and beckoned him. "The lad's awake, sir," the sailor said. "He took a good knock, but he's sturdy and will be sound again soon enough. He's asking after you, sir."

Dalton took a slow look along the decks of Fury, assessing everything. His eyes paused at the midships rail where four shrouded forms lay, wrapped in canvas; then he turned away for one more look back, this time not at where the frigate had gone, but at where two more *Furies* had gone to the deep. Then he nodded. "Thank you, Mister Fisk. Please relieve Mister Locke at helm, and hold us at this course. I shall be below for a bit."

"Aye, sir."

Billy Caster lay in a bunk in Dalton's own cabin, his pale face lit by lanterns and by the gray evening light from an open transom. His head was wrapped in swathing, and he had plasters on one cheek and a forearm. As Dalton stooped to enter the little cabin, the boy's eyes brightened. "I didn't lose any of the musters and ladings, sir," he said. "I was afraid I had, but Mister Fisk found them."

"Well done, Mister Caster." Dalton looked at his head wrappings, then sat on a bench beside him. "We shall be in

Chesapeake again soon, and it will be well to have our accounts in order."

"Mister Fisk said we lost some of the men, sir. Who . . . ?"

"Aye." Dalton sighed and lowered his head. "Misters Nelson, Leaf and Popkin in the fore, and Mister Waverly in the tops, all to be buried at sea at first light of morning. There'll be memorials, as well."

"Memorials, sir?"

"Mister Hoop." Dalton sighed again, his voice thin. "And Mister Claremore. It was the shot that scored you, lad. It took out our port stern chaser . . . and them with it. The pair of them, and the cannon. They went over the side. We searched for them. We found two men from the corvette, but Mister Hoop and the cook are gone."

Billy's eyes grew moist, and he looked away, then back. "Still, we won, sir."

"Aye, we won the day. *Valkyrie* is run off, and the corvette is sunk."

"And *Fury*, sir?"

"In need of carpentry and smithing, a rigger and a sailmaker. But she's sound enough. We'll put her together again."

For a time the boy lay still, thinking about it. Then he asked, "Sir, did we . . . did we do what we came to do?"

Dalton stood, crouching slightly to avoid the low beams, and stepped to the transom. He leaned there, looking out, his eyes bleak and hooded. "Maybe we began it," he said finally. "But far more needs to be done."

"*Valkyrie*, sir?"

"Aye, *Valkyrie*. That pirate, and other pirates." He seemed to be speaking more to himself than to Billy. "War breeds confusion, Mister Caster. Where there are fields of honor, the plunderers abound. They are the pestilence that war brings, breeding on chaos. War may always be with us, just as kings and councils are, but piracy must be addressed somehow, even in wartime." He turned from the transom, though his eyes still seemed to gaze at distances. "I've wondered whether kings and councils, even at war, can't agree to address such matters."

"I've heard of it being done, sir."

Dalton blinked. "Ah? And have you, now?"

"Mister Claremore told me of enemies joining forces to fight pirates."

"A very civilized notion." Dalton nodded. "I wonder if our kings and councils are as civilized as was *Fury's* cook."

Long after his captain had returned to the upper decks, Billy Caster puzzled over the nature of things . . . and remembered the words of a one-armed cook who later joined a giant to smash an iron ball into the bow of a pirate ship.

Epilogue

In the late spring of the year 1778, Governor Patrick Henry of Virginia received a petition calling for the establishment of a coastal patrol, declared noncombatant in matters involving the disagreement between the English crown and the Confederated Colonies, to serve as a deterent against acts of piracy on the high seas.

More or less simultaneously, similar petitions were received by members of the Continental Congress at Philadelphia, and by ministers of His Majesty George III of England.

It became a matter of some debate, the idea that opposing forces in wartime might under certain circumstances agree to, and act jointly upon, the reduction of criminal elements that plagued them both.